HE LOVE ME HE LOVES ME NOT

AIMEE BROWN

Boldwood

First published in Great Britain in 2022 by Boldwood Books Ltd.

Copyright © Aimee Brown, 2022

Cover Design by Alice Moore Design

Cover Photography: Shutterstock and iStock

The moral right of Aimee Brown to be identified as the author of this work has been asserted in accordance with the Copyright, Designs and Patents Act 1988.

Every effort has been made to obtain the necessary permissions with reference to copyright material, both illustrative and quoted. We apologise for any omissions in this respect and will be pleased to make the appropriate acknowledgements in any future edition.

A CIP catalogue record for this book is available from the British Library.

Paperback ISBN 978-1-80426-807-0

Large Print ISBN 978-1-80426-803-2

Hardback ISBN 978-1-80426-802-5

Ebook ISBN 978-1-80426-800-1

Kindle ISBN 978-1-80426-801-8

Audio CD ISBN 978-1-80426-808-7

MP3 CD ISBN 978-1-80426-805-6

Digital audio download ISBN 978-1-80426-799-8

Boldwood Books Ltd
23 Bowerdean Street
London SW6 3TN
www.boldwoodbooks.com

This one's for you, Dad. The first book you won't see released. I put your name in it so now you'll live forever.

1

DAX

Saturday Afternoon...

'What did Kevin say?' Brynn, my cousin and wedding planner extraordinaire, asks.

I turn to her as she sets her bag onto one of the pristine, white bamboo folding chairs lined up like soldiers on parade – all perfectly spaced and mostly empty, as we're still thirty minutes from the ceremony.

'First things first...' I say. 'Kevin is a real assjack. What d'you see in that guy?'

Why she would have ever dated him in high school is beyond me. He's a far cry from her husband,

Jake. Kevin is a narcissistic forty-something, white, balding man with a beer gut. Jake is a funny thirty-something black guy with a six-pack. They're worlds apart.

But Kevin, unfortunately, owns the building I want to lease. The building that once held my late father's florist shop.

I remember spending entire days in that shop helping my dad put together floral arrangements and going out on deliveries. I'd love to have my shop in a place filled with so many memories of him.

'So, he didn't age well. We can't all be Adonis with a talent for flowers,' she says with a roll of her eyes.

'That's right,' Jake says. 'Not everyone can age as well as us.' He steps up beside me, pulling at the lapel of his jacket with the confidence he never lacks.

Once again, Brynn rolls her eyes dramatically. A move she often uses when Jake and I are together. He's one of my best friends and I'm the one who set the two of them up. Somehow, he swept her cold heart off its feet, and they're now living in wedded bliss and have added a new character to their lives by way of their two-year-old daughter Zoey. The pair of them run a wedding planning business together. Brynn is the brains, and Jake is the brawn.

Besides blood and weddings, Brynn and I don't

have much in common. When I let my floral ambi-
tions loose into the family email gossip chain, she
called me immediately, offering to help me break into
the business. It's been two years since I started
spending my every day with flowers, and I don't
regret it.

'What happened?' she asks.

'He wants to sell instead of lease. Thinks he can
make more of a profit.'

'So, offer more,' she says, as though I've got a
money tree growing in my apartment.

'I'd have to sell a kidney to come up with the
money I'd need, Brynn. He seems to think the place is
made of gold.'

'How much is he asking?'

'He's undecided, but he's thinking one sixty-five,
nine, nine, nine.' I repeat his words. Which included
way more nines than the building is worth.

'For a run-down business that hasn't been updated
since I was born? Greedy bastard. That's just wrong.'

'Yep,' I say, turning back to the wall of roses I'm
finishing up. 'I can't afford that with the shape it's in. I
have sixty-five thousand dollars to my name, and
Mom has graciously put in fifty grand. That's still
many nines away from what I'd need to buy.'

'Finance it!' she suggests.

'The problem is that the building isn't worth that much. I couldn't get a loan in the shape it's in. There's no way I could make repairs and upgrades paying what he wants.'

'Dax, *honey*.'

Great. I've activated her mom voice.

She grabs the flower from my hand. 'They've leased the place since your dad had it. Nearly two decades. I doubt this opportunity will come back up when you can afford it, and the building isn't going to fix itself. If it's that important to you, you've got to make it happen now.'

I grab back the pink blossom. 'I'm doing everything I can.'

A heavy sigh leaves her lips. 'What if we talk to him?' She motions between her and Jake.

'Be my guest.'

The grin growing on her face tells me she's got other plans.

'What?'

'Tell him,' she says to Jake.

He shakes his head. 'I'm not telling him. It was your idea. You get to sweet-talk him into this one.'

I drop my head. 'What did you two do?'

'*Well...*' She drags out the word, now squinting one

eye closed as she considers her words. 'Two ideas. Don't be mad.'

Don't be mad? That's not a great lead-in when it comes to Brynn. Her ideas never end up good for me. She once convinced me to join a charity auction to make some money for the business. I delivered flower arrangements to a retirement home weekly for two months. If you've never tried to escape a building full of elderly women thrilled to see a single young man, you've never really lived. That's a joke. I've never been groped so much in my life. Talk about dirty. Damn. The jokes and innuendos nearly went to my head. I had no idea eighty-something-year-old women were that horny.

'Whatever it is, just say it.'

'I need you to stay through the ceremony today. There's been a change of plans, and I've already promised, so be prepared to make it happen.'

'Continue,' I say.

'The bride saw a viral Facebook video, and she's requested a similar event.'

'What's that got to do with me?'

She grits her teeth together in an awkward grimace as she pulls her phone from a pocket in her dress. 'Maybe just watch?'

What the hell did she sign me up for that she can't even put into words?

I take the phone she's now handing me, pressing the play button on the video she's loaded. The most ridiculous song ever blasts through the speakers.

A man appears at the end of the aisle, flinging his floral print suit jacket open and revealing a belt bag that he unzips with a flair I've never witnessed before. He grabs handfuls of flower petals, blowing them off his hand like a kiss towards women in the crowd. Christ. I can't help but laugh as he makes his way down the aisle, dancing, charming the women, and embarrassing the men.

'You're not expecting me to do this, are you?'

'No,' Brynn says. 'I'm expecting you to be better than that.'

Our eyes meet. She's got to be kidding.

'The bride requested you specifically.'

'Why me?'

'Because you're hot to trot,' Jake says as if I should know this.

'He's not wrong,' Brynn says. 'Look at you. Tall, dark, more than handsome. If we weren't related...'

'Ew.' I throw my head back in disgust, and Jake looks even more horrified.

'Jesus,' he says. 'That's a scene I didn't need in my

mind's eye. Like I don't already feel like a troll standing next to this overly tall, bearded dreamboat, you gotta go and say something like that?'

'I've never *actually* thought of it,' she reassures him. 'He's my cousin. That'd be gross. I'm just saying *that's* why the bride chose you. You're pretty.'

'I'm pretty,' I repeat her words, shaking my head. 'You're serious about this? You want *me* to be the flower boy?'

'It is your business name there, big fella. Not much of a stretch,' Jake says, slapping my back.

Brynn is starting to visibly panic that my answer will be no. 'Think of the single women who will be watching,' she says to entice me. 'We all know you're going to hand your card to some single, beautiful bridesmaid before the day is over, who will then offend your neighbors when you ravish her before she disappears into the sunrise, never to be seen again. Maybe this will help flush her out?'

'You're trying to bribe me with my own easiness?'

'Is it working?'

She makes my bachelor lifestyle sound much dirtier than it is. I don't *always* take home bridesmaids. I glance down at the stack of buckets at my feet, one of them still half full of flowers. I toss the single bloom still in my hand into it. This is how she sees me, eh? It's not as if I didn't know; it's just weird to have her use her low opinion of my love life to tempt me to do this.

'Don't even pretend you're embarrassed. When you look the way you do, it's your freaking job to sleep around. Lord knows I would.'

Jake rubs his temples. 'What the hell did I marry?'

'You like it,' she says with a wink.

So, maybe I've had a slight problem with the ladies in recent years. Puberty passed me by in high school, so when I finally went through it and grew into my own skin, I noticed women looking my way. Things got fun. It's not a crime.

'Do I have to walk down the aisle to "Stroke Me"?'

Jake bellows a laugh. 'Why *wouldn't* you want to?'

'What would you pick?' Brynn asks, ignoring him completely.

'Oh!' Jake says suddenly, his eyes on my T-shirt. 'I've got the perfect song.'

'What?'

'You'll have to trust me.'

'Nope,' I say. 'I absolutely do not trust you.'

He laughs. 'You probably shouldn't trust me.'

'Is he going to do it?' A voice interrupts us.

I turn to see a gorgeous woman wearing a long blue formal dress walking our way.

Brynn glances at me, a single eyebrow raised. '*See*,' she mouths. '*Bridesmaid*.'

All eyes are on me as they await my answer. I drop my head, blowing out a breath. I can't believe I'm about to say this.

'He'll do it,' I say. 'But only because the bride requested it. I can't possibly turn her down on her big day. Can I?'

The bridesmaid grins. 'I know I'm excited,' she says with a wink.

We all watch as she walks away, stopping to glance back at me with a grin before she disappears into the house where the bridal suite is. Of course, I grin back like the hussy I apparently am.

'Hell yeah, she's excited,' Jake says mostly under his breath. 'Later, she'll be yelling your name in your overly clean bedroom with her naked ass pressed against your freshly ironed sheets.' He slaps my ass as though I'm headed into a football game. 'Who irons their sheets anyway?'

'I send my laundry out,' I remind him. 'I don't iron them myself. That said... maybe she will. Don't be jealous all you have to go home to is this.' I motion to Brynn, who cocks her head, a pinch-lipped grin on one side of her face.

'Not funny,' she says, now digging through her

bag. 'I bought you this. I can't even believe they sell them again.' She pulls something from her things and hands it to me.

'She wants the stupid waist bag and everything?'

'Jake, go get the petals he brought in earlier.' She ignores my question.

'On it.' He salutes Brynn as if she's his drill sergeant. Which isn't that unbelievable.

'The flower wall looks amazing, by the way. You almost done?'

I glance back at the wedding backdrop. An ombré fade wall of pink roses as tall as I am. This thing has taken me hours to complete.

'Looks good. Just need to clean up.'

'We'll take care of that.' She glances behind her. 'Guests are arriving. Time to get you prepped to shake that booty down the aisle. Don't hold back. I want twenty-eighteen Matthews-style barbecue-party-Dax front and center.'

'I never should have invited you to that.'

The Matthews are my mom's neighbors. One half of the two of them, Penny, was a late eighties, early nineties, pop star. We're talking international tours, photos in *Bop* magazine, and MTV videos. There are so many things a guy of my age should know nothing about (like *Bop* magazine) that I'd consider myself an expert in because of the Matthews.

Growing up I spent a lot of time there; honestly, I still do because their son River has been my best friend since I was four.

'By the way,' Brynn says a few minutes later as she shoves flower petals into the bag now securely strapped around my waist. 'The second thing I needed to tell you is that a woman is here from *Here Comes the Bride* magazine.'

'You the town herald now?'

'Not usually, but she's here to see you.'

'Why would she be here to see me?'

'Here, wear this.' She hands me Jake's black suit jacket.

'Doesn't really go with jeans, does it?'

She laughs under her breath, shaking her head as though I'm the biggest dummy here. 'It's going to make those jeans so hot you won't be able to touch 'em. Your ridiculous shirt choice is kind of perfect too. It's almost like you knew what was coming.'

I glance down, reading the text upside down. *I'm sexy, and I grow it.* Shit. I forgot I was wearing this one.

'At least it's got flowers on it.'

Flower pun T-shirts are kind of my thing.

Everyone I know has them made for me or buys them whenever they come across them.

'Anyway,' Brynn says. 'She's here because she's looking for a contestant for an upcoming YouTube show called *Battle of the Blossoms*.'

'What's that?'

'It's a floral competition. Winner gets a full spread in the magazine and... fifty thousand dollars.'

'*Fifty* grand? Where do I sign up?' I ask, jokingly.

She blows out a noticeable sigh of relief. 'I'm glad you said that because I kind of already did.'

'*Brynn*,' I say firmly as if I have any control over her. 'We've talked about this. You're banned from setting me up for things. Dates, events, *anything*, unless you talk to me first.'

'I know, but this was too good to pass up, so I figured asking for forgiveness would be easier than permission. Your performance here might be what puts you in the running. Don't hate me for it, either. We're family. You can't hate family.'

'Uh, you can totally hate family,' I say, more than irritated. 'I'm doing it right now.'

'Lucky for me, we don't have time to discuss it.' She turns her attention to the wedding party, now getting everyone lined up, motioning for the musician to start the music.

Are you kidding me? She's just going to send me out there with this little info? If I wasn't actively living this moment, it might be funny. It better be funny when it's over, or I'll never listen to another of her suggestions again.

'I got you, man,' Jake says in a near whisper as he walks over to me. He adjusts his jacket I'm now wearing. 'When the beat drops, bust a move. Make me proud.'

'Why do I feel like you're about to do me dirty?'

'Probably cause that's our thing, sugar.' He pats the side of my cheek, a goofy grin on his face.

After seven bridesmaids walk the aisle, the original song cuts with a scratch, and I feel in my gut I'm in for something I'm not ready for. A new song starts, and I roll my head dramatically towards Jake, now standing off to the side of the venue. He's bouncing to the beat, his face lit up like a jack-o'-lantern as he thrusts his hips as if he's in a nightclub. He did *not*.

My shirt screwed me. 'Sexy and I Know It' is playing through the speakers. Loudly. Here I thought 'Stroke Me' would be embarrassing. He's as good as dead as soon as this is over, and I hope the look on my face is sending him that warning.

Guests are now chattering with the music change; heads turn my way.

'*Go,*' Brynn hisses. '*Do it.*'

There's no getting out of this now. I blow out a breath and unbutton the jacket as I step forward. Matthews-party-Dax. Summoning Matthews-party-Dax.

'*Dax!*' Brynn is shooting me daggers.

Here goes nothing. I toss a handful of flowers over my head and do some kind of spin. The crowd ahead of me bursts into laughter, Jake whistling like an idiot from the sidelines. I find the beat and groove my tall, dorky ass down the aisle.

Right about now, I'm thankful for the other half of the Matthews. Dr John Matthews, OB/GYN. An ex-professional dancer who has given his son and me quite a few lessons in the art of dance over the years. Today that little detail of my life is serving me well.

Flower petals are thrown, hips are thrust, upper body rolls are performed. My dignity has taken a hit, and I'm not at all proud of what's going down, but the hoots from the bridal party are oddly inspiring. Once I reach the end of the aisle, every groomsman is now dancing with me in their places, and I toss one more handful of flowers over my head, leaping out of the ceremony space on my way to kill Jake. God help me if I get more requests for this.

2

HOLLYN

Saturday Evening...

'Hot-cha-cha, lady!' Mercy says through my screen with a grin.

I've got my phone held out in front of me as I walk to the restaurant I'm meeting Tristan at.

'Are you sure white wouldn't have been better? Considering the situation and all?' I glance down at the dress I bought this morning, especially for this occasion.

'Black was the better choice. You look hot,' she says with an obnoxious wink.

'Thank you, BFF.'

'My pleasure,' she says. 'I can't believe he's going to propose. You sure you want this? I mean, he's kind of a wang.'

I laugh nervously, but inside I'm internally screaming. Not like I'm in a horror movie or anything. Well, maybe a little like that. A proposal is a big deal, especially considering I wasn't expecting it. I kind of thought Tristan wanted to shack up forever instead of making it official, seeing as we've been dating for eight years. I'm sure these pangs of anxiety bouncing through my insides like a pinball machine are entirely normal.

'I see that question has activated your overthink button,' Mercy says, obviously knowing the many faces of me well. She should. We've been best friends for twenty years. 'Let's see your surprised face.'

'You think I need to practice my surprised face?'

'Did you think you'd walk in there and act like it was any other day? You can't let him know you found the ring receipt. Where's the shock in that?'

'OK...'

I'm not an actress. In fact, I suck at lying altogether. Just ask my parents. Instead of lying, I pretend I have nothing to say. It's not truly a lie if it's an absence of information, is it? I don't even know the proper reaction for this moment because I don't know how I feel about it. Do I gasp? Cry? What *is* the correct response to a proposal eight years into a relationship?

I give her a wide-mouthed, wide-grinned gasp.

She scrunches her face. 'That was a little too *not-so-surprise birthday party*. Try again.'

I switch to a more reserved, about to cry, hand over my mouth shocked look.

'You look terrified, but so would I if that tool asked me to spend forever with him. Maybe it'll depend on the words that come out of his mouth? I don't exactly have high hopes for him.'

'Mercy, stop,' I say. 'God, why am I so jittery?' I ask her, adjusting my dress. 'Why's my ass sweating?'

'You've got the ass sweats? Yikes.' She laughs. 'I'm sure everyone is nervous when they get asked to put one man on a pedestal for the rest of their lives. I'll never personally know because: *No. Thank. You.*'

'You really think that?'

'Not *think*, Hols. *Know*. Never, ever in a million fucking years will I get married.'

I laugh to myself. 'I meant about the nervous part.'

'Oh! For sure. My friend Annie said it was the most unrestful moment of her life and she helped pick the ring.'

'How'd she get through it without being on pins and needles?'

'In her defense, she's much more normal than us. She's only got the usual anxiety. Not our shared *my family is so fucked up I'd literally rather die than spend a holiday together*.'

Yep. We both have that. Mercy's anxiousness stems from a rough childhood, whereas mine is from being the daughter of a woman constantly in the spotlight. I've never been able to live up to my famous musician mother, and that's created some issues I wish it hadn't.

'She said after she calmed down, she just knew,' Mercy continues, her face now scrunched in disgust. 'She felt it in her bones or some shit. Sounds painful if you ask me.'

Mercy can't have a conversation without everyone around her knowing exactly how she feels. She's honestly herself. No hesitations and no apologies and I love her for it.

My phone dings with an incoming text. 'Maybe that's finally Vic!' I glance at the notification box. 'Never mind. Just River.'

River is my younger brother. We talk every day. Mostly so he can annoy me or gross me out with some meme he insists is hilarious.

After moving to Seattle, I pulled away from my

parents. I needed a life of my own. One where I wasn't constantly in the shadow of my mother. I could never let River go, though. He keeps me sane and makes me feel like I'm not alone.

'Is icky Vicki ghosting you out of jealousy or what? I know she always thought she'd be the first of the two of you to get married, but when you're a bitch—'

'She'd never do that. Something's off, though. First, she dumped Isaac. Then she stopped calling. I may need to set up an intervention soon.'

'Didn't realize there was an intervention for being hoity-toity as fuck.'

Mercy doesn't love Victoria and vice versa. The three of us have kind of a best friend triangle. I met Victoria in college; we were roommates and got close enough I'd consider her my Seattle BFF. While Mercy is more like the sister I never had. She's got no reason to be jealous, but I get it. Vic gets more facetime than Mercy since we live in two different states.

I stop in front of the restaurant – one of my favorites, FireFly – and take a deep cleansing breath, but it doesn't cleanse much. I can do this. It's just me and Tristan taking our relationship to the next level.

'Remember when you met Tristan?' Mercy asks.

The day I met Tristan, I was a sophomore in college, and my eyes were glued to him the second I walked into American Literature 101. To my surprise, I beelined to a seat in the front row. Usually, I'm a back-row kind of girl. But the man was Clooney gorgeous. A real silver fox. I wanted to be closer to him. He seemed to have obvious life experience, which is what I wanted. Life experience that wasn't mine and I needed to know more.

More is what I got when I found myself in his office a few weeks later, hiding in his closet, half-naked, hoping the Dean didn't walk around his desk and see my bra hanging off the handle of one of his desk drawers when he stopped by for a surprise visit to check in on Tristan's classes.

Yep, I was a student, and he was my professor. It was all very Aria and Ezra of *Pretty Little Liars*, college edition. Sure, he was nearly twenty years my senior, but we were both adults, and it was love at first sight.

'I loved him the moment I saw him.'

'Not possible,' Mercy says. 'But I remember. It was puke worthy.' She sticks her finger in her mouth as if forcing herself to vomit. 'Here you are, eight years later. I might not like him and think you can do a thousand percent better, but if you're happy, I support you in saying yes and becoming the next Mrs Hollyn Wells, the *third*.'

Ugh. When she says it like that, it makes me

second guess everything. I've tried to forget that Tristan has been married before. Twice. I'm seriously dating Ross Geller.

'Do you still feel what you felt all those years ago?'

'Um—' Do I? I think I do. I know love isn't all clouds and rainbows forever, but love is love. Right?

'Hello? I think you froze.' Mercy shakes her phone, the screen bouncing around her hotel room.

'No, I'm here. Just—' Freaking out, wondering if I should do this? How do you even feel something in your bones? 'I'm panicking, Merc. What if this isn't right?'

If I fall into a complete panic attack on the sidewalk, I will die.

'Deep breaths, Hols.'

I follow her orders, leaning against the corner of the brick building, taking long deep breaths in through my nose and out through my mouth. Just like my therapist has suggested.

'Don't you think you'd have figured out you didn't love him before now? Eight years into it?'

'You're right,' I say. 'I'm sure you're right.' I hope.

A car pulls up, Tristan sits in the cab's back seat.

'He's here.'

'Follow your heart!' she says. 'Don't you dare ask

icky Vicki to be your maid of honor either, or you'll have hell to pay.'

'Of course it's you.'

She smiles wide. 'Good luck!'

I shove my phone into my bag and turn to Tristan as he gets out of his cab, an anxiety-ridden smile plastered on my face.

'Sweet pea.' He greets me with the name I hate. My dad calls me sweet pea. Or he did when we were on speaking terms. 'Shall we go in?'

'I'm ready.' My voice wobbles as I say it, causing him to study me, searching for the reason.

Pull it together, Hollyn. You've been doing wife business at girlfriend prices for eight years. Time to move this roller coaster into the next bend or make an emergency exit. Now is the time.

FireFly is one of those multi-experience restaurants with many mood settings within one building. Romantic rooms with fireplaces and lit candles. Outdoor garden seating. Even a library room filled with books and leather.

My favorite is the one we are being led through right now. It's dimly lit with large boho basket light fixtures, flickering candles under colorful glass shades, cushioned bench seats lined with pillows, and vintage décor that makes you want to spend hours sitting and chatting with whomever you're with, forgetting that an outside world exists.

I hang my bag from the back of my chair and sit across from Tristan. He immediately opens his menu, ignoring me entirely until his phone buzzes with an incoming text. He glances at the screen but doesn't put down his menu or respond.

'Wine?' a server asks as she approaches our table.

'One rosé and one Chardonnay,' Tristan answers without looking away from his menu.

'Please and thank you.' I finish his sentence for him.

Our server gives me a gracious grin. I'd been a server my entire adult life until recently. I know how jerk-ish people can be, and I hate that Tristan can sometimes be one of them.

Tristan glances over his menu at me. 'You know I hate when you do that.'

'And you know I hate when you don't. It's polite, that's all. She's not beneath you.'

His eyes flick from me back to his menu. I don't need the menu. I already know what I want. I'm a woman who prefers the comfort of things I know I love than the surprise of things I might not. The fettucine here is either to die for or soggy as if it was premade and reheated. A tad hit and miss, but my fingers are crossed for the former.

'Flowers?' A man selling individual roses stops at our table. He glances between the two of us, but Tristan waves him away without so much as looking up at him. I give him an apologetic shrug.

Romantic gesture missed. I'm not surprised. Tristan isn't exactly romantic. He *was*; when we first started dating, he'd do all the things. Open my doors, share desserts, hold my hand, the works. He's since gotten over all that.

'How was your meeting?' I ask, setting the menu aside.

'Unremarkable.' He closes his menu, setting it atop mine as the server delivers our wine. She takes our orders and leaves us with our drinks and my anxiety. 'Your day was...?'

'So far, so good. I bought a new dress specifically for tonight.'

His eyes dart to my chest, the ruched sweetheart neckline in his gaze, my breasts now the object of his almost absent look of approval. 'Very nice.'

The buzzing of another text causes him to furrow his brow and he grabs his wine, taking a large swig before setting it back on the table. When he reaches into his inside jacket pocket, my heart starts to pound.

This is it. Deep breath, Hols. It's just a proposal, not a bomb. Every serious relationship eventually moves into engagement territory.

He pulls an envelope from his jacket, handing it to me. My name, Hollyn Matthews, scribbled across it in his nearly illegible handwriting.

'What's this?' I ask, not expecting him to do it via love letter. Maybe he's more romantic than I expected?

'A menagerie of things, really.'

I open the envelope, pulling out a handful of documents. I glance through the papers quickly.

'I don't understand.' I look at him. 'What *is* this?'

He has an unfocused stare as he gazes at the items in my hand. 'Hollyn, I think we've reached the end of our current situation.'

OK... even I'll admit this proposal is not oozing with romance.

'I've sold the apartment. We took a bit of a hit, but that's your share.'

'You *sold* the apartment? Where will we live?' I ask, glancing at the check. 'Fifty-nine thousand dollars? And fifty cents?' My voice raises with each word. He did not just give me a check for barely a third of what I paid, *in cash*, when we bought it seven years ago. Did he?

'Tristan.' I lower my chin. 'I put my entire trust

fund into that condo. My parents are still pissed. One hundred and fifty thousand, cash. Where's *that*?'

He shrugs, suddenly more interested in his wine than our conversation.

I glance through the papers and find a... plane ticket? SEA–PDX, one way, dated for tomorrow morning. This isn't a proposal.

'A one-way ticket home? Wait, *what*?'

'We're breaking up, Hols,' he says flatly, void of all emotion. 'I've moved on.' He waves a hand my way as though I'm a fly, annoying him.

And the coaster is out of control. We're no longer moving into the next bend. I'm free-falling down a drop by myself without a seatbelt.

'I'm sorry, *what*?!' I ask again, shaking my head, hoping to shake it right into understanding what the hell is going on. 'I thought you were going to propose tonight.'

He burst out an awkward laugh. A few people seated around us glance over. '*Propose?*' he asks, as if the word is poisonous. 'What on earth would give you that idea?'

A shattering sound echoes through my head, causing me to look around for whomever just dropped their wine glass. But nobody in the room is reacting, so it must just be my heart.

'I found a receipt for the ring.' And not just any ring. A seventeen-thousand-dollar engagement ring. The receipt actually had the word 'engagement'.

He closes his eyes, pinching the bridge of his nose with his finger and thumb. The same move he does when he's been caught doing something less than honest. Finally, his face softens, and he drops his hand to the table.

'You're going to make this harder than it needs to be, aren't you?'

My jaw drops. 'If asking what the hell you're talking about is that, then I guess I am.'

He sighs heavily. 'As I said, I've moved on.'

'You've moved on?' I repeat his words slowly, allowing them to sink into my head. He's moved on? As in, to another woman? The nerve of this bastard. 'The ring was for someone *else*?'

He lifts a single shoulder. 'I'm sorry, Hols. But a proposal was never on the table for us. You're not exactly marriage material.'

Not exactly marriage material? Jesus, Tristan, why don't you tell me how you really feel?

'You're a bit immature for something as serious as marriage. Honestly, you were more my back-up plan. Fun for a while, but always the sweet good little girl who waited at home for me. I appreciated that. It's always nice to come home to a bed that's not empty, especially with someone as beautiful as you in it. But I'm over it, and now it's time for me to move on.'

My heart pounds in my chest and head like an EDM song. I *hate* EDM. I shake my head, probably looking like a deer in the headlights, not knowing what to do or which way to flee. *I was his back-up plan?* Did he seriously wait eight freaking years to tell me this?

The server delivers the dishes we ordered, setting each plate in front of us. Damn it. Soggy. Now I'm *really* mad.

'You cheating bastard,' I say, the panic from earlier quickly filling my chest like smoldering hot lava. It hurts like hell and is pissing me off like nothing else.

'Let's not get overly emotional,' he says, motioning with his hands for me to calm down. 'We're in public.'

I nod, pulling my napkin from my lap and tossing it onto the table. Sweet, good little girl, eh? That's about to change.

'*You* chose to do this in public, Tristan. Not me.' I stand from the table, grab my wine glass, and toss the contents in his face. I don't like rosé anyway.

Oh. I laugh to myself. I've never done that before, but it was liberating.

'Hollyn!'

Heads turn as the surrounding diners definitely hear what I'm now hearing.

'You're acting like a broken-hearted teenager.'

'Am I?' I ask, throwing my purse strap over my shoulder. 'I guess this won't surprise you then...' I pick up his plate and dump it onto his lap, giving it a good shake, so I don't waste any. After all, it's not cheap. 'Eight years, Tristan. You wasted *eight* years of my life.' I grab my plate and do the same.

'*Hollyn!*' he roars this time as he stands, allowing the food to drop onto the floor at his feet. Now that's a waste.

The server practically runs to our table. 'Is there a problem?'

Tristan growls something unintelligible as he storms from the table towards the bathrooms.

'No problem at all,' I say to her. 'Don't mind him. He's got zero table manners. A real animal in a de-signer suit.' I laugh, but it surfaces as more Cruella de Vil than Sleeping Beauty.

'I'm gonna need a bottle of your most expensive champagne to go. And an entire chocolate cheese-cake. I don't even care if they're individual slices pieced together to form an entire cake, just make it happen?'

Who am I right now? I can't eat an entire cake!

The server grimaces as she looks at the mess I've just made, but eventually, she nods.

'Wait,' I call as she walks away. 'Make that three bottles?' Might as well make it count.

'Sure.' She nods, her eyes wide.

'I apologize for ruining your evening,' I announce to the room of diners all here for an atmosphere Tristan has most definitely ruined. 'He's... uh – moved on and proposed to someone else after stealing nearly a decade of my life.' I do a curtsey for reasons I'm not sure of and walk away from the scene towards the front of the restaurant to pick up my newly placed to-go order.

'Charge everything to this.' I hand her Tristan's credit card. The card he loaned me this morning when I told him I was buying a new dress for tonight. *How about a dress on me*, he suggested. How could I possibly refuse that? I thought I was purchasing the outfit I'd be going home engaged in. Apparently, he knew it was the dress I'd be flying home in. A consolation prize for him being the jerk of a decade.

'Actually, charge every order in the house tonight to it. He's a very giving person.'

'Sure...' she says, hesitation in her voice.

'And run it through the shredder when you're done as well. He's a real security freak.'

She nods as one of her fellow servers hands me a box filled with three bottles of champagne and an entire chocolate cheesecake. Dinner is served.

'If he by chance asks questions, answer them all with these three paltry words and let him know they're absolutely from me. *Go. To. Hell.*' I smile sweetly, or maybe insanely; it's hard to tell at this point.

'Yes, ma'am.'

And with that, I put on the brave face of a woman who's just been dumped and exit the restaurant into a world I no longer know.

* * *

Twenty Minutes Later...

I'm sitting on the steps to my building, the box of food sitting next to me. I pull my phone from my bag, redialing Victoria's number, but this time it doesn't even ring; it just goes straight to voicemail. I hang up and type out a text.

Where are you? Kind of having the worst day ever.

If I ignored her like she is me, she'd be livid. Where the hell is she?

I look around the street at random people meandering by, living life, and probably not feeling as if they wished they could disappear like I do.

I gotta call my brother. He'll be so thrilled. I dial his number and lift the phone to my ear, my hand shaking. Emotions are quickly surfacing.

Don't lose it now, Hols. You can hold it together for a few more minutes.

'What up, loser?'

At the sound of his voice, a sob emerges before I'm ready.

'Hols? What's wrong?' His voice is full of worry.

'He dumped me,' I cry into the phone.

'Shit. Why?'

'I found an engagement ring receipt.' I bite my lip hard in a desperate attempt to hold back a hideously ugly public cry. 'But it was for someone else.'

'The ring was for someone else? Jesus, Hollyn. You really know how to pick 'em. What a fucking prick.' He's angry. I knew he would be.

'Yeah,' I say meekly, tears spilling over and streaming down my face. 'I thought he was going to propose, Riv.'

'Why the fuck would you want him to propose?'

'I love him. Or I thought I loved him? I dunno. I don't think I know what love is anymore.'

He grunts. 'Whatever you two have isn't love. Trust me. I know you've put a lot of time into this douche, but he's a real blowhole. The guy has cheated *multiple* times. Just get on a plane and come home already.'

'I *am*, River. I kind of have to. I lost my job a few months ago, and I haven't been able to find anything.'

He sighs heavily into the phone. I can almost see him pulling the phone from his ear and dropping his head into his hands out of frustration.

'We talked about this, Hollyn. I can't help you if you lie to me. You lost your job? Why'd you wait months to tell me?'

'Humiliation, probably.' God, I am a complete failure. 'I had enough savings to get me through a few months. I thought I'd find something before then. You sure you want honesty?'

'Well, I'm your brother, and you're obviously calling me for help, so yeah, I'm sure I want honesty.'

'He sold the apartment too.'

'If you're coming here, you don't need it.'

'That's not the problem, Riv. I put my entire trust fund into that apartment when we bought it, and he only gave me fifty grand back.'

'*What?*' he snaps, his voice dripping with irritation. 'He *stole* the money you paid for it?'

Did he *steal* it? Obviously, he's going through something right now, but is he *steal-from-his-girlfriend* evil? I didn't think so. At least not until right this second.

'I don't know. Maybe the sale hasn't gone through yet? Maybe he forgot? I don't know how condo sales work.'

'You don't forget that kind of money, Hols. That fucker pocketed it, I'm sure of it. He's been manipulating you for years. Of course the bastard stole it,' he growls into the phone. 'Stay where you are. I'm coming there.'

'No!' I say, standing from the steps. That's the last thing I need. Once, when he came to visit me, he ended up in jail when he and Tristan got into it.

I put the phone on speaker, set it on the top of the cheesecake in the box, and head into my building.

'Let's just give him a bit. In case something is going on with the sale I don't know about.'

'I don't mind coming up there and kicking his ass. I'd *love* to do it.'

'Yes,' I say. 'I know. But the last thing I need to deal with is you in jail, *again*.' I jab the elevator button. 'If I thought that would help, trust me, I'd be on board. I just...' I pause, shoving away my emotions. 'Can you pick me up at the airport tomorrow morning?'

'Hello, Hollyn.' Mrs Hunt from the third floor steps into the building, waiting for the elevator with me. 'You alright, dear?'

'Is she ever?' River answers for me.

Mrs Hunt's eyes move from me to the box his voice is coming from.

'Sorry,' I say. 'My brother.' I scrunch my face, shrugging my shoulders.

'Yes, I'll pick you up,' River continues. 'But you can't just blow this off. He needs to do the right thing. I'll get Dad on him.'

'*No!*' I yell as I step into the elevator, scaring Mrs Hunt half to death. 'Sorry,' I say to her quietly. 'No Mom or Dad. Please, River. I can't cope with them right now. Give me some time. I'll deal with it. I promise. I'll figure something out.'

River's silent on the other end of the line for too long.

'Please, Riv?'

'That fucker's got one month before I step in. *One month.*'

Mrs Hunt raises a judgmental eyebrow as River swears.

'Sorry,' I say again. 'He's crude as can be, no manners at all.' I glance at the box. 'Deal,' I say to River. 'One month.'

'Wait,' he says. 'If you don't want Mom and Dad to know you're here, where exactly do you plan on staying?'

A minor detail I hadn't yet considered. 'With you?'

He laughs, suddenly stopping. 'You're serious? I don't exactly live alone. Dax is here too.'

I forgot about Dax. 'It won't be for long. You think he'd mind?'

River sighs. 'He'll deal. It's an emergency. You can stay in my room.'

'No way are we sharing a bed.'

'That's a big no from me too, dumbass. I'll stay with Summer for a few.'

'Summer?' I ask. 'Who's Summer?'

'A girl I'm seeing.'

'I didn't even know you were seeing anyone.'

'How's that feel to have the person you're closest to in life *not* tell you everything?'

Shame fills my insides like static. 'I get it. I'm a selfish jerk. I know.'

'As long as you know.'

I roll my eyes. 'I'm sorry,' I say, sincerely feeling bad that I'm interrupting his life because I can't figure out how to be good at this adulthood gig. It's just way more complicated than I expected it to be.

'Just get your shit and get the hell away from that loser before he sweet talks you into overlooking his asshole ways again. Everything will work out. OK?'

I nod as if he can hear me, the tears surfacing again as the elevator doors open, Mrs Hunt stepping out. The doors slide closed again and the elevator continues onto the fourth floor where my apartment is.

'*Hello?*' River says after a beat of silence a tad too long.

'OK,' I half cry.

'Jesus. You're a mess.'

'I know. It's pathetic. I don't know what I'd do without you.' I start to cry again as I step out of the elevator.

'Stop crying, Hols. You're not the only one bad at life.'

'Thank god.' I force a sad laugh.

'See ya tomorrow ya pain in the ass.' He hangs up without giving me a chance to say goodbye.

For a moment, I stare at my front door as I pull my keys from my bag. This may well be the last time I see this place. The place I've called home for seven years. Sometimes life sucks.

3

DAX

The Next Morning...

'What's this?'

I glance at the time when he walks into our apartment. Seven-thirty in the morning. Rarely is River up at dawn. How did I not hear him leave?

'Coffee.' River sets the tray with two coffees on the kitchen island. 'Blueberry scones, courtesy of Summer.' He puts a pink bakery box down. 'And... bacon.' He carries one of the coffees and the white Styrofoam box containing the bacon to the couch.

'You know I love it when you talk dirty to me,' I

say, grabbing a coffee and scone. 'What's this for anyway?'

'I need a huge favor,' he says.

The last time River needed a huge favor, it was one in the morning, and I had an overnight guest. He knocked on my door, yelling, 'You got a rubber?' Not at all mood-killing, considering.

'It's Hollyn.'

'Hollyn?' My voice is awkward as I freeze, scone midway to my mouth. 'Is she alright?'

River looks up from his bacon, his gaze locked on mine. 'What the hell was that?' he asks. 'You had the "I still love her" look all over your face.'

'No, I didn't.' I shake my head. 'It was just the uh, scone, catching me off guard.' I take a big bite to prevent talking myself into a hole.

Maybe I had a bit of a crush on Hollyn in my younger years, but I was twelve. And thirteen, and fourteen, and fifteen... you get it. She doesn't know. I never had the stones to actually tell her, so we were only ever just friends. She couldn't really see past me being her little brother's bestie, and a two-year age difference, when you're in high school, seems a bigger deal than it is. I'm totally over it.

'OK...' he says with a disbelieving laugh. 'Anyway, remember the manther she thinks she loves?'

Manther, the word River calls old guys who date much younger women. Man plus panther. I've learned not to ask questions.

'Ah yes, Professor Twats McGee,' I say with a laugh. 'What was his name? Trinity?'

Riv laughs. 'Close. Tristan Wells.'

'Right.' I knew his name. I'm not a fan. 'Good old Professor Wells, giving private "tutoring" to women half his age and treating a student list like a Tinder profile. Do *not* tell me she's marrying that douche. Your dad will end up in prison.'

Dr Matthews isn't much older than Professor Dickbag. The summer after her junior year of college, she and Tristan spent a week with her parents. Until that week, I'd never seen Dr John drunk *and* pissed. I was honestly a little scared we would end up a part of a news story before the happy couple finally left town.

'She thought he was going to propose; turned out he was, just not to her.'

'What?' I nearly choke on my scone. 'Back up. He proposed to someone *else*? In *front* of her?'

Jesus. I may not know her well anymore, but I know she doesn't deserve that.

'That I don't know. You know how I am with crying women. I may not have heard every word she sobbed through. But I know her flight will be here in an hour, and I have a meeting at the same time that I can't miss. Potential donors for the documentary flew in last night for this presentation. I can't pick her up, and I was hoping you'd do me a solid?'

River's a film guy. He's done a few commercials and a half-dozen music videos. Now he's working on his biggest project yet – a documentary about his mom's life.

'What about your parents?'

Not that I wouldn't love to see Hollyn again. I would. *That's* the problem. It took me a long time to get over her, and it was painful enough that I'd rather not go through it again.

He shoves another piece of bacon into his mouth. 'That part she was clear on. No Mom and Dad until she's had time to process what happened. She and Dad haven't spoken in years, and you know Mom and Hols. They've got this weird thing about Hollyn making poor decisions and never visiting, dropping out of college for a guy, and a list of other stupid shit I couldn't care less about.'

I nod. Penny and Hollyn's relationship has been complicated for as long as I can remember.

'Maybe Mercy could pick her up?' I grab my phone, ready to text her.

'She's in Los Angeles, remember?'

'Right.'

I now remember. Mercy and I do a lot of work together in the wedding world. She's a foul-mouthed,
musical genius who plays multiple instruments and is
hired for nearly every wedding in the city. She didn't
play at the last one I worked because she's currently
touring with a group of classical musicians playing
cathedrals on the west coast.

This isn't leaving me any options. I could order
her an Uber, as could River. But who wants to be wel-
comed home after being gone nearly a decade with a
stranger arriving to pick you up? I can't do that to her.

'I guess I can pick her up, but considering I haven't
seen her in years, don't you think that will be a tad
awkward?'

'If she didn't want awkward, she should have
picked a better week to get dumped.'

'Please tell me you didn't say those words to her?'

I don't have any sisters, but I know a thing or two
about how to talk to women, and that isn't a sentence
that would ever leave my lips.

River's eyes meet mine. 'Not out loud or anything,'
he says, his mouth full. We're beyond manners in our
relationship.

'I don't know how you landed Summer, but may
the force always be with you.' I stand from the

barstool I'm perched on, snatching a piece of bacon from the box he's hoarding.

'Fine. I'll pick her up. Where should I drop her off?'

He suddenly chokes on a sip of coffee. 'Here?'

'*Here?*' I ask. 'As in the couch? Because there are only two beds in this apartment, and they're both slept in nightly. By us.'

'She'll stay in my room. I'll spend a few days with Summer to give her some space. You know how well I do with crying, heartbroken women.'

I blink rapidly, choking out an irritated laugh. 'What am *I* supposed to do?'

'I dunno. Women love you. You'll figure it out.'

'If murder wasn't illegal...' I mumble, lifting my coffee to my lips.

'You might be as tall as a damn tree and have more muscle than me, but I'm faster; you'd never catch me.' He laughs until he registers I'm not thrilled about any of this.

'You're *mad*? For *real*? *Why*? It's Hollyn. The same girl you had on weekly rotation as you Lone-Ranger style romanced yourself through high school.'

'Those words better have never left your lips before or after right this second, or I absolutely will catch you. I was a horny teenager.'

He lets out a belly laugh. 'Yeah, weren't we all.'

'You're kind of putting me in a tough spot here.'

'Why? You aren't seriously still in love with her, are you? I thought you'd moved on. If you haven't, now might be the time.'

I sit on my sectional, resting my head against the back. This is going to be a disaster; I just know it.

'You can get anyone you want. Why would you still have a thing for my sister?'

'I don't still have a thing for her.'

It was a childhood crush. The feelings have completely resolved. I haven't thought about Hols in years. I'm just shocked to know she's coming back. That's all.

'Then pick her up without living out any past fantasies and bring her back here. I'll deal with her as soon as my meeting is over. I'll owe you.'

'You'll owe me alright. You're also going to promise me right now that you'll never tell her about any of this. Or anything else embarrassing about me you have in that man bun-covered head of yours. It was a childhood crush. It's over.'

'You don't like my hair?' he asks, obviously offended, reaching up and touching it.

I shrug.

'Well, la-de-fucking-da. We can't all be as pretty as you.'

He grabs his coffee from the table, swipes a scone from the box on the island, and heads towards the front door.

'Cross your fingers for me. If I don't get the funding, this documentary is dead in the water.'

'How about you cross your fingers for me? The guy who has to go pick up a woman I haven't seen in years after what sounds like the worst night of her life.'

'Done, ya baby.' He flashes crossed fingers over his shoulder as he walks out, then reveals just one finger as he closes the door.

Thank god I never got that actual brother I sometimes wanted. River's enough to deal with.

I tap my phone, checking the time. I've got one hour to get to the airport in rush hour traffic. Perfect. What better way to spend a Sunday morning?

I'm wandering my apartment, gathering my shit, when it hits me. Flowers. Duh. I'm a florist. Flowers fix everything, at least momentarily; this I know.

I head into my room to my makeshift floral storage. I bought six full-size wall coolers in preparation for having a shop of my own one day. Three of them are in my mom's garage, where I have shipments delivered. The other three are filled with flower stems for upcoming weddings and currently live along my bedroom wall.

I scan my stock. I need a friendly flower. Nothing romantic. They've got to say, hey old friend, sorry you've been fucked over by an old dude, but welcome back.

Roses? Too romantic.

Sunflowers? Too big.

Chrysanthemums? Nah.

Daisies? Yes. But not the standards. Gerbera. Mixed colors that will most likely at least make her smile.

As I'm wrapping the bouquet in paper, there's a knock at my door. I grab my keys from the counter and open the door to a face I don't recognize.

'Can I help you?' I ask, stepping onto my porch, holding the flowers under my arm as I lock the place up. 'Gotta make it quick; I'm on my way out.'

'Dax Hartley?'

'In the flesh. Let's walk.'

The woman follows beside me. 'I'm McKenzie Reynolds with *Here Comes the Bride* magazine. Your cousin Brynn gave me your address.'

I stop at the top of the stairs, turning towards her. This is the woman that was at the wedding yesterday. I never got a chance to meet her as after my little performance, it was a race to get the hell out of there before I booked myself in all the bride's friends' and family's upcoming weddings. As the flower boy.

'I was at the Altman wedding yesterday. Let me first say your performance was outstanding. The flowers were beautiful as well.'

A laugh surfaces. My performance, eh? It felt less outstanding and more embarrassing, to be honest.

'Any idea what you want to do with your talent?'

I rub the back of my neck, a little confused by her question. 'What is *be* a florist?' I give the obvious answer *Jeopardy*-style as if it's still a mystery. 'I'm not following.'

'Sorry,' she says. 'I'm here to discuss you competing on *Battle of the Blossoms*.'

'Right,' I say, remembering the vague mention of it. 'I don't know much about it.'

'I'd love to have dinner and discuss.' She bats her long fake eyelashes as she waits for my response.

Is this a business meeting or a date? Knowing Brynn, she's probably combined the two.

'Honestly, I don't even know if I'm interested. This was Brynn's idea as I need cash for a business venture.'

'That's what I was hoping you'd say. I see you're on your way out, but here—' She pulls a business card from her bag, extending it in my direction. 'Call me this week. We'll talk.'

I take her card, staring at it as she jogs down the stairs to a car waiting for her. I suppose it couldn't hurt to talk to her and see what this is all about. I mean, I do need money.

Suddenly, I notice the flowers in my hand.

'Crap, Hollyn.'

I pull my phone from my pocket and check the time. I'll need to fly through traffic to make it on time.

* * *

At the Airport...

I grab the bouquet from the passenger seat. Do I need a sign? Probably not, but what the hell. I wouldn't be me if I didn't embarrass her right off the bat. I rifle around the back seat of my car, grabbing a piece of cardboard from a box I used to hold some flowers I picked up from a vendor last week. I carefully choose my words just in case she truly doesn't recognize me or thinks I'm some weirdo here to kidnap her. For all I know, she looks nothing like she used to. Maybe *I* won't recognize *her*?

I stop just outside the gates, glancing through the arrivals board.

SEA-----Delta-----3758-----8:45-----D9-----Arrived at 8:42

It's eight-fifty now, so she should exit at any time. I unfold the sign and stand off to the side, watching people greet their friends and loved ones. One couple embraces. A woman runs past me to a group of people, all squealing at the sight of her. A few seemingly lonely businesspeople meander by.

'Meeting your wife?'

I glance back at the woman the voice belongs to, only to realize she's speaking to me.

'No. Not my wife. My best friend's sister.'

'Ooh.' The forty-something woman lets out a throaty groan. 'Even better. The brother's best friend. It's only my favorite romance trope.'

'Romance trope?' I ask, having no clue what the hell she's talking about.

'You know, the guy falls for his best friend's sister plot... in movies and books?'

'No. This definitely isn't that. We've never dated. Just doing my friend a solid.'

Her eyes lower to the flowers and sign in my hands. 'You sure about that?'

I glance down nervously. 'Yes. Very sure. I'm a florist; flowers are what I do. She just got dumped, and I have no idea what to say, so I was hoping the flowers could speak for me. Bad idea?'

'Adorable idea. Very best friend's brother tropey.'

She thinks this is *romantic*? I glance down at my sign that is very *not* romantic and probably a little offensive. I turn away from the stranger, trying not to overthink what she's just said. There's probably no way Hollyn will see what she sees. Right?

Stop thinking, Dax.

I focus on the passenger-only hallway in front of me. More families. More business folks. Couples. *Hollyn.*

My heart slows in my chest as I watch her walk my way. Wow. Still beyond beautiful. For a moment, the airport halts to a stop, and only she exists, somehow moving in slow motion and getting prettier with each step.

Fuck. This was a bad idea. My mouth feels suddenly full of sand as I attempt to swallow away the feelings I thought were long gone.

As she walks, she pulls her long wavy, honey blonde hair over one shoulder, tucking the opposite side behind her ear, then adjusts the bag that's literally half her size, hanging off one shoulder.

Hollyn's always been pint-sized. Five-three, five-four, something like that. At nearly six-five, I stand about a foot taller. Besides the oversized sunglasses hiding her eyes, she doesn't look much different than she did the day she graduated high school.

She glances around, probably looking for River. But instead of telling her *I'm* here, I stand glued to the floor, mesmerized by her. How is she still this pretty? The freckles, the dimples, all of it makes me forget I can even speak.

Pull it together, Dax. You're a grown man now. Not the once dorky Dax she used to humor with late-night conversations when you spent the night with her brother.

Finally, I lift the flowers into the air when she's within hearing distance. 'Hollyn.'

4

HOLLYN

On Hollyn's Side of the Airport...

Longest. Night. Ever. The last twelve hours have felt as if they've taken a year to get through. I haven't slept at all, and truthfully, I think I'm still a little drunk from last night. If I'm not careful, the cheesecake will make a comeback.

I walk past the bathroom, wondering if I should stop and freshen up since I haven't seen my brother in a few years. Nah. It's River. He'll understand I've had the day from hell. I pull the prescription sunglasses from the top of my head over my eyes. Contacts weren't even possible this morning after spending the night sobbing into a never-ending glass of champagne. My glasses are buried in my carry-on bag, so these are my only option. It's a blessing, really; they hide my red, swollen eyes.

'Hollyn.'

A guy saying my name stops me in my tracks. *Who is that?* He's got a bundle of colorful daisies raised over his head, and he's waving them in my direction like a flag flying in the wind.

'Most annoying girl I've ever met?' I read the sign in his hand aloud. '*What?*'

The sign reads like River, but unless he's grown significantly and dyed his blond hair dark brown, that's not him. I squint as I stare down the corridor, walking as slowly as possible while figuring out who this is yelling my name.

'Hollyn Matthews,' he calls again, a giant grin on his face.

'Oh, man,' I say under my breath with a sigh full of nerves.

Dark hair, short thick beard, I-work-out-but-not-every-day muscles, taller than nearly everyone around him, and a voice that could melt the panties off every woman in the room.

Damn it, River. You sent Dax?

OK, so it's not ideal considering my current situation, but at least *someone* is here to pick me up. I remember Mercy once mentioning Dax had finally grown up in a way she one day noticed, but I didn't think much about it after that. She wasn't wrong.

Here goes nothing. I plaster on a grateful smile and lift a hand as I exit the passenger-only area.

'Hi,' he says, an awkward grin on his face. He waves his sign my way with a laugh then offers me the flowers in his other hand. 'These are for you.'

He brought me flowers? I can't help but smile. And to think Tristan wouldn't even buy me a single rose last night.

'Thank you,' I say, taking them from him. 'I suppose they make up for the insult.' I glance at the sign he's now folding in half and tossing into a garbage can nearby.

'I thought you'd enjoy that,' he says with a smirk. 'Let me take your bag.' He removes it from my shoulder, throwing the strap over his.

'I should have known River would hand this job off to you.'

Dax shrugs. 'You know River, always doing five things at once.'

'What is it this time? Kidney donation? TikTok

needed his attention? Arrested in a Mexican jail since I talked to him last night?'

He bellows a laugh. 'Donor meeting.'

I raise an eyebrow, more than confused.

'For *money*,' he blurts, 'not organs.' He touches the back of his neck uncomfortably, a shy smile on his face. 'You know, the whole Penny Candy documentary he's working on. He's looking for funding.'

I've been here five minutes, and already there's mention of my mom's alter ego. A name she still goes by even though the eighties have been over for decades. Think Tiffany meets Mariah Carey, and you'll have Penny Candy, the once famous pop star.

'I hardly recognize you,' I say, staring up at him.

How on earth did he grow into this? Is that a bicep? And a tattoo? Wait, I glance at his forearms – *two* tattoos? A single stem rose on the outside of each.

When he notices me inspecting pretty much every inch of him, I glance away. He's precisely the kind of man I'd do a double take at if he walked past me just to admire him from afar. He was nineteen and beyond awkward the last time I saw him. There's not much of that kid left.

I breathe in deeply, smelling something pleasant. Is that *him*? I sniff again. He's wearing cologne? Not the usual I-forgot-my-deodorant smell he and River used to sport. His hair was longish and wavy and now it's short and messy, the braces are off, and the scrawniness seems to have been dropped off at the gym – *jeez, Hols, look away.*

He's no longer the skinny, dorky kid who used to help River terrorize everything I did. This guy is cool, tattooed, bearded, smells nice, looks nicer, *and* brought me flowers. I'd say his dorky days are behind him. Well done, puberty. I applaud you.

'How was your flight?'

'My flight?' I almost forgot I was just on a plane. 'It was fine. Completely void of all the horrific things that go through your head as you board. Thankfully.'

'Good.' He nods. 'You got any baggage?'

'You have no idea,' I say, nervous laughter escaping my lips.

He doesn't get it immediately, but as my grin grows, he catches on. 'Oh.' He laughs. 'I meant *actual* bags in the baggage area. Not piles of internal luggage you'll unpack in my apartment later.'

'I've got both kinds, thank you very much.'

Suddenly he looks uncomfortable. He attempts to hide his shy grin by glancing down at his shoes. That's the Dax I know. He was always unsure of himself.

The two of us follow the overhead signs towards the baggage claim silently. We exchange glances here and there. I think I'm in shock that this is the kid who used to shove me into my parents' pool, fully clothed, every chance he got. Then he'd giggle like a little girl while I tried to chase him down and return the favor.

'We should probably grab a cart,' I suggest, nodding at one a woman has just abandoned. He grabs it, tossing my bag onto it.

Every brand and color of suitcase that exists rolls by on the baggage carousel as we watch. I glance down at the flowers in my hand. Tristan's words come back to me. *Flowers die, Hols. You want me to have death delivered to you, so you feel loved?* Yeah, what a charmer.

'Thanks again for these,' I say, lifting them to my nose. They look as though they should smell of cotton candy and saltwater taffy but nope, nothing. 'I haven't gotten flowers from a guy in years.'

He frowns. 'That's shameful. You should have.'

That makes me smile again. I honestly expected to be standing here dreading every moment of being home, but somehow, I'm not, and I'm pretty sure it's because Dax is the one who picked me up. River would probably already have me in a headlock, attempting to make me miserable as brothers do.

I spot one of my bags out of the corner of my eye. 'There's one!' I run over, pulling it down one-handed.

It lands on its corner, falling over and nearly taking me out with it.

Dax is quick as he reaches around me, steadying me with one hand and grabbing the bag with the other. He stacks it on the cart, moving my carry-on bag on top of it, taking the flowers from me, and setting them on top.

Another of my bags rolls by. I pull it off the conveyor belt with both hands, but Dax again takes over, stacking it on the cart with the others.

'I'm sorry to hear you and the professor called it quits.'

His voice is somehow soothing. Everything he says seems effortless. Cool. Controlled. Even a bit suave. I could listen to him read the phone book.

'*He* called it quits, and here I am. Really, it's probably for the best. Things hadn't been great for a while. I'm sure after I drown myself in sappy romance movies, sparkling wine, chocolate, and all the anxiety-ridden overthinking one can do, I'll see it was never meant to be.'

Dax nods, obviously a tad uncomfortable with the topic of conversation. I get it. I've been uneasy since I left the restaurant last night.

My last bag rounds the bend of the carousel, so to save him from listening to my heartache, I point. It's my biggest bag and closer to him. He grabs it one-handed, stacking it on the cart with the others. I could barely lift that one with two hands, and he just man-handled it like it was full of feathers.

'Is that it?'

'Everything else will be shipped to my parents next week. Right after they find out I'm here, I hope.'

'So, you're here for *good*,' he says, pushing the cart towards the exit.

'Wasn't what I'd planned, but it looks that way.'

'Well,' he says, glancing down at me with a shy grin. 'At least you look good, right?' He stops at the au-tomatic doors, motioning for me to exit first.

He's even a gentleman? Things *have* changed.

'You're a liar, but I appreciate it.'

'It's not a lie. You do look good.' He pushes the cart through the doors behind me. 'You've hardly changed at all. How'd you manage that?'

'Exactly,' I say. 'I've stayed the same, and you've done an impressive one-eighty.'

A grin grows on his face, and once again, he glances at the ground below him as if I've embar-rassed him.

Suddenly, his phone rings from his pocket. 'Hang on.' He answers it. 'Now, what'd you do?'

No hello. It must be River. I stand on the sidewalk

next to him, waiting out his phone call and breathing in the Oregon air. It's drier than the air in Seattle. The whole place feels lighter.

'Sorry,' he says. 'Brynn, my cousin, entered me into some reality competition, and they like me!' He acts surprised.

'What, are you the next *Bachelor*?' I joke, but I can picture it, and I shouldn't.

He bursts out a laugh. '*The Bachelor* is still on? Jesus, I thought for sure that'd be played out by now. No. *Battle of the Blossoms*. A floral competition put on by *Here Comes the Bride* magazine.' He lifts his shoulders, his lips pressed into a straight line. 'That's all I know about it. Not sure I'll be signing on the dotted line yet.'

'Floral competition? Really?' I didn't see that coming. 'You mean you didn't buy these at Safeway on your way here?' I grab the bouquet from the cart, once again lifting them to my nose only to realize they still have no scent. God missed an opportunity there.

His face drops to stone-cold serious. 'I went out early this morning, hiked the canyons, and picked those stem by stem just for you.' A grin slowly grows on his face as he watches my reaction to his blatant lie.

I bite my lips together to stop the ridiculous smile

I can feel trying to take over. Yep, he's definitely *The Bachelor* material.

Dax winks, and my grin turns into an awkward laugh.

'Sorry,' I say. 'I just—River never told me, and I hadn't imagined you taking over your dad's business in a million years. You were always mister sports star. Baseball, basketball, swimming. I assumed you'd go pro. And if that didn't work out, I thought for sure astronaut.'

He laughs to himself. His cheeks reddening by the second as I talk about his past life is probably the most adorable thing I've ever seen. Here is this gorgeous sweetheart of a man who used to regularly freeze my bras when he'd stay the night with my brother, seemingly embarrassed to hear me talk about him in the way I am.

'Meeting you now, in the ten minutes I've known you again...' I shrug, glancing down at the daisies in my hand. 'Florist seems to fit this Dax.'

'Trust me, I never saw it coming either. Kinda hit me out of the blue one day, and I ran with it.' He pushes the cart across the road into the parking garage. 'How about you?' he asks. 'What are you up to these days? It seems like there was something you wanted to do when you were young. What was it?'

I spent the plane ride overthinking, coming up with answers for the questions I'm sure are headed my way. None of which I ended up with actual answers for. At least nothing that sounds like I have my life together and didn't give it all up for some stupid boy and the idea of love at first sight.

Eight years as a 'professional' server, now in-between jobs, doesn't sound as impressive as it did two bottles of champagne in.

Like an idiot, I made Tristan my entire world from the moment we met, and I didn't think through what might happen if he destroyed it. Now that it's imploded, I realize I have no idea who I am, no plan, no job, no skills, only every one of his left shoes.

Yes, I stole all his left shoes and tossed every roll of toilet paper into the dumpster before I left. I had to do something, and it was the only way I could think to dampen his coming days. It brings me great joy to think of him on the toilet, no toilet paper in sight, and no left shoes to run to the store in. A minor setback that I'm sure he'll blow by as though I never existed.

'I wanted to professionally fangirl Justin Timberlake.'

Dax drops his head with a laugh. 'That sounds right.'

'Probably would have done more for me than

what I actually did. I didn't even graduate college. Dropped out with nine months left to go, so I don't have more than a high school diploma. I'm sure I'll end up back at Mom's record shop like when I was eighteen. She'll be so proud.' Disappointment hangs in my voice as I attempt to shrug it away.

Dax frowns as he clicks a button on his keys, his car coming to life and the back hatch opening without him even touching it.

'I'm sure she'll be happy to have you back despite all that.'

'We'll soon find out.'

He shoves a bag over the back seat, so there's room for everything. He piles the rest into his trunk, barely able to close it once it's all been loaded.

'Let's get you back to the apartment. If I'm reading you right, you've got some self-loathing and man-hating to start on.' He winks, a sly grin on his face as he slides into the driver's seat.

I don't know how the next few weeks will go down, but there isn't an ounce of me looking forward to any of it. Even though Dax has made me smile more than I expected, there's still the lingering issue of starting my life over at twenty-nine. I don't even know where to begin.

5

DAX

Five Days Later...

I called the woman from the magazine. McKenzie. I need the money, and the only other way I have of getting it would offend my mother.

We're at a steakhouse in downtown Portland having a meeting so she can sweet talk me into partaking in this competition. Little does she know this forty-dollar steak is helping already.

'Let's talk about your audition,' she says.

I stop, my fork full of mashed potatoes midway to my mouth. 'My audition?'

Considering I know exactly nothing about an audition, I can only assume Brynn had a hand in this part. McKenzie slides an iPad to the center of the table, pressing play on a video she's loaded.

'Watching it live was so much better.'

Oh no. I glance up at her, then back at the video playing. No, no, no. She recorded this? Shit. I laugh nervously to myself or maybe *at* myself. There I am in all my glory, throwing rose petals and dancing my ass down the aisle of the Altman wedding last weekend.

'You've proven to be quite popular on the website.'

'It's on your website?' I nearly drop my fork.

'Of course. Viewers have already voted you as favorite potential contestant. We had many submissions and had to find a way to narrow it down from twenty-five to five. Honestly, I knew you'd make it the moment you stepped into that aisle. It was perfect,' she says with a chef's kiss. 'The flower wall, the flower boy, the essay has all—'

'The *essay*?' I interrupt her, now confused.

'Brynn sent in an essay as your application weeks ago and your story really moved us. When it came time to pick our top twenty-five, you were in my top two.'

Brynn. I sit my fork on the edge of my plate, rubbing the back of my neck.

They were moved by my story? I don't even have a story. I'm just a regular guy struggling every day to keep his business going. What the hell did she tell them?

'I uh...' I pause, suddenly nervous. 'I'm confused. You're talking about things I didn't even know existed. Truthfully, I'm not even sure I want to do this. I'm already booked through the entire summer.'

'Completely understand,' she says, grabbing her wine glass. 'Let me explain the basics of the show.'

'It's a TV show?'

'YouTube. Online is now more popular than traditional television according to many surveys.'

I had no idea.

'Listen, I get that you're busy. We intentionally chose wedding season because this isn't the kind of reality show where you're sequestered for months until it airs. We're trying a new format. You'll compete right from your hometown for five weeks against five other florists with weddings you've already booked. We cover the cost of everything, even what the couples would owe you for your services, so you won't be losing money. Not only does this help get them on board for changes, but it encourages them to allow us to film. Free wedding flowers.' She cocks her head.

'What engaged couple could refuse that? More honey-moon money.' She laughs as if the idea is genius.

'These are your actual clients and your business name on the line; we respect that, Dax. We also understand wedding orders take time to create so we won't disrupt that. We'll only be judging you on one centerpiece, per wedding, that you'll have three hours to create on-site.'

'*Three* hours?'

The Altman flower wall took me over four hours to build and I have a feeling to compete against other talented florists, I'll need more than flower walls.

'That's the catch. Some of these creations are time-consuming and difficult to manage on your own in a short period. We get that. Which is why you'll choose *one* assistant. Someone from your life who has no experience in the industry. Show us how you manage someone else because, should you win, we're investing in your business with a fifty-thousand-dollar prize.'

An assistant without floral experience? Not exactly helpful and probably more of a hindrance than anything else. How am I supposed to train someone on the job while competing?

'Ian, a cameraman, will follow you around while

you work. Those clips will be part of the show. Every other week, at the end of each challenge, we'll talk about your designs, and on Sundays, you and your assistant will fly to another contestant's hometown for judging from a pro. Our judge, Jillian Winston, is one of the most well-known wedding florists in the industry. She'll give her advice based on the videos Ian takes while you create these arrangements. Episodes are uploaded Monday evenings, which will include you and your assistant at the wedding, Jillian's thoughts and her predictions on top and bottom two. Viewers will have seventy-two hours to vote for their favorite florist, *American Idol*-style. A contestant team can be in Jillian's predicted top two and still be voted off by fans so don't get comfortable. Jillian will announce the viewer voting results live with a short show recap every Friday.'

I'm staring across the table at her with a single eyebrow raised, trying to process everything she's just said.

'Basically, you create floral masterpieces for your weddings like you always would, we film it, you and your assistant fly to another contestant's hometown to meet with Jillian, she discusses your arrangements by video in front of you, the other contestants, and the cameras. She'll then have a word with each of you, give advice, tips, then predict her top two and bottom two. After that it's up to how much the fans like you as to whether you stay or go.'

'This is a lot.'

'It seems overwhelming, but you're just competing for a cash prize that we expect you to invest back into your business. Brynn tells me you're hoping to buy back your father's old floral shop?'

'Yeah.'

What didn't Brynn tell them? I drag a hand down my face as I think this through as quickly as possible.

'Let's say I decide to do this. How long would all this take, from start to win?'

'Should you win, I'd think we could have a check to you just after the finale.'

We're in the first week of April. That means I could own my dad's shop by June if things go my way.

'Any idea who you'd choose as your assistant?'

'Most of my friends would probably offend your audience,' I say with a laugh. 'So, no.' I grab my beer, taking a long sip. 'You really think I've got a chance at winning this?'

She grins. 'I wouldn't be here if I didn't.'

Weeks of challenges. Risking my reputation if I

lose. The clients I've earned will have to put their faith in me that I don't screw up their vision of the most important day of their life so I can attempt to grasp at my dreams. That's a lot of pressure.

I cut into my steak. I can feel McKenzie's stare boring through me as I dip a hunk of meat into the lake of A.1. Sauce on my plate. I have to do this. If there were another option, I'd take it. But at this point, unless I'm prepared to do Kevin some kind of favor, I've got nothing.

'What do I need to sign?'

* * *

Back at Dax's Apartment that Night...

'Hey,' I say when Hollyn walks out of River's bedroom.

Besides occasionally hearing her in there crying, I hardly know she's here. I haven't worked up the nerve to knock and make sure she's OK. I figured if I could hear her, she's at least alive. I'm entirely out of my comfort zone in this situation, and River seems to have dropped off the face of the planet.

'Oh.' She stops suddenly at the sight of me, surprise on her face. 'Hi. I thought you were gone for the evening?'

'Nope. It's a wild Friday night for me.'

'What are you playing?' she asks, walking to me, glancing at the game controller in my hands.

'*Madden.*'

She grins. 'Still a gamer, eh?'

'You can take the boy out of childhood...' I say with a wink, pausing my game.

'Riv said you like to entertain the ladies. I figured you were out doing that, so I ordered food.'

'He said that did he?'

Fucker. Why he continues to tell her my business, I don't know. He's hardly even talking to me right now since he's too caught up in being Summer's new temporary live-in boyfriend while avoiding his broken-hearted sister.

'River likes to act like I'm the town madam, but I swear, I'm not charming the panties off ladies any more than he is.'

She laughs, biting her bottom lip in a way that makes me wish I wasn't going commando under these sweats. I suddenly feel naked in public.

'Way more info than I need,' she says with a chuckle. 'Do you like Chinese food? Cause I probably ordered enough if you want some.'

'I don't know if you remember this, but I used to eat dinner at my house and then come to yours and do the same.' I shrug. 'I can always eat.'

'And that's why you're seven feet tall?'

I laugh. 'Six four,' I correct her. 'And a half.'

The smirk on her pretty face pokes at the old feelings I'm trying to avoid. If I pretend they aren't surfacing again, maybe they'll go away?

'Sorry,' she says, rolling her eyes playfully.

As she stares at the game I'm once again attempting to play, my eyes wander. Her hair is piled on her head in a messy bun. She's wearing black-framed glasses, and not a stitch of make-up is on her face.

'*What* are you wearing?' I ask, pointing at the colorful leopard print blanket with sleeves she's got wrapped around her like a robe.

She glances down, scrunching her nose. 'A Snuggy.' She pulls it tight around her. 'Lame, but comforting.'

I nod, my eyebrows raised as I acknowledge her insanity. She has a blanky? I'm gonna bank that info for later.

'The mourning is going well?'

'Ugh.' She blows out a heavy breath. 'Tristan is an asshole. My best friend since college has disappeared for whatever reason. And I'm spending half my time feeling bad that I haven't once offered to pay you for eating your food and taking over your Netflix account.'

'If it weren't you, it'd be your brother.'

I look back at the TV, focusing on my game, if only to get my eyes off her.

She sits down not far from me, adjusting herself until comfortable. Yes, my eyes are on my game, but I'm struggling to play even remotely as well as I would if she wasn't here. Usually, right about now, when I suck this bad, I'd be yelling at the TV as if it was its fault, but her Snuggy has ridden up above her waist, and now her tiny shorts are burning a hole in my brain.

'You suck at this,' she says.

I laugh out loud, tossing the controller her way.

'Give it a go,' I say, standing from the couch and heading into the kitchen if for nothing else but to stand behind the open fridge door to cool off the hormones she's sent sizzling through me.

'When's Mercy back in town?'

She looks up, her eyes suddenly wide. 'I'm disturbing you.' She sets the controller on the couch and gets up, heading back to River's room. 'Sorry.'

'No!' I half yell, surprising even myself. I shut the

fridge, hurrying around the island towards her. 'That's not what I meant. I just... uh—'

'It's alright,' she says. 'I know I'm imposing on your life. I bet River never even told you I was staying here before I arrived.'

I shrug.

She nods. 'I thought so. It's fine. I'm supposed to call Tristan back anyway.'

Call Tristan? Why?

'Hols,' I say, wondering if I should say this as it's not my place. If River were here, I'd suggest he do it. But he's a pussy, hiding out with Summer, leaving me to deal with this.

'Maybe you shouldn't be talking to Tristan? He can't be easy to get over when he's still in the picture.'

Her face drops, her shoulders following, and things go from awkward to worse when she starts to cry.

I'm going to kill River.

'I'm sorry,' I say. 'I didn't mean to—' I reach out to her, but she steps away quickly.

'No,' she says, cutting me off in a shaky voice. 'You're right. I shouldn't be. I don't know how to get over it. Clearly, I'm an idiot. Can you just put my food in the fridge when it gets here?' She snorts back another cry, wiping her eyes with the corner of the

Snuggy as she walks back into River's room, closing the door behind her.

'Sure,' I say a full ten seconds after she's closed the door. 'Smooth, Dax,' I tell myself as I walk back to the couch. Here I thought I was good with women.

6

HOLLYN

Four Days Later...

River sits next to where I'm lying on the couch, pulling my Snuggy from me, revealing a salsa-stained tank top underneath as I stare at the TV.

'Go take a shower, ya slob. You're scaring Dax.'

'What?' I sit up, glancing across the room at Dax standing in the kitchen as though he's intentionally avoiding me. 'I'm scaring you?'

River's room got too depressing, so I moved into the living room a few days ago. I've now taken over the couch, TV, and pretty much the entire apartment. Dax hasn't been around much, so I figured it was OK. Has he just been avoiding me?

'Scared is a strong word,' Dax says. 'Worried seems more fitting.'

Yesterday, he brought me tacos and tequila and suggested I drink away my feelings. It was the first time we'd really hung out, and considering we both laughed, I thought everything was cool between us.

I glance to the coffee table where the still-open bottle sits. I didn't even use a glass. Jesus. How did I let this break-up spiral so far out of control? Oh, that's right. When I realized *Victoria* was the other woman. My so-called friend. I don't know for sure, but she's blocked me on social media, which doesn't scream innocence.

'I worried you?' I ask, blowing hair that's escaped my bun from my face.

'Damn girl,' River gawks. 'Your breath is rank. What *is* that?' He covers his nose and mouth with his hand, glancing around the room, his gaze landing on the tequila bottle.

'*Tequila?*' He lifts the bottle. 'I haven't drunk tequila since that time it tried to kill me. Where the hell did you get this?'

I glance at Dax, who raises a guilty hand slowly.

'Sorry,' he says, an oops-I-did-it-again grin on

half his face. 'In my defense, Mercy suggested it. Obviously, I never should have listened to her. I thought maybe it would take the edge off and cheer Hols up. I didn't expect our girl here to just pop the top and drink it right from the bottle.' He cocks his head, but instead of looking mad, he seems impressed.

River glares. 'No more booze,' he says sternly.

'OK, *Dad.*'

Dax laughs under his breath, stifling it when River shoots him a glare.

'Get your ass in that bathroom and do something about all this, or I'm calling Mom and telling her you're here.' Riv pulls his phone from his pocket, tapping the screen and flashing Mom's contact photo at me.

'No!' I jump from the couch. 'Not, Mom. OK, I'm over it.'

I can barely deal with myself right now. I'm not ready for Mom yet.

'Over smelling like a men's locker room?'

'Over *Tristan*,' I correct him.

'After eight years, you've mourned for a week and a half, drank part of a bottle of tequila, and suddenly you're over him. Somehow, I doubt that. You smell like garbage, woman. Take a shower. Dax and I have reputations to uphold, and you're dragging us down with your self-loathing bullshit.'

Well, this isn't at all embarrassing. Having Dax call my brother and rat me out. Jeesh. He could have just told me I smelled like garbage himself.

Twenty minutes later, I'm out of the shower, sitting on the toilet, a towel wrapped around my chest as I slather lotion onto my skin. I can hear the two of them talking in the other room.

'I think you should tell your parents,' Dax says.

River shushes him.

I shove my ear against the door to hear them better.

'I already did,' Riv says, his voice now lowered.

Dang it, Riv.

'She doesn't know yet, but we're going out tonight. All of us,' River continues.

No, we're not.

'How exactly are you going to convince her of that?' Dax asks.

'I called help. Mercy's back in town, and Hols would never say no to her.'

He really thinks he's got this all thought out, doesn't he? Like he's somehow got the upper hand.

Dax laughs. 'That'll go over like a lead balloon.'

At least *someone* knows me. *How* are these walls

this thin? I wonder what they pay for this place. It can't be much.

'I have a plan,' River says. 'I'll get her to Mom and Dad's after, and Mom will have her set up in her old room before I can even ask. *Voila!* I'm sleeping in my bed again, and our apartment no longer smells like BO. You're welcome.'

'Thank you?' Dax asks in an unmistakably skeptical tone. 'I don't know, Riv,' he says. 'I don't think she's going that easily.'

'Or maybe you don't want her to go?' River asks. 'This entire scenario is like your teenage wet dreams come true.'

'*What?*' I ask myself out loud, forgetting that they can likely hear me if I can hear them.

The two of them go silent. Suddenly, the fridge ice maker starts grinding away.

'Your childhood...' River fades out, the sound of them moving around the kitchen making noise interrupting his words. 'Sleeping in the next room, a thin wall being all that separates you.'

For a second, all goes silent again, and I almost think they've left the apartment.

'If you don't shut it, I'll wrap this towel around your neck and—' Dax growls, his voice loud enough to make out every word.

I swing open the bathroom door, hoping to prevent River's murder.

Both of their heads snap my way.

'Everything cool out here? I thought I heard something going on...' I walk down the hall, towel still wrapped around my chest and barely long enough to cover my upper thighs. I stop in front of River's door.

'Yeah,' Dax says nonchalantly. 'We're cool.'

River nods. 'We cool.' He says the words in a tone of voice I haven't heard in a while but know well. The we're-up-to-no-good tone. Maybe staying here wasn't the best idea. I forgot what these two are like together.

'What are you doing?' River asks Dax, whose eyes flitter from me to River quickly.

'*What?*' Dax asks. 'Nothing.'

Dax looks back at me, an eyebrow raised, an uncomfortable smile on his face. '*Ow,*' he says suddenly, looking at River.

I glance at River, who lifts a shoulder as if he has no idea what his problem is.

'You two are weirdos.'

'I gotta go,' Dax says suddenly, grabbing his keys from the counter and practically running through the front door, slamming it behind him.

'What was that about?'

River shakes his head, waving a hand towards the door. 'Just Dax being Dax.'

'I meant *you*. I could hear you two talking.'

'You *could*?' He tosses his head back as though he's shocked. 'Then it's not new news when I tell you we're going to see Mercy perform tonight.'

'No, it's not *new* news,' I snap.

Of course, the whispering between him and Dax that I couldn't quite make out *is* new news I'd love to know. But I'll save my questions until later.

'And no Mom and Dad, Riv. You promised.'

He fills his cheeks with air, blowing it out slowly. 'That's gonna be a problem. They never miss Mercy's shows. She's like the daughter they never had.'

I roll my eyes, now heading into his room. 'They *have* a daughter, buttface. They just preferred Mercy.'

'Oh, come on. Don't be all jelly; they loved you too.' He leans against his door frame, his arms crossed over his chest and wearing a stupid smug smile I wanna smack.

Mercy is the musical daughter our parents always wanted and they've always been her biggest fans.

'Fine,' I huff. 'I could never deny her their support. But no more shenanigans.'

'I can't promise no shenanigans, Hols. It's practically my middle name. Now get dressed and look respectable. I may want to pawn you off on someone for the night, so I can sleep in my own bed.'

I laugh. 'Your sister doesn't do one-night stands, so don't even try it,' I say, closing his door in his face.

If he thinks I'm going to do whatever he's got planned, he's forgotten who he's dealing with.

* * *

Later that Night at a Downtown Bar...

'This is exciting,' Summer, River's girlfriend, says from across the table. 'I've never seen her perform.'

'She's amazing.'

The two of us stare at one another across the table, unsure of what to say since this is our first meeting.

'How long have you and River been together?'

'Two months. He's such a sweetheart.' She swoons in a way I've never seen a woman do over River.

'*Really?*'

River, a sweetheart? There's something I never thought I'd hear. He's the guy who will take a photo then laugh before telling you your skirt is tucked into your underwear.

'Yeah. I really like him.'

'That's great. *Someone* should,' I say behind a hand as River walks up. Summer laughs.

'What's so funny, girls?' he asks, sitting three drinks on the table.

'Just you.'

'Believe nothing she told ya,' he says to Summer as he sits next to her, draping an arm over her shoulders. 'She's a big liar who lies.'

'Mature,' I say, grabbing my drink. 'What's this?' I hold up the fruity-looking drink, inspecting it as if I could tell what's in it based on looks alone.

'*That* is called a 1-900-FUK-MEUP.' He laughs. 'It reminded me of you.'

I drop my head towards the table. Brothers are just fantastic. God couldn't give daisies a proper scent, but he approved little brothers.

'Hey, I have like, one minute.' Mercy is suddenly at our table, yanking me from my chair and hugging me like I've just come home from war. 'Do *not* leave here without me. Got it?'

'I would never,' I say in return.

Mercy and I met in the first grade. She was the kid always by herself, eating a PB&J sandwich with milk made specially by the lunch lady for kids whose lunch tabs were never paid. My heart couldn't take it, so I asked my mom to make an extra daily lunch for my new friend. When you're six, anyone who has anything in common with you becomes your best friend. At that time, we had lunch in common. It became so much more than lunch over the years, though. She's my chosen family.

Tonight, she's playing with her ex and business partner, Dylan Santiago, in their classical cover band, Violated. She's a musical prodigy who plays five instruments as though she was born doing it. Violin, cello, guitar, ukulele, and piano. She grew up in foster care from a young age. Her first foster home was with a college music professor who got her started on violin. She fell right into it, spending every moment she had in the band room perfecting whatever song she was learning. Honestly, she shocks the pants right off anyone who hears her perform. She's mesmerizing.

She looks the part of a sweet and innocent classical musician but has the mouth of a girl running a wild outlaw biker gang. I've always said she puts the ass in classical, and she's never disagreed.

'Hello, Portland!' An employee of the bar is standing on stage, stringed instruments on stands behind him. 'Tonight's talent was well requested. Please welcome Violated to the stage!' The room applauses.

'Sorry we're late.'

The hair on my neck stands when I hear her voice. She's my mom so of course I'd know her voice anywhere. The fact that it immediately makes me disappointed in myself isn't completely her problem.

'There she is!' She pulls a chair to my side. 'My baby girl!'

'Hi?' I say uncomfortably.

'Give me a hug, Hols.' She doesn't wait and wraps her arms around my shoulders, squeezing me within an inch of my life. A few people stare, obviously knowing exactly who she is since she's well known by the locals. I've always been glad we lived miles outside the city because of it.

'Look at me,' she demands, touching my chin like she did when I was a kid, forcing me to look at her and listen.

We share the same pale skin, blue eyes, and freckles. Even our hair color is the same, but hers is shoulder-length, curly like River's, and currently filled with dark pink, blue, and purple streaks. She's wearing giant silver hoop earrings, and her colorful outfit and make-up look nothing like any of the other fifty-something-year-old women in the room. She doesn't look a day over thirty-five, and she doesn't act a day over twenty-five.

'Tristan is a dick,' she says. 'Just a big ol' capital D

followed by an ick. An absolute wanker of a guy that you are too good for. Got it?'

I nod, a shy smile emerging on my face. Maybe I missed her a little.

'Thanks. Can we not talk about him tonight? I'm trying to move past it.'

She lifts both hands to shoulder level as if the police have asked her to. 'Perfectly fine. His name won't leave my lips again.'

I don't believe that for a second.

'We're here to see our girl perform.' She claps loudly as the rest of the room settles. 'Woo-*hoo!*' she bellows, then whistles the same obnoxious two-fingered whistle she'd use to call River and me home for dinner with as kids.

Mercy's now laughing to herself. She probably can't see us with the lights, but she knows exactly whose woo-hoo that was. I'm sure of it.

After a few silent moments of her and Dylan getting into position, the notes of Billie Eilish's 'Bad Guy' fill the room. Dirty song for the first choice, but I would have been surprised if Mercy hadn't gone for a shock value right from the go. That's who she is.

The grin on my face couldn't be more enormous as she plays. She makes it look so easy. I tried it once;

it wasn't. I haven't seen her perform live in forever, and I suddenly feel bad about that.

On my list of people to apologize to are my parents, River, Dax – after this afternoon – and now Mercy. I've left her behind for way too long.

As soon as her instrument is back on the stand when their set is over, she hops off the stage and beelines right to me.

She's four inches taller than my five-three, and gorgeous. Big green eyes, lightly tanned skin, shoulder-length straight dark hair, and the curves every woman wishes she had. She ended up precisely the woman we both wanted to be as little girls.

'You were outstanding!'

'Why, thank you, darling,' she says. 'Maybe I'll let ya buy me a drink.'

'I don't think that'll be a problem.' I link my arm through hers and lead the way to the bar.

'Hello, handsome,' she says in a seductive voice to the bartender. 'A tuaca sidecar, *extra* cherries.' She holds two fingers in the air.

He rolls his eyes, a half-cocked grin on his face that says he enjoyed her flirting.

'Anyway,' she continues, not acknowledging what I just witnessed. 'We sold out. As soon as the venues were announced, tickets lasted ten minutes. I can hardly believe it.'

'I can. You're a rock star!'

'Hardly.'

'How're things with Dylan? Is it weird to be broken up and still working together?'

She shakes her head. 'Dylan and I were never right together. He always wanted to "fix" me. Why did you never tell me how annoying that is?'

I frown. I would have, trust me – that's the kind of friendship we have – but I never actually knew Dylan. Tonight is the first time I've ever seen him in person, and he didn't exactly run over to meet me.

'Because I'm a terrible self-centered friend who chose a man over the people I'm closest to for nearly a decade.'

'Stop,' she says, her eyes on the bartender.

'I'm serious,' I say, taking a sip of the drink I'm still nursing because it's way stronger than I expected. 'I owe you so many apologies. I've been a jerk. Worse than that, actually. What's worse?'

Mercy cocks her head, a sly smile growing. 'I believe the words you're looking for are Professor Tristan Wells.'

I laugh to myself. She's not wrong.

'We all do stupid shit, Hols. Me included.' She

stops, choosing her words slowly. 'For instance, the guy that just made my drink, we, uh, banged one out in the bathroom last week, and I told him to pretend like it never happened. Cause it never will again. It's not personal, just business. I had needs, and he was there. What the hell, right?'

'*Mercy!*'

She shrugs. 'When you start noticing the new Jake from State Farm in a way you wish you didn't, you know it's time to find a real man to take care of things. The boy got lucky.'

I whip my head around to take a second look at him. He's cute. I don't know why she'd cut him off already. But that's Mercy. She doesn't do 'love'.

'You little minx,' I joke.

'Icky Vicki was never this much fun, was she?'

'Not even a little bit.'

'Now tell me how you're doing. Like *really* doing?'

I take a giant breath, blowing it out slowly. 'Honestly, I don't know. One moment I'm fine; the next, I'm in a ball of tears wishing the floor would swallow me whole. There were so many red flags I ignored, Merc. *So many*. What's wrong with me?'

'Nothing's wrong with you.'

I scrunch my face at the sound of her voice before finally turning to my mother. I kind of thought she'd work the room, somehow finding her fans everywhere she goes like she always has. But, nope, here she is joining us at the bar.

'You simply picked the wrong guy,' Mom continues, taking my drink and helping herself to a sip. A big sip. 'It happens. I slept with my first agent when I was sixteen – a total felony on his part. But it felt like something I needed to do to get to the place I thought I wanted to be. The sex was fine.' Mom scrunches her nose the same way I do when displeased. 'But fine doesn't last a lifetime. Take my advice and find the guy who can piss you off, then rock your world after. That's where the good sex lives.'

I glance around the room, looking for a garbage can I can puke in. Mercy raises a single eyebrow, a crooked grin on her face. She enjoys my mother's mouth far more than I ever have.

'If I had to guess,' Mom continues as if I'm not wishing I could burst my own eardrums right now. 'You and Tristan's love life was just fine?'

She wants to talk about my sex life?

'Maybe...' I finally say.

'I knew it. You need passion, Hols. Someone who makes your toes curl, your panties wet, and your heart melt.'

'Oh, god,' I groan to myself, dropping my head

into my hands as Mercy laughs next to me. 'Please stop talking.'

Welcome to my childhood full of embarrassment, oversharing, and zero inhibitions.

'She's not wrong,' Mercy says. 'You got caught up in a moment that should have lasted eight minutes, *not* eight years. It happens.'

'Has it ever happened to you?'

Mercy laughs. 'Well, no. Mostly because I don't do long-term relationships. For good reason. That being: most men are just boys in overgrown bodies. *Men* are far and few between. It's like finding a particular feather in a heap of nearly identical feathers.'

Mom laughs, nodding as though she gets it.

'I don't even think Tristan ever lasted eight minutes,' I say mostly to myself.

At one time, the sex was good but, looking back, that feels like forever ago.

'See,' Mom says. 'Lesson learned. Time to move onto bigger, better, and *younger* things.'

'Hello, Hollyn.' Dad stops in front of me, giving me a once over, then a quick hug – the kind you'd give a distant family relative you don't know well.

I was beginning to think he'd never say hello as he's been sitting at the table chatting with River, pretending I don't exist since he got here. He's been mad at me for a long time, and if I had to guess, once he finds out I've lost my trust fund I'd say he'll stay mad for a long time to come.

'Hi, Dad.'

No response, just a polite smile.

'Did you tell her yet?'

'No, John, I haven't told her yet,' Mom says.

'We don't have all night. We're meeting Jim and Deborah for drinks in twenty.'

'Fine.' Mom turns to me, handing my drink back. She looks at me with a frown.

'Sweetheart, we've turned your room into a recording studio. Mommy is making a comeback.' She beams. 'River mentioned you need a place to stay. Unfortunately, we've decided you staying with us isn't the best idea.'

'Nor is you working at the shop,' Dad adds.

Mom gently touches his chest – her cue for him to shut up and let her handle this. 'We love you, *of course* we love you. We're your parents. But it's been hard for us to watch your life from a distance while you had no interest in making us a part of it. So, since you're nearly thirty, it's only fair for you to make this transition back home on your own.'

I glance between the two of them. I'm not sure what I thought they'd say, but I'm sure this isn't what

River expected. Yeah, we have our problems, but them turning their back on me never crossed my mind.

'I deserved that.'

Mercy, sweet friend that she is, laces her fingers through mine and squeezes my hand.

'I don't expect you guys to fix this for me. I made the decisions to get into this hole, and I'll figure out how to get myself out. For the record, though, I am sorry I've been such an awful daughter.'

Mom nods her head, acknowledging my apology as Dad pulls her towards the exit by her hand. And just like that, they walk out the front door without so much as a goodbye.

'Well, I didn't see that coming,' River says, now standing where Mom had been.

'What do I do now? I'm sure I've overstayed my welcome with Dax. The guy's afraid of me.'

'Dax is *afraid* of you?' Mercy asks, clearly confused. 'Giant, muscly Dax fears tiny, petite you?'

'In his defense, she stunk. *Badly*,' River says, a matter-of-fact look on his face. 'Like *bad*, badly.'

Mercy raises both eyebrows, looking at me questioningly.

'It's a story I don't want to get into right now, because... humiliation.'

'Dax is the nicest guy,' Summer says, interrupting

the tension of Mercy silently looking for an explanation to all this. 'I'm sure he won't mind you staying a little longer.'

I look to River. He shrugs. 'Can't hurt to talk to him.'

'Sure, I'll talk to him. I can move into a hotel for a while if nothing else.'

I can't depend on my friends and family forever. I'm an adult. And sometimes adults have to figure their crap out on their own. Especially when they've left everyone behind for so long.

7

DAX

Later That Night...

What in the hell is that? I open the glass shower door to figure out what I'm hearing. The walls in this building are so thin I've followed conversations between the neighbors downstairs for months. It's not going well for them.

The shrieking continues, so I turn off the water and hop out, wrapping a towel around my waist before throwing open the bathroom door.

'Hollyn?' I see only her back as I walk out. I

thought she was going to her parents' house after Mercy's show tonight?

'Dax!' Sydney, a woman I have a friends-with-benefits situation with, is backed against the front door, holding a handful of long stem roses I had in a bucket of water, swinging them like a sword in Hollyn's direction.

'This nutjob woman came after me with a lightsaber!' Sydney yells. 'Who even has a lightsaber?'

That'd be River. He owns many. I glance at Hollyn, who's now looking between Sydney, and me, confused, as she holds her hostage with a blue lit-up lightsaber, now making fight noises with each swing.

'I may have more than a few trust issues, but I'm *not* a nutjob,' Hollyn says to Sydney defensively, swinging again. 'I'm just a woman who doesn't want to be murdered!'

For a second, the scene in front of me is so confusing all I can do is listen as I catch up.

'You thought a *toy* would keep you from being murdered?' Sydney hollers back, jumping onto my sectional, swinging the roses at Hollyn, petals flying across the room, hitting me in the chest.

'A toy sword versus flowers; yeah, I'm good,' Hols says.

I brush petals from my shoulder, starting to laugh as Hollyn looks my way.

'Wait,' she says. 'You *know* her?'

I nod, grabbing the lightsaber lifted over her head. It blasts sounds of a battle from its internal speaker as I lob it onto the couch, pointing at the flowers Sydney is holding. She tosses them onto the ottoman, stepping off my couch as she does.

'I invited her here, Hols. This is Sydney.' I motion to Syd. 'Syd, this is River's sister Hollyn. She just got back to town.'

The two women look somewhat deflated and although they don't exactly hug, they each acknowledge the other's presence without weapons.

'What are you doing here?' I ask Hollyn. 'River said you were staying with your parents starting tonight.'

Her face drops. Oh, no. Don't start crying again.

'Seems I've caused too much damage to stay there.'

They said *no*? Wow. I guess I didn't realize things were that bad between them. That had to hurt in her current condition.

'I was going to talk to you about staying here a while longer, but you were in the bathroom when I got here, and after meeting your weirdo neighbor wearing a robe not closed enough' – she motions to-wards Roger's apartment – 'I got scared when I heard someone struggle with the lock. That guy invited me in for a cup of jungle juice. What even is that? Poison?'

'Never drink anything Roger gives you,' I warn her.

'Clearly, this is a bad time,' Sydney cuts in.

'Give me a minute, and we'll talk,' I say to Hollyn before following Sydney out the front door.

'Dax!' Roger greets me with a toothy grin. 'Looking *good*, my man. Double digits tonight, eh? *Noiiice...*'

The look on Sydney's face as Roger talks tells me River and I tolerate way too much of what this guy says.

'Not now, Roger!'

'Hear ya loud and clear, boss.' He locks an imaginary lock over his mouth, tossing the invisible key over his shoulder.

'I didn't know she'd be here tonight, Syd. I'm sorry.'

She sighs. 'It's not a big deal. Just didn't expect to battle my way into a guy's apartment.' Finally, she laughs about it.

'You know I'm not this guy, right?' I swing a thumb Roger's way. '*Two* women? Come on. Hollyn's only here temporarily. Her boyfriend dumped her; she's on the outs with her family. She's not in a great place.'

Sydney's eyes move from me to Roger. 'Wanna close that robe, ya freak?'

Roger glances down, readjusting himself. 'Don't let Bob the boner scare ya, baby. He likes you, is all.'

My god.

'Roger!' I growl, shutting him up instantly.

'It's not a problem, Dax. I'll call you later this week,' she says, heading down the stairs.

'You are a *machine*,' Roger says with a hip thrust once she's out of sight.

'Listen, Rog—Bob, whoever you are.' I stop in front of his door. 'No more creep factor with the women. You need to be fully clothed. You scared Hollyn.'

'Is Hollyn the pretty blonde one? Cause da-yum, she's boiling if ya know what I mean.' He licks the tip of his finger, touching his shoulder with a ssss.

'Don't talk to her or look at her like that. *Ever*,' I warn him. 'She's River's sister. You don't want to piss off River, do you?'

Roger thinks River is his best friend. Probably because River sits out here and has a beer with him once a week, humoring him with conversation.

'No, I do not,' Roger says.

'Coverage head to toe around the ladies, then. Capiche?'

The irony of my saying this as I stand on my porch in only a towel isn't lost on me.

'Ten-four, buddy.' He points a finger gun at me, blowing its tip afterward.

When I walk back into my apartment, Hollyn's lying face down on the couch, groaning into a cushion. Red rose petals are scattered all over the living room, and half a dozen desecrated stems lie on the ottoman.

'Did I just cock block you?' Hols asks, her words muffled by the cushion her face is pressed into.

'Yes, you did.'

She should be laughing with me at this entire situation right now. It's funny. But she's not. What do I do here? Obviously, she's not doing well, and yet again, River is nowhere to be found.

'God,' she groans. 'I'm sorry.' She finally turns her head, resting the side of her face on the cushion and looking at me. Her eyes move from my face to my towel, an unmistakable smirk surfacing.

'You do realize you're wearing only a towel and have shampoo in your hair?'

'Give me ten minutes. I want to show you something.'

Maybe she just needs some words of encouragement? I can handle that. I'm almost positive she thinks she's hit rock bottom. Anything supportive and uplifting that comes out of my mouth will surely help whatever mindset she's in.

'Where am I gonna go?' she asks. 'Nobody wants me around because I'm a self-centered jerk.'

'That's *not* true.' She really feels that way? 'Ten minutes, Hols. Don't attack anybody else, OK?' I earn another smile as I back down the hall to finish my shower.

When I walk into my living room ten minutes later, she's on the couch, legs crossed beneath her, the TV blasting. I grab the remote and click off the show she watches repeatedly.

'Come on,' I say, grabbing my keys. 'Want to see a piece of your past?'

She looks at my hand now extended her way. 'It's after midnight.'

'Do you have a curfew I don't know about?'

'No,' she laughs.

'Then what's the hold-up? We're grown-ups now, Hols. We can do anything we want.'

Finally, she takes my hand.

* * *

Twenty Minutes Later...

I type a code into the garage entrance, parking on the top floor, and do the same to get into the building. I'd rather not go through security on the ground floor because he'll call up to Jake and announce my arrival. The last thing I need is him or Brynn knowing I secretly come up to the roof of their building.

'Where are we?'

'Best rooftop in the city, and I just happen to have access. One more floor,' I say, leading the way up the stairs to the roof, stopping just inside the door that leads to a little-known garden.

'Eyes closed,' I say, turning to Hollyn when we're both on the landing.

'Nope.' She shakes her head. 'I hate surprises. They make me anxious.'

'You hate surprises? That's new.'

She lifts both shoulders. 'Blame Tristan because every surprise he ever gave me was really for him. Including him ambushing me with a publicly humiliating break-up.'

Ah. Tristan created some fears and insecurities, did he? Why am I not surprised?

'How about we don't say his name for a while?'

Hols crosses her arms over her chest, her cheeks pink. 'Fine.'

I open the door and step through, holding it for her so I can see her reaction. Her eyes grow wide as she steps onto the roof, her arms dropping from their defensive stance to her sides.

'Whoa,' she says, walking through an arbor covered in vining flowers and twinkle lights.

Boxwood topiaries line one side of a plank wood walkway, and thousands of colorful wildflowers are growing in raised boxes on all four sides. Lights are wound up potted tree trunks, some currently blooming with sweet-smelling flowers. In the center is a seating area around a gas fire pit, and a pool is off to one side, the water glowing. Not a soul is up here, considering it's late, which is what I was hoping for.

'This is—' She strolls the edge of the wildflower boxes, her fingertips grazing the tips of ornamental grasses along the edge of the beds, her eyes on the city lights flickering all around us. 'Magical. How'd you find this place?'

'I created this place,' I tell her, glancing around at my work.

'*What?*'

I shove my hands in my pockets and nod. 'Tried

my hand as a landscaper for a couple years. My cousin lives in the building and tipped me off they were taking bids, so I took a chance, threw my name in the hat, and voila! Magical rooftop garden I now escape to whenever I need to think.'

A smile grows on her face. 'It's beautiful, Dax.'

'Grab a seat; it gets better.' I point to a couple of double lounge chairs in a corner. Then I flip a hidden switch that shuts off all the overhead lights, leaving only the lighting along the rooftop edges and the pool light aglow.

I sit down next to her in the oversized lounger, leaving enough room between us that it doesn't seem as though I've invited her up here to seduce her. The last thing I want is her uncomfortable around me.

'You can see the stars better from here,' I say, pointing to the sky.

She looks up, her smile growing. 'Well, well, if it isn't astronomer Dax. Never thought I'd see you again.'

'He still exists. I just usually do this by myself nowadays.'

'What?' she asks, surprise in her voice. 'You mean you're not sweeping women off their feet by the dozens, impressing them with your extensive knowledge of flowers *and* constellations?'

'Nope. I only ever did this with you.' I stare up at the sky, the memories I haven't allowed myself to think of now playing through my head like a movie.

'You're still into it, though, aren't you?'

I nod. Now probably more than ever. 'It's peaceful.'

'Stars, flowers, and magical rooftop gardens. I don't think I'd have ever guessed this is who you'd become. You're way cooler than I thought you were.'

I chuckle. 'Only took you decades to see it.'

She rolls her eyes, shaking her head as she looks back up at the sky. 'Which Greek god are we meeting tonight?'

'It's not an ideal time to see it but right there' – I point at a constellation I'm sure she doesn't see – 'is Cepheus, the King of Aethiopia. To his right is his queen, Cassiopeia. She was a woman obsessed with her own beauty. We're talking disturbing levels of vanity here. The two of them had a daughter, Andromeda. This story's about her.'

Hollyn wraps her arms around herself as if she's cold.

'Here.' I pull off my jacket, handing it to her.

'What? *No*, I couldn't,' she says, refusing it.

'Yes, you can,' I insist, laying it over her like a blanket. 'I dragged you up here in the middle of the night; please, use it.'

'What about you?'

'I'm fine,' I say, a smile on my face to reassure her.

In reality, it's so cold my balls have tucked in for the night. But that's the furthest thing from my mind right now. Somehow sitting this close to her is sending sparks through my insides.

When she glances back up at the sky, I continue my story. 'Cassiopeia's vanity didn't stop with her. She deemed Andromeda more beautiful than all the Nereids. This, of course, pissed off Poseidon, Greek god of the sea, because his wife, Amphitrite, was the eldest of the Nereids.'

'Pissing off a Greek god seems risky.'

'That it was.'

God, this is as nerdy as I get. No one else can *ever* witness this. The only reason she is, is because we used to do this as teens.

Hollyn's brain moves at lightning speed, especially at night, which means more often than not, she couldn't sleep. I'd hear her open her bedroom window from River's room when I'd sleep over, and I'd sneak out onto the roof with her and tell her the stories of the constellations. Then she'd talk about whatever was bothering her, and word by word, I'd fall more and more in love with the girl.

To her, those nights were probably completely innocent. But I've relived all of them a million times, looking for moments I missed where I should have told her how I felt. You can't change the past yet I can't help but wonder how different our lives might be had I worked up the courage to tell her before she left for Seattle. Would she be sitting here, broken-hearted over a guy who probably never really loved her anyway?

Story, Dax. You're telling the woman a story. Don't get lost in the past.

'No one could be more beautiful than his wife. So, Poseidon vowed revenge for Cassiopeia's declaration offending his wife and ordered Cetus, a minion sea monster, to attack the city the king and queen ruled. He informed Cepheus the attack would stop only when Andromeda had been sacrificed.'

I glance over at her. She seems completely lost in the story and stars above us.

'Cepheus had had it with Cassiopeia's nonsense. He also answered to Poseidon, so like any good king would, he agreed to sacrifice his daughter to save his city and chained Andromeda to a rock so she couldn't flee her fate.'

'Jesus, Daddy Cepheus. That's a little extreme.'

'The gods were brutal as fuck.' I laugh to myself.

I stare up at the constellations I've spent too much time learning about. So much of my free time is lost staring out a telescope on my private balcony back home. It's an easy escape from whatever I've gotten myself into at times. Something about the stars is so calming. Romantic even if you blow by the murder and chaos in the stories. As a teen, I thought my little hobby would help me talk to women, but Hollyn was the only one interested enough to listen to me.

'Onto the hero of our story. Perseus. One of the most celebrated heroes in Greek mythology.' I point to his constellation and Hollyn's head follows my finger. 'He was on a mission to kill Medusa.'

'I feel like we need tense background music.'

I chuckle. 'He succeeded in killing her and as he flew home on his Pegasus, with Medusa's head in a bag—'

'*So*, romantic.'

'Every day, I hope to find a severed head to present to a woman, yet the opportunity still evades me,' I joke, making her laugh.

I missed this. Her laugh. Her commentary. She's always made my stories better.

'Anyway, Perseus came across a chained Andromeda before Cetus did. He fell in love and struck a deal with her father. If he could save her, he could marry her. Unfortunately, like real life, it wasn't that simple.'

A breeze blows by, sending her perfume right to me. Peonies mixed with vanilla. It's filling my head with memories I've never allowed myself to forget but refused to look at either. They're buried in the back of my heart where I needed them to stay to get over her when she left. Now they're storming my head, looking for a way out, and it's overwhelming me in a way I didn't expect.

'You alright?' she asks, glancing over at me.

'Yeah, sorry, lost in my head there for a minute.'

Find your words, Dax. Story.

'Um, Perseus slayed Cetus, no problem. But after, he learned her parents had promised Andromeda to her uncle.'

'Ew.'

'They liked that bloodline pure. But yeah, *gross*. To marry her, Perseus needed to kill the uncle too. He was outnumbered, but eventually, he pulled Medusa's head from the bag and turned the uncle to stone, winning the battle and taking Andromeda away from her family to marry.'

'And a severed head saved the day after all. Romantic in a way I hope I never experience.'

I laugh. 'Note to self: don't bring Hols a severed head as a romantic gesture.'

'Well, it might be useful if it can turn people to stone. I've got a list.' She glances over at me, a sly smile on her face. 'I missed this.'

'Me too.'

'Wanna know something?'

I nod. I want to know everything.

'Anxiety still plagues me at night, and sometimes, even all these years later, I imagine lying on my parents' roof with you, listening to your stories.' She flashes me a shy grin. 'You never aged in my head, so you definitely didn't look like the man sitting next to me now. But somehow the memory of you, *this*, helped?'

My memory has helped her. I would have never guessed that. Not in a million years.

'You know you always could have called me. I'd have told you the stories over the phone.'

'That's not as easy as it sounds when you're lying next to another man.' She sighs, still staring at the sky above us. 'Ya know, now that I've had time to think on everything, I don't think I've been happy for a long time. I was afraid to do something drastic because I like comforting things and changing the world I'd come to know would have led to chaos. My head can't handle chaos.'

'I get that. Constellations are calming for me. That's why I like astronomy. When I'm overwhelmed, I look at the stars and they remind me that there's a huge world out there; I'm for sure not the only one looking to the skies when I feel like I've lost control of my tiny piece of it.'

I missed having these talks with her. She's the only one I've ever been able to talk to like this.

'You're different. But the same? Like a piece of my past that has somehow gotten smarter, but you're still Dax, ya know?'

'I am still Dax.'

'Have *you* ever been in love?'

'Um...' I swallow hard, rubbing my neck nervously. 'Yeah,' I finally say. 'It's painful.'

'That's what Mercy says, too.'

'I guess she and I have that in common then.'

'What happened?'

'To what?'

'The girl you loved. Where is she?'

'She uh—' I can't answer this without telling her it's her. Unless I make it vague. Maybe I'll finally find the courage to tell her if she gets it. If she doesn't, I probably never stood a chance.

'I never told her. We were friends. There wasn't a good time, and, in the end, I realized she didn't feel the same way.'

She frowns, touching my forearm. 'I'm sorry. She doesn't know what she's missed.'

I drop my head before glancing back at the sky; a few wispy clouds backlit by the moon move through the constellations. I'm not sure if her response makes it better or worse.

Change the topic, Dax. Move on before you say something stupid and make her uncomfortable. She's never seen you as more than River's best friend. Nothing's changed.

'What do you want to do, Hols? Now that you're back.'

'If you're asking me what I want out of life...' She glances out at the city around us with a sigh, pulling her knees to her chest. 'I wish I knew. Now that I'm here, I realize everyone around me knows what they want, and I feel like I'm treading water in the middle of the ocean.' She glances at me. 'What about you? Do you know what you want?'

I nod. 'Remember the floral competition I mentioned at the airport?'

'Yeah.'

'Winner gets fifty grand, and I'm hoping to buy my dad's old shop, so I signed on the dotted line.'

She smiles sweetly. 'You want to buy your dad's old shop. That's adorable, Dax. And you made the show! Congratulations. How exciting.'

'Nerve-racking seems more fitting.'

'You're kind of proving my point,' she says.

'How's that?'

'River's pouring himself into this documentary. Mercy's a musical genius running her own business. Mom's making a comeback. You fell in love with flowers and have this floral competition.' She frowns but tries to smile through it. 'I have nothing. My family hates me. I'm sleeping in my brother's bed. I have no skills. Every relationship I thought I'd built in Seattle has vanished. I've done nothing but focus on myself for the last decade and ended up with zilch because of it.'

'Your family doesn't *hate* you, Hols.'

She shakes her head, pressing her chin into her knees. 'I don't even know who I am anymore.'

That's heavy, but I'm sure if I was in her position, I might feel the same way.

'Want to know what I see?'

'Sure,' she says, glancing at me curiously.

'I see a woman who has every opportunity at her fingertips. You can do anything you want. Strained relationships can be repaired. If it's any consolation, I don't feel any differently about you than when we were teens. I'd bet money your parents feel the same way, and if they don't, they will.'

She smiles sadly, touching my hand momentarily. 'How'd you get so smart?'

'It's that damn growing up thing,' I say. 'Truthfully, I miss talking to you. River isn't the same. You're the only one I've ever let see this side me.'

'The dorky side?'

I laugh. 'Yeah. Dorky Dax to your rescue. I mean the side of me that has feelings. I don't let those loose often. You're one of the only people who've gotten a look in here.' I touch my chest.

Her smile is adorable in a way that makes me long to kiss her.

'In that case, I owe you an apology. I'm sorry I worried you before. Once I find something to fill my days, like a job, I'll be alright.'

'A job,' I say mostly to myself. 'You need a job.' A light bulb goes off in my head. 'Of course. I don't know why I didn't think of it before. I need an assistant for the show.' I sit up, turning towards her. 'You like flowers, Hols?'

'Yes?' she asks it as a question, clearly confused.

'I get to choose someone to help with challenges that will happen in a time crunch and they aren't allowed to have floristry experience. What would you think if I asked you?'

She lifts an eyebrow, staring at me.

'I'd be with you every step of the way. I can teach you everything you'd need to know.'

'*Me?*'

'Why not? It could be fun. Maybe you'll find yourself in the process?'

The two of us stare at one another.

'I know it seems like I've got no worries,' I tell her. 'Like I know exactly what I want and how to get there, but that's not entirely true. This show, putting myself out there for strangers to judge, scares me. Maybe I'm not as good at this flower thing as I think I am? I don't know, but I've got a lot riding on this, and if I fail, I'll only be able to blame myself. But if you were with me...' I hesitate, a goofy grin growing on my face. 'I could blame you.'

I'm obviously kidding but watching her smile at my words makes me feel better about all of it.

'My future rides on this show, Hollyn. It'd be nice to have someone with me that I trusted.'

'You trust me?' She sounds surprised.

'I've got no reason not to.'

'We don't know each other anymore, though.'

'Call it a gut feeling.'

8

HOLLYN

Moments Later...

'What do you think?' he asks, his head cocked, a hopeful smile on his face.

I think it sounds incredible. Dax makes me feel like I'm not a total loser. But I can't do that to him. I'm a mess. I'm the last person on earth who could help someone else reach their dreams. Especially considering I've got no dreams of my own currently.

'I don't know,' I say. 'What if I hold you back? If I messed up and made you lose, I couldn't live with myself.' I stand up from the lounger, walking to the edge of the flower gardens, staring at the surrounding city.

Lights twinkle in the buildings around me. The air is heavy from the rain earlier. The silence of the night is deafening to a girl who can't stop her thoughts as they spin through my head like a tornado. Honestly, I prefer listening to Dax talk about stars.

'Right now, I'm just a pain in your butt. What if you feel that way about me as your assistant too?'

'I don't feel that way about you now.'

I heave a sigh. 'I'm selfish, Dax. I'd sink you.'

'No, you're not. You're temporarily lost. It happens to all of us. You can be whoever you want to be.' He says it in such an upbeat way, as if it's an absolute fact. 'But you're right,' he says. 'You came here to start over, not help me with my dreams.'

God. Now I feel bad. He looks as if he's lost faith in me, like everyone else. Maybe I need to be focusing on someone else? Isn't that the opposite of selfishness? Perhaps I sh—

Suddenly, my phone rings in my pocket which is weird since it's well after midnight. Nobody calls me, especially not at this hour.

I pull it out and see my dad's face is on the screen. Something's wrong. I flash my phone at Dax, who stands, taking a step towards me.

'Dad?' I put the phone on speaker so Dax can hear in case it's something terrible.

'Hollyn,' Dad says. 'Tristan is here.'

What? Why?

'He's refusing to leave until he sees you. This man has never even so much as called us on the phone. You need to take care of this before he ends up in the hospital. Or worse.'

'What does he want?'

'I don't know. But get here before I end up in jail.'

'Come on,' Dax says. 'We'll be there in fifteen, John.'

'Thanks, Dax. See ya soon, kid,' Dad speaks directly to Dax as if I'm no longer a part of the conversation. I didn't realize they were still close.

'You can just drop me off,' I say as the two of us jog down the stairs towards his car.

'No way am I dropping you off to deal with that dumb fuck in the middle of the night alone. I'll be right there with you.'

I've invaded his world, taken over his TV, cock blocked his booty call, and said no to his request to help with the show. Why would he help me after all that? The man is a mystery.

The times I've ridden with Dax over the years, he's been the perfect driver. Not this time. If I ever wanted to experience the death ride of a lifetime, that was it. We made it to my parents' place in less than fifteen minutes and, sure enough, a rental car is parked in front of their house.

'Listen.' Dax reaches over, touching my arm. 'I'll be right behind you. Tell me if you feel you've lost control or are scared and I'll take care of this loser.'

I nod, taking a deep breath before opening the car door. Tristan is sitting on the step of my parents' porch, leaning against one of the posts. I glance back at Dax, who's now walking around his car and leaning against the door I just exited.

'What are you doing here?' I ask Tristan as I walk his way, my arms crossed over my chest.

He jumps from the porch, stumbling down the step but regaining his footing quickly. I stop a dozen feet from him. His tie hangs loosely around his neck, and his hair is ruffled. What has gotten into him?

'I came for you, sweet pea.' His voice is gentle, but I'm not buying it.

'Please don't call me that,' I say. 'I take it she said no?'

'Why would she say no?' He laughs as though I'm some kind of idiot. 'I gave her a two-carat rock. The only answer was yes.'

A two-carat rock? Jesus.

'Who is she?' I don't want to know, but I do.

He shakes his head. 'Doesn't matter.'

'How long, Tristan? How long's it been going on?'

'Two years.'

Two years? My heart feels like it falls apart, if there's anything left to break. How did I not know this? Am I *that* clueless?

'So, the longtime girlfriend you were seeing behind my back said *yes*, is currently *wearing* your ring, but you're *here. Why?*'

'Ask your brother.'

I shake my head. My brother? 'What's River got to do with this?'

'He thinks I should give you another chance.'

That doesn't sound like River at all. 'He hates you. Why would he want that?'

'That's what I thought, too,' he says. 'Then I got to thinking... you're kind of a pain in his ass, always calling him with your problems. Perhaps he hates you more?'

My heart practically stops.

'He's drunk, and he's lying, Hollyn,' Dax says calmly from behind me.

'Who's this?' Tristan suddenly notices Dax and walks towards him. My heart starts to race in my chest.

'He's not a part of this. Leave him alone.'

Tristan ignores me, his eyes locked on Dax's. 'A pretty boy, eh? Seems a little young for ya.'

'You mean *you* seem a little *old*?' Dax shoots back.

'I prefer the term mature,' Tristan responds.

'Well, I prefer the term dick bag.' Dax stands away from the car and takes a few steps our way. 'I know for a fact River does too. No way did he call you and ask you to come here and take her off his hands. What *really* brought you here?'

'I'm not here to talk to some Neanderthal who thinks he's tough. I'm here to talk to Hollyn. Come on.' He grabs me by the upper arm, his fingers digging into me, leading me towards his rental car.

'Ouch.' I attempt to pull away from him. 'I don't want to talk, Tristan. There's nothing left to say.' The more I pull from him, the tighter his grip gets. 'You're hurting me!'

The front door swings open and Dad appears on the porch with a baseball bat. He runs down the path towards Tristan, swinging as if someone has lobbed him a pitch.

'You touch her one more time, and you'll never walk again!' Dad yells.

'*John! Wait!*' Dax yells, running to Dad and

catching the bat mid-flight before Tristan loses his kneecaps. 'I'll take care of it.'

Dad and Dax exchange glances, before Dad steps away and watches the three of us.

Tristan turns his gaze to me. 'Bodyguards, eh? You're nothing but a pathetic little girl.' He shoves me, knocking me to my knees in the grass.

'Hols.' Dax is immediately at my side, helping me up. 'I'm gonna kill him,' he says partly under his breath into my ear.

'*Don't*,' I say. 'I can get rid of him.'

Dax heaves an obviously frustrated sigh.

'I guess you don't want that money after all,' Tristan continues.

'Wait,' I say, stepping up to him, Dax moving with me. 'You're admitting you stole the money?'

'I'm not *admitting* anything but it's something we can talk about.' He nods at his car. 'Along with you calling *off* the investigation.'

'What investigation?'

'The college is investigating me for sexual harass-ment. I can only assume it's because you've put in a complaint.'

'*Or* maybe it's one of the girls you've harassed?' I suggest. 'Tristan, *you* broke up with *me*. So, I left. I haven't reported anything. I just want my money back.'

'Then let's go talk about it,' he says, getting closer to me by the word.

'She's not going anywhere with you,' Dax says, stepping in front of me.

'Nobody asked you,' Tristan barks.

I've never seen him like this. He looks rabid. Eyes glazed over. Shirt half untucked. Absolute anger oozes from him. He's in trouble with the school, and he's losing it.

'Let's go.' Tristan reaches for my arm again, but before he can grab me, Dax swings, hitting him in the face with his fist and knocking him to the ground.

'Oh my god,' I say with a heavy breath. 'Dax.'

Tristan groans, sitting up, his nose now bleeding. '*This* is what you want? A scrappy punk?'

I glance at Dax, tears in my eyes. I can't believe he just did that. I take another step, now practically standing behind him, in case Tristan tries anything else. Dax grabs my hand, giving me the courage to say what I need to say.

'You came here without an invitation, Tristan. Stole thousands of dollars from me. Cheated so many times I can't count them, and you proposed to someone else. You destroyed me. We have nothing to talk about. I was just your back-up girl until you met someone more marry-able. Your words. Remember?'

He laughs to himself, but it sounds a hint un-hinged. I've never feared Tristan until right now but the sudden echo of sirens headed in our direction makes him visibly panic. He jumps up, running for his car. Dax takes one step and knocks him back to the ground, grabbing his keys that fly across the sidewalk.

'You're not leaving here in this condition; you could kill someone,' Dax growls.

The police fly in, running from their cars. One straddles Tristan, the other grabs Dax and shoves him against his car.

'Not him!' I yell, running towards Dax. 'He didn't do anything wrong. You can't arrest him.'

'Ma'am, step back unless you want to be arrested too,' an officer commands.

'Hollyn, listen to him,' Dax says.

'No! They can't blame you for this. *He* attacked me.' I point to Tristan. 'Dax *saved* me.' I touch Dax's shoulder. 'Dad?' I glance back at my father for help.

It takes us a few minutes but eventually we sort things out, and the officer removes the cuffs from Dax's wrists. We spend the next twenty minutes going over everything with the police and I agree to press charges, so they haul Tristan away to sleep it off with the instructions that he will be on the next flight home.

As the police drive away, Tristan in the back seat staring me down, I practically collapse on the curb because the anxiety in my chest is suffocating me and I suddenly need a break. I focus on my breathing as Dax sits down next to me, leaning his shoulder into mine.

'You're stronger than you think you are, Hols. You did the right thing.'

9

DAX

Later That Night – Back at the Apartment...

'I'm so sorry,' Hollyn says again when we walk into my apartment.

This is about the thirteenth sorry since we left her parents' place. When the door's closed, she locks all three locks.

'I never expected him to—'

'I know, Hols,' I interrupt her. 'We're good. It's not the first fight I've been in.'

Although it's the first time I've been cuffed and nearly arrested for it. Tristan tried to press charges, but once the police realized he was beyond wasted and had put his hands on Hollyn, they decided charges weren't warranted. At least not towards me.

I knew the moment he grabbed her arm, by the sheer terror on her face, he'd never done that to her before. Thank god. Her fear triggered something inside me that I hadn't felt since high school. I couldn't let him hurt her.

Hollyn walks across the apartment, my jacket still hanging over her shoulders. Slowly she pulls it off, tossing it to the ottoman and dropping onto the couch.

'What would he have done if he'd have got me into his car?' she asks, her eyes wide. 'What if he doesn't go home? What if he comes here?' She glances at the door, getting up to check the locks.

I stop her, my hand on her wrist. 'You're safe here, Hols. I'd never let anything happen to you. If Tristan walks through that door at any point, they'll be the last steps he ever takes.'

She forces a crooked smile.

'Had you not been there tonight—'

'Your dad would have taken care of it. Are you sure you're alright?'

She nods, tears sliding down her face. 'I'm just—'

She shakes her head, as she wanders to River's room. 'I'm tired.'

I watch her walk into River's room, partially closing the door behind her, as I sit on the couch, staring at the ceiling for a moment. I can't believe that just happened. What a fucking psycho. What the hell was he talking about, money and investigations? The guy had gone off the rails. Even Hollyn seemed like she didn't recognize him.

River's door opens suddenly. Hollyn's now wearing pajamas as she climbs into the bed. She pulls the covers to her chin, but doesn't turn off the lamp, just stares at the ceiling.

'What are you doing?'

'I uh—' She sits up, the blankets dropping off her, revealing the tiny tank top she's now wearing. 'It's dumb.'

I walk over to her room, leaning against the door frame. 'I'm sure it's not dumb.'

She lifts her shoulders. 'I'm scared.' She bites her lips together. 'I keep wondering what he'd have done if I'd gotten into that car with him?' She wipes away tears before they can fall. 'What if I'd been alone?'

'You weren't,' I remind her.

'What if when they let him out, he comes over here to finish what he's started?'

'What would make you feel safe right now?' I ask, honestly not knowing how else to answer.

She glances around the room, her gaze finally settling on me. 'Could you uh...' She bites her bottom lip. 'Please don't think I'm suggesting this romantically or in any kind of sexual way, but could you maybe... sleep in here?'

'In *here*?' I repeat her words, looking around the room filled with half-unpacked bags. Hardly any floor space for my giant frame to even fit. 'Like on the floor?'

'Or on the bed? Just for one night. I'm sure I'll feel better when I know Tristan's back in Seattle.'

'Huh,' I grunt, pulling out my phone and glancing at the time. Two-thirty in the morning. What could *possibly* go wrong with me in her bed after two in the morning? Other than *everything*.

'Me sleeping in your bed will make you feel safer?'

She nods. 'Too much to ask?'

'No,' I say. 'I can, just uh – give me five minutes to turn things off and change.'

I flip off the lamp in the living room on the way to my room. This is fine. *Everything* is fine. I'm just hopping into bed with the woman I've dreamed of for fifteen years. I'm sure nothing will happen.

I drag a hand down my face, rubbing the side of

my neck as I stand in the middle of my room, figuring out what to wear to this little sleepover. Snowboarding gear would work. No accidents are happening through that. She might think I'm weird, though.

God damn it, River. He invited her here, and now, almost two weeks later, I've faced every old feeling I've ever had, almost been arrested, and just laid her ex across her parents' front lawn. Now I'm faced with the ultimate challenge.

I throw on some sweats and a T-shirt, grab my pillow and a blanket, and head back to her room. She's still got the lamp on as she watches me toss my pillow onto River's bed and lie down next to her.

She flips off the lamp, and we both lie in the dark, silently listening to one another breathe. We've been lying there five minutes when she becomes restless.

'You, OK?'

'Can I just uh—'

She moves closer, pressing herself into my side, her head on my shoulder and her hand on my chest. For a moment, I lie awkwardly still, hardly even breathing as she settles in. Thank god it's dark in here because I probably look like I've just witnessed a car accident. Never in a million years did I expect her to touch me in this way. Hesitantly, I rest my hand on her back, and she relaxes into me.

Breathe, Dax. She's just scared, and you're the only one here. This is completely innocent.

'Thank you,' she says after a few minutes of silence. 'You saved me tonight, Dax. If your offer still stands, I want to help you with the show.'

'We don't need to talk about it now.'

'I'm serious. I'm here to make a change, which means I need to do just that. Let me do this for you. Please.'

Without thinking about it, I touch her hand on my chest. 'OK.' I stroke the back of her hand with my thumb. Things just got way more complicated.

* * *

The Next Morning...

'Dax.'

River's voice wakes me up. I open one eye, his less-than-thrilled gaze meeting mine.

'What the *fuck* are you doing in here?' he asks in an obnoxious whisper.

I glance over at Hollyn, still sound asleep, my arm cold and dead underneath her.

'Shh.' I pull a single finger to my lips as I slowly remove my arm from beneath her and jump out of bed, dragging River into the living room with me, closing the bedroom door quietly, so we don't wake Hollyn up.

'It's not what it looks like.'

'It looks like you fucked my sister in my bed,' he thunders.

'Will you shut up?' I half yell back. 'Do you truly think I'd do that? Something happened last night, Riv. Not between her and me, but me and Professor Cocksucker. She was scared, and asked me to sleep in there. What was I supposed to do? I couldn't possibly say no. She was terrified.'

'I'll bet you couldn't say no,' he says sarcastically.

'Trust me, if something was going to happen between your sister and me, I'd talk to you about it.'

His angry face fades, and a smirk grows. 'Dad says you whooped him good.'

'I was pissed. He tried to tell her *you* wanted her to go back to him.'

'*What?* No. I filed a complaint with the college. An investigation has been opened on his "extracurricular activities".'

That explains part of Tristan's anger.

'Listen,' I half hiss. 'I was just trying to help, and now I'm in this in a way I never wanted to be. All because of you.' I take a deep breath; I smell her. I lift the neck of my shirt to my nose. Jesus, that perfume is gonna kill me.

'I almost got arrested last night, Riv.'

He laughs.

'It's not funny.'

'It's a little funny,' he says, pinching his fingers together.

The knock at the door is almost a relief. The last thing I want to do is think about the fact that I hardly slept last night. Mostly I just stared at the ceiling, worried about a million things.

I pull open the door to Brynn.

'You did it!' she says excitedly. 'I knew you'd love this idea. I'd have brought you flowers to celebrate, but who brings a florist flowers?' She laughs, setting a bouquet of fruit cut into flower shapes on my kitchen island. 'When do we start?'

'*We?*'

'Well, yeah. You need an assistant, right?'

The door of River's room opens, and Hollyn walks out. My gaze goes right to her. Her hair is wild. She's wearing her black-framed glasses, and one leg of her sweats is pulled up around her calf. Yet she's still completely gorgeous.

'Who's this?' Brynn asks, looking between River, me, and Hollyn. 'She's cute,' she whispers.

'What are you doing here?' Hollyn asks River.

'Dad called this morning. I thought I'd stop in and see how you two were. Had ya a little fight, did ya?' He jumps around his sister, throwing pretend punches at her while laughing.

'Shut it,' Hols says, shoving him into the wall as she walks towards the bathroom. 'It was way scarier than that.'

'That's Hollyn, River's sister,' I tell Brynn. 'She's staying here after a break-up. She uh...' I stall, almost afraid to say the words I'm about to say. 'I asked *her* to be my assistant.'

The incredulous stare from Brynn isn't making me feel better about any of this.

'In my defense, I didn't know you wanted to do it.'

'It's not that I *wanted* to...' She grabs a piece of pineapple from the edible flowers. 'I just assumed you'd choose the gal who got you the gig.'

'Sorry. You have a baby, a business, and a husband. I thought you were booked. Hols needs a job, and I have a spot for her.'

'So, you're paying her. Like an employee?'

I grab a strawberry from the arrangement, shoving it into my mouth and hoping for a sudden allergy. One simple, not quite fatal, allergic reaction would do. Is that too much to ask?

'I hadn't exactly thought that far ahead.'

'And you two are...' Brynn motions the index finger of one hand through the O shape of the other. 'Don't you think that will complicate things?'

'She's only staying here until she gets on her feet. There is no...' I motion the crude gesture back to her.

'*Yet.*'

'*Ever.*'

One thought that went through my mind like a news ticker last night has been decided; I can never sleep with Hollyn. We've already complicated things enough, and if I want a chance at buying back my dad's store, I can't get overly involved with her.

'I know you,' Brynn says. 'She's gorgeous; you're easy. Give it time.'

I shake my head, pulling her all the way into the kitchen with me, so River won't overhear us.

'You're wrong about this one. She's River's sister. We have a rule we don't sleep with each other's exes or family. She's just gotten out of a terrible relationship that came to a head last night. Is she beautiful? My god, *yes*. But this is strictly business, Brynn. I can't expect you to give up your responsibilities; you've already done enough. Don't you think?'

She shrugs, pulling a spike of cantaloupe from the edible bouquet. 'I suppose I have. It's not a big deal. Actually, it means I could coordinate watch parties. *Oh*, I kind of like that more.'

'A party planner is going to plan, am I right?'

'You're totally right,' she agrees. 'This is good.' She grins. 'But I've gotta get. I just dropped Zoey off at daycare so I could clean the house. Keep me in the loop!'

'Will do,' I say, following her across the room and closing the front door behind her as she leaves.

'This is a busy apartment,' Hollyn says, emerging from the bathroom. 'Was that another woman with an arrangement?'

'That was my cousin, Brynn. The one that signed me up for *Battle of the Blossoms*. She was under the impression I'd choose her as my assistant.'

Hollyn looks concerned. 'Is she mad? I understand if you'd rather choose her. I could help River with the documentary.'

'No, thank you,' River says as he walks out of his room, as if spending time with his sister would be the worst thing.

'Why are you even here?' she asks him.

'Needed some things.' He lifts the gym bag in his

hands as proof. 'And I wanted to make sure you two were still alive. Then give Daxy here a high five for beating down Professor Buttpipe.'

He raises a hand to me, but I shake my head. He frowns.

'Seriously,' Hols says to me. 'Choose whoever will help you win. Don't risk your dad's shop for me.'

My phone dings on the counter next to me, an incoming text popping up on the screen. McKenzie from the show. I sent her an email as I lay awake last night to let her know I'd picked my assistant.

'I've pretty much made it official already. This is someone with the show. She wants to meet up tomorrow afternoon and go over everything before the first challenge this weekend.' I glance at my phone. 'She says you'll need to sign some paperwork too.'

'Sure,' Hollyn says, a slight grin on her face.

'Gotta go,' River interrupts us. 'Mom's expecting me.' He walks into the kitchen, pulling a fruit spear from Brynn's bouquet.

'You two better behave. I don't want to walk in here and find you in each other's arms again. Got it?' He waggles his finger at me as though *I'm* the culprit here.

Hollyn's eyes go wide as she grimaces. 'It was completely innocent, Riv. We're not horny teenagers.'

Well, *some* of us aren't anyway.

'He was mad?' Hollyn asks as soon as the door closes behind him.

I shake my head as I pull the toaster from the cabinet. 'Not *mad*. More surprised?'

'I'm sorry,' she says meekly.

'Stop being sorry, Hols. You did nothing wrong.' I sigh, leaning on the countertop with my hands.

'River lives by this stupid bro code thing. We aren't allowed to get involved with each other's exes or families.' I look at her. 'I think I agree with him. We shouldn't cross that line. You're just getting out of a relationship, and I have this competition to focus on.'

Hollyn hops up onto one of the barstools across the island from me. 'I could never... with *you*? No. Totally out of bounds.'

'You don't need to say it like I'm repulsive.'

'You're far from repulsive.' Her eyes go wide. 'Wait, I didn't mean it like *that*. I meant last night I was... humiliated? Terrified? You made me feel safe, Dax. That's all.' She glances up at me with just her eyes.

Be still my heart.

'I need to know we're on the same page, Hols.'

'Totally. I'm on the page...' She opens her hands like they're a book, pretending to read it.

'Good. So, tell me, what do you know about flowers?'

'I know what they are.'

'Wanna go on some deliveries with me this morning? Get a feel for it?'

'Sure, that could be fun.'

She's the most annoying girl in the world, just like your sign at the airport said, Dax. She is not sexy as fuck in these blue sweats, tiny tank top, and nerdy glasses. She's just a girl you used to know who now sleeps in the room next door. Still, I suddenly need air.

'Get dressed and meet me in the parking lot in thirty.'

10

HOLLYN

Moments Later...

I feel better this morning. Not like my soul's healed or anything; that'll take some time, but better. Even considering I hardly slept a wink. And not only because a guy who'd just put himself in danger to protect me was sleeping with his arm around me either.

Most of the night was spent mulling over everything that could have and did go wrong. I put Dax in a position I'm sure he regrets. I knew it the moment he made his 'we shouldn't cross that line' speech. That said, volunteering to help him with the show feels good. As though I have a purpose.

He asked me to help with deliveries this morning, and it's the least I can do. Plus, maybe today will end up a jump start to the training I'm most definitely going to need.

As I walk to the parking lot, I spot Dax at the most adorable delivery truck I ever did see. It looks like an old UPS truck that he's converted into a mobile florist. It's navy blue, with colorful flowers and vines painted all over it and his business name, The Flower Boy, is written in romantic scrolly lettering along each side.

'Dax!' I say, the hugest grin on my face. He closes the double doors at the back when he hears my voice. 'This is seriously cute.' I run my fingers along the outline of a painted flower.

'It does the job. The girl who painted it did me well.'

I raise a single eyebrow, a half-cocked grin on my face.

'Not in the way you're picturing, perv.' He laughs. 'Get in.'

We both climb into his truck. I breathe in deeply as I get settled, glancing into the back, the flowers making me smile immediately.

'It smells so good in here.'

'Perk of the job.'

He fidgets with the radio, eventually settling on a station playing a Justin Timberlake song. Dax glances over, waggling his eyebrows.

The memories of my youth are coming back to me quickly. He and River competed to get the louder stereo systems in their cars back in their teens and River always won. But the summer before my senior year, Dax pulled ahead. He'd been working evenings for a pizza delivery place, and with his charm, I don't doubt he killed it in tips alone. He dumped every dime he made into his car and stereo.

I was the judge that year. Usually, it was some other friend of theirs, but this day, I was the only one home when Dax finished installing the last speaker in the trunk of his car. So, on a hot July afternoon, we started the competition in my parents' driveway.

My job was to sit in the passenger seat of each vehicle with them and decide whose stereo gave me a bigger headache. River played some rapper I was offended by and demanded I shut up when I objected. Dax read the room and turned on the air conditioning while he blasted Justin Timberlake's 'SexyBack' because he knew I was smitten. As if his attention to the heat outside and the judge's music preference wasn't enough, the dancing in his seat as he performed the song into his makeshift microphone cell phone sold me. I laughed a lot that day and stayed in his car with him for far longer than I needed to.

I glance over at him as he drives. Why can't life be that simple now?

'Do you remember the stereo wars of twenty-ten?'

He laughs. 'Oh yeah. We were nerdy as fuck, weren't we?'

'*Were*, yeah.' I bite my lips together to prevent the goofy grin from taking over my face.

'We had fun back then. Didn't we?' he asks, side-eying me.

I nod. 'Made me smile just remembering it.'

He turns up the song, singing terribly. 'Still bad?'

'Somehow worse?' I laugh, encouraging him to get louder.

'Stop number one,' he says once we're in the city, pulling up to the curb in front of an office building.

We both get out, walking to the back of the truck. He pulls a bouquet of rainbow roses before closing the doors.

'Wow! These are gorgeous. *How* are they rainbow-colored?'

'It's actually really cool,' he says. 'I order them like this, but I've read up on them. It's a white rose, dyed by injecting color through the stem as they grow to create rainbow-colored buds. These are headed to a woman who's just come out to her family. Her dad wanted her to know how much she's loved.'

I put a hand to my chest. '*Really?*' That is the sweetest thing I've ever heard. 'If this is what you feel every time you do this, I can see why you chose this profession.'

'We haven't even gone in yet, Hols. Don't start crying already.'

'Right.' I sniffle away the tears threatening to emerge. 'I can do this,' I say, taking a breath and following him into the building and to the second floor.

'Hi,' he says to the receptionist. 'I have a delivery for a...' He rechecks the order. 'Teagen?'

The woman nods, almost immediately even more emotional than I was. I lift a hand to my mouth, so I don't cry with this total stranger. Crying at ridiculous things is kind of who I am. Commercials, YouTube videos, Instagram reels of complete strangers, they all get me. This is no different.

Dax sets the flowers on the counter, turning them, so the card faces her.

'You're incredible, Teagan. Never change who you are. I hope you have the best day ever.' He says it as if they're old friends and he's so sincere that she walks around the counter and hugs him.

Shut. Up. Heart. He's just doing his job.

'Thank you,' she says.

He turns to me, raising his eyebrows with a goofy grin as we head to the stairs and it takes me until he's nearly at the bottom to pull myself together. Eventually, I follow him through the door he's holding for me.

'What do you think?'

I think I'm half-stunned into silence and I swoon a little too visibly, making him blush. 'I'm not trying to make this weird, but *wow*, you're charming as hell, Mr Hartley. Seriously, you're good at this.'

'Swept off her feet on delivery number one. You're going to have a long day.'

'How did I never see this side of you before?'

'Not sure it existed until long after you'd left town, and I'd finally grown into my awkwardness.' He opens my door for me and I climb in, grinning like a loon as I do.

'Don't go falling in love with me now.' He winks, closing the door as my heart does a flip, then swan dives right into my stomach with a splash.

'I like this, Dax,' I say as we drive through the city. 'I'm sorry I missed the transition, though.'

'Consider yourself lucky. That was a rough couple of years.' He fidgets with the radio station for a moment. 'I'm still the same guy you used to know. Totally nerdy, but now I know who I am.'

'Nah,' I say. 'You're different. Better.' I flash him a smile, lacking the brainpower to use any other words.

He grins shyly. 'I think you're better too, Hols.'

'*How?* I'm a mess.'

'You're raw. You've got nothing to hide and everything at risk. You're surviving after heartbreak. That's honorable.' He glances over as though he sincerely believes this.

'How come you don't have a girlfriend?'

Might as well make this as awkward as possible, right?

He shrugs, thinking about his answer before speaking. 'I guess I put my career first. Women don't love that. Then there's the fact that I haven't found anyone I want to get close to. I dunno. Maybe one day, some woman will sweep me off my feet when I least expect it.'

'I don't doubt you'll do the sweeping.'

'Ha!' He bursts out a laugh. 'I let the flowers do the sweeping nowadays.'

'Is that your move? Bringing women flowers to entice them to come home with you?'

'No.'

'No, you don't bring them flowers, or no, you don't

woo them at all?' Hard to believe after just watching him talk his way into a hug by a stranger on the first stop.

'Both?' He glances at me with his brows drawn together. 'In my opinion flowers are for the women I have feelings for, that mean something big in my life. I hope this doesn't hurt the image of me you're building in your head, but I don't hand them out willy-nilly to the women I have casual relationships with.' He pauses momentarily. 'My dad brought flowers to my mom every day they were together. I didn't understand it at the time, but I do now.'

'But you brought me flowers?' I say, thinking back to the daisies that lived in a glass of water on River's dresser for the few days I kept them alive. 'I'm almost certain I'm just some casual girl living in the bedroom next to yours.'

'Oh, Hollyn,' he says, a small sigh leaving his lips as he shakes his head. 'You are an entirely other story.'

I wonder what that means? Don't overthink it. It's probably completely innocent. I look back at the flowers behind me. They line one side of the van, arrangements kept safe in wooden boxes that line the floor. Everything is so pretty. Him included.

'This next delivery is probably the most adorable thing I've had the pleasure of doing. They're for a nine-year-old girl who recently won the state spelling bee.' He pulls up in front of a brightly painted school. 'Her parents thought these would make her day.'

He pulls a bouquet from the back of the truck, much like the one he brought me at the airport. Bright orange and hot pink daisies, with grass weaved in to look like ribbons. He made that and it's gorgeous. I can hardly believe this is the Dax I knew.

'That's so pretty.'

'You're going to swoon every time I do this, aren't you?'

'Afraid so,' I say, lifting a single shoulder. 'I'd stop it if I could, but... nope, I can't.'

Dax stops at the front desk, explaining what he's here for and the receptionist calls the young girl, Hilary, to the office. Moments later, as Dax and I stand in the main hall, a young girl appears at the top of the stairs. She's got dark brown skin, shoulder-length curly hair, and wide eyes. She approaches hesitantly, so Dax kneels.

'Are you Hilary?'

She nods excitedly.

'I heard you won the spelling bee this week. Is that true?'

'Y-E-S,' she spells out her answer. How freaking cute is she?

'Wow.' Dax chuckles, glancing at me then back to her. 'Congratulations. You should be proud.' He hands her the bouquet, and she lets out a little squeal. 'Your mom told me your favorite colors were pink and orange. I hope I did OK?'

'I love them!' she says, taking them from him and staring down at them like I did at the airport. 'Thank you!' She runs back up the stairs, a massive grin on her face when she glances back at us.

When Dax turns to me, I've got one arm crossed over my chest and one hand over my mouth. He rolls his eyes with a laugh.

'Thanks, ladies,' he says to the office crew as we exit the school.

I rub my forearms, hoping to get rid of the sudden surge of goosebumps covering every inch of me.

'Cold?' he asks. 'I brought a hoodie if you want it.'

'My god,' I say with a groan. 'You're too much. I don't get how you don't have women lined up around the block to date you?'

He throws his hands in the air as if he's got no idea what I'm talking about, which doesn't help.

'You were right,' I say, trying not to make eye contact for fear of my heart jumping right from my chest and sprinting to him. 'This is fun. Watching *you* do this is fun.'

'I'm sure what you did for a living was fun too. I can't imagine you picking something boring.'

I let out a laugh. 'I was a waitress. For eight years, I delivered food and drinks to people. Most of the time, without even a thank you. Then I got fired. Nothing fun about that.'

'You got *fired*?' he asks. 'For what?'

'I told a guy to eff off after he grabbed my ass.' I roll my eyes as I say it and Dax's grin grows. 'I'd already asked him not to touch me once, so when he tried it again, my inner Mercy came out, and the words rolled off my tongue way too easily. He had the last word and got me fired while he watched.'

Dax's laughter stops, and he looks over at me, his face serious. 'Should have punched the prick.'

'I considered it. Trust me.' This time I laugh. 'This, delivering flowers to people, it's something else. Pure joy. People are sincerely happy to see you.'

'Pure joy,' he repeats. 'I can't argue with that.'

We do deliveries for a few more hours before I get a text from Mercy asking me to meet her for a late lunch. Dax drops me off at the restaurant before he heads home, and truthfully, I'm sad to see him go. Because of him, I haven't thought about Tristan even once today.

*** * ***

Lunch...

'Why do you look like you've just floated over here on cloud nine?' Mercy asks as she walks in.

I haven't been able to quit smiling since I got into Dax's truck this morning. My cheeks hurt, and my heart has done more than a dozen flips with every delivery we made. I've never witnessed someone so perfect for a job. And someone so *not* perfect for it – I spent most of the day blinking back tears.

'I delivered flowers with Dax this morning.'

'Oh...?' Mercy asks, squinting as if she's trying to look inside me.

'It was so...' I stare out the window, looking for the right word to describe it. 'Enchanting? He's *very* charming. I didn't expect that.'

'Shit,' she says. 'He's kicked Tristan's ass, mesmerized you with his constellation bullshit, wooed you with flowers, and now you're in love with him, aren't you?'

Her question snaps me back into reality. I'd texted her early this morning to tell her what happened last night and she was shocked. So shocked her responding texts were just gibberish.

'What? No! I'm *not* in love with him. He's River's best friend.' I glance at the menu secured under the tabletop glass, scanning it for something that will fill my mouth, so I don't say something stupid.

'*However*,' I continue, avoiding direct eye contact with her, 'I did agree to help him while he takes part in a floral competition. *Battle of the Blossoms*?'

Mercy raises an eyebrow. 'He made it, did he? I figured he would.' She studies the menu too then looks up at me.

'Be careful, Hols. Dax is kind of, well, let's just say he's got a way of luring the ladies in with his pretty face and enchanting words but never makes them serious. Not that there's anything wrong with how he lives his life. He's single and allowed to do whatever and whoever he wants. Just know, the man could charm the panties off a mannequin at the half-empty mall. I don't want you to get hurt again.'

'I'm not going to get hurt because I don't have those feelings for Dax. He's just a nice guy. We're friends.'

'Trust me. I know the Dax you don't, and he can separate his feelings from sex. You can't.'

I want to argue with her, but she's not wrong.

'He can't be *that* bad. I met a girl he's sleeping with the other day. She seemed relatively normal. I think her name was Sydney? And, truthfully, *met* might be a strong word. I had her pinned against the wall with one of River's lightsabers because I thought she was an intruder.'

Mercy bursts out laughing. 'I'd have paid money to see that. Syd's still flavor of the month, is she? She's made it longer than I thought she would. Personally, I think she's too serious for Dax. I mean, he posts videos on TikTok with your father. *Dancing.* Sydney is always stone-cold sober. They just don't work.'

He's done videos with my dad? I don't do TikTok because social media makes me anxious, so I cap it at a few and ignore the rest. I know my dad, though, and he's never left the professional dancer within behind. He even put himself through medical school while working as a back-up dancer and he's been in dozens of music videos. But him and Dax? I had no idea.

'Why have you never talked about him if you two are so close?'

'We *aren't* that close. We both work in the wedding and funeral world, and because we all grew up together, we're in one another's friend circles. I watched as he went from dorky Dax to the tattooed, flower-loving, bearded love guru he is now. If you've ever listened to me about anything, let this be it. Don't get sucked in.'

I can tell she's serious. Mercy doesn't give advice like this unless it's for your own good and I trust her.

'I hear you,' I say. 'I promise I won't fall in love with Dax. My heart can't take another fall. From here on out, I'm treating love like I would if someone offered me drugs. I'll just say no.'

'Good,' Mercy says. 'Did Professor Assbag go home?'

I nod. 'Texted me a photo of the inside of the plane this morning. Told me to enjoy the pretty boy and fuck off.'

Mercy shakes her head. 'The boy's got some stones; I'll give him that.'

'Speaking of stones, his mystery woman got a two-carat one. Two freaking carats, Merc.' I roll my eyes, angry all over again.

'Whoa.' She stares at the menu. 'I feel dirty as hell just knowing that. You dodged a bullet. Possibly a literal one after what he pulled last night. I'm glad Dax is good for something. He should have beat him within an inch of his life.'

I don't dare tell her Dax and I slept in the same bed last night. To Mercy, that's one step closer to me riding him like a bronco in a rodeo.

'Back to your new gig with your favorite fuck-boy.'

'I'm his *assistant*, and I don't know what the job entails yet, but I'm nervous. Hopefully, I'll just be handing him flowers. That's probably all I'm good for.'

'Stop. They're flowers. How hard could it be?' she asks. 'Maybe you'll be wiping his brow as he creates flower arrangements like he's performing surgery. He takes all this pretty seriously.'

'I'll know more tomorrow. We meet with a woman from the show, McKenzie, to sign the papers. If he wins, he's putting the money towards buying back his dad's old shop. Isn't that sweet?'

'Adorable,' she says flatly. 'If he wins, do you get part of the winnings?'

I hadn't even thought about that. 'No. I couldn't. I wouldn't. This is his dream. I just...' I hesitate. Ever since last night when I dumped my trash on Dax, I've been thinking about this. 'My old life wasn't making me happy and I'm here to change. I felt like me doing this favor for Dax, without expecting anything in return but a distraction from my failed attempt at life, would maybe help me figure out who I am again? What I want out of life.'

'You're trying to be self*less* instead of self*ish*. It's a good start, Hols. Just be careful with Dax.'

'I promise. I'm not looking to fall in love.'

11

DAX

The Next Day...

'Your job, Hollyn, will be to support Dax in whatever way he needs during the challenges,' McKenzie says.

I requested she meet us at my mom's because Hollyn knows nothing about flowers and we're going to practice once McKenzie leaves. I'm sure she'll learn quickly. She's smart.

'You're his new bitch, Hols.' River laughs from the edge of the garage.

It would be just my luck that he pulled into his

parent's place right as she and I pulled into my mom's next door.

Hollyn shoots him a glare.

'Ian is the cameraman we've assigned to you,' McKenzie continues. 'He'll follow you around during your challenges, asking questions as you work. We want to know *ev-er-y-thing*. From what kind of team leader Dax is to what you thought of his ideas and direction. Is he a terrible boss? A great one? If the challenges are affecting your relationship, tell us. The more honest you are, the more viewers will fall in love with you and the more votes you'll get.'

'*Relationship?*' Hollyn asks, her eyes darting from McKenzie to River to me.

'We aren't an item,' I say, motioning between Hollyn and me, saying the words I know she's thinking.

McKenzie laughs as she massages her forehead with her fingertips. 'I never insinuated it was a *romantic* relationship. It could be friendship, working, rivals, even family. I don't care. No matter what it is, how it plays out will make you an OK, great, or terrible team. The relationship between you may make or break you.'

'They're childhood frenemies, both competing for my attention, who aren't allowed to date because he's my best friend, and she's my sister. Bro code rules,' River says, filling McKenzie in on everything she never wanted to know.

McKenzie stares at him, a confused look on her face. '*Who* are you, and *why* are you here?'

'He's River, and he's nobody. Wasn't even invited,' Hollyn says, irritation dripping from her voice.

River glares her way. 'I'm a production guy eavesdropping on a show in production. It's research.'

'What do you produce?' McKenzie asks.

'Local commercials, music videos, and currently a documentary about a once-famous pop star.'

She nods, clearly not impressed. 'Well, you helping the two of them with anything to do with the show is completely against the rules and will get them kicked off, so choose your visits wisely.'

'He won't be helping,' I say quickly. 'In fact, he was just going home.' I speak directly to River, pointing at his parents' house as though he's a dog who's followed me off the property.

'Is this show like *The Real World*?' River asks as he backs away. 'Because everyone bones in that show, and no boning allowed.' His eyes are right on me.

'Go. Away,' Hols says to River, pleading with her eyes.

'Riv!' Penny calls his name from their front door. 'Come film something for me.'

He shoves his hands into his pockets and walks away, leaving us to get back to McKenzie and the instructions on our first challenge, which happens tomorrow.

'Now that we have some peace,' McKenzie says, 'I went through your file for the Brightly wedding. Did you talk this through with the couple?'

My responsibility is to discuss a plan of action with my clients for anything the show throws at me and, to my surprise, they've all been more supportive of this venture than I expected.

'Yes.'

'I love that it's taking place at The Wooden Shoe Tulip Farm. Tell me your ideas.'

'Well...' I glance at Hollyn, suddenly nervous. 'The ceremony is going to take place outdoors, with the fields and sunset as the backdrop. It'll be very colorful, so the wedding party florals are simple, all white. The tulip fields are the ceremony showstopper.'

'And for the reception?' McKenzie asks. 'This is where we want to see drama.'

'Perfect, because what I have planned is easily the biggest piece I've ever done. It's a white tent reception so I'll reverse the look of outside inside the tent. Colorful tulips suspended from the ceiling will match the fields outside just above the guests' heads.'

McKenzie claps her hands together with a grin. 'I love it. The white against the rainbow of tulip fields, then the color against the white tent is perfect. Whimsical meets classic. What do you think, Hollyn?'

Her eyes are wide, and her grin even wider. 'Sounds beautiful, but complicated. We're going to do that in *how* many hours?'

'Three,' McKenzie reminds her.

'Honestly, I can't picture it, but I'm *sure* Dax can handle it.'

'You're a brave man, Dax. Think you two can pull this off?'

'I'm sure of it,' I say with a confidence I probably shouldn't have considering I don't know how well Hols and I will even work together yet.

'This is it from me,' McKenzie says. 'We'll converse via video chat and emails from this point on. You have my info, so let me know if you have concerns, questions, or need anything at all. Both of you.' She glances between the two of us. 'Now point me towards the café with the strongest coffee in town.'

* * *

Hours Later, Still in the Garage...

'Oh my god,' Hollyn groans, midway through her third bouquet as we prep for tomorrow.

A song once made famous by her mother blasts from her parents' backyard. To me, it sounds like our childhood dancing around us. To her, it's clearly the most annoying thing ever.

'*What* are they doing?'

'We could take a break and find out?'

'No,' she says, wincing as the song gets louder. She keeps her cool for a few more minutes until she suddenly drops the bouquet onto the table.

'Let's go.' She storms through Mom's garage, to her parents' driveway, and into the backyard, me hot on her heels. We both stop as we reach the edge of the pool.

I laugh, but Hollyn has a dropped jaw and a wide-eyed, horrified look on her face. Penny is doing the dance routine she did in this song's video, and River is singing it at the top of his lungs into the end of a pool net he's using as a microphone, bouncing around as if he's on stage as they prep the pool for the upcoming summer. A camera on a tripod not far away is catching every second of their performance on film.

'Christ on a cracker,' Hollyn says, staring across the pool at them.

'I know you missed this,' I say, nudging her with my elbow, now copying the moves I know well because I've been a part of this family since I was four.

She glances at me and laughs, shaking her head. '*What* are you doing?'

I lip sync the words to the song, pointing at her in the right spots. 'River, your dad and I sometimes make videos. The three of us dancing. We're supposed to film this one next week.' I shrug, shaking my ass to the beat. 'River and I, we get the likes.' I wink.

'It's cause we're pretty,' River yells, doing the moves with me from across the pool. 'We're gonna kill this one.'

Hollyn sighs heavily. 'You know when you're born into a family, and you wonder why?' She stares at me, her grin growing by the second as I dance. 'Why *this* family? Why *me*? Why *that* kid next door?'

I laugh out loud. 'I do know that feeling, but probably not as well as you do considering...' I motion to her mom and brother both dancing like no one's watching.

'This is one of those moments. And you're not helping.'

I continue dancing, mainly because it's making her smile. She used to not care what other people think, now she's lost all confidence in herself and is standing on the sidelines looking in.

'Come on, Hols. Dax will teach you the moves!'

'I *know* the moves, Mom. I'm your daughter, re-member? That said, no thanks.'

'Stop being uptight and get your tiny little ass over here and have some fun.'

'Yeah, Hols,' River says. 'Pull the stick from your ass and loosen up.'

'I don't have a stick up my ass.' She looks at me, eyebrows raised. 'Do I?'

I pinch my fingers together. 'Usually, when Justin Timberlake is singing, you're singing with him. When we dance, you dance. Right now, you're pretending you're too cool to be this dorky.'

A gasp leaves her lips, but the smile on her face says she's not mad. I dance towards her, getting even more animated the closer I get, my recent flower boy performance flashing through my head. She's going to see that video at some point, and I doubt I'll ever hear the end of it.

'You know you want to,' I say, exaggerating the moves even more.

'Sometimes I hate you,' she says through a grin. The same smile that's always said *you've lost your ever-loving mind, but I don't hate you.*

'It's fun. You should try it. Very stress relieving. Like having sex,' I say, waggling my eyebrows.

'You're the expert on that, aren't you?'

'Wouldn't you like to know.'

'I feel like I'm at a high school dance,' she says as River makes his way to us.

'You can't admit we're a little good?' River asks.

Hollyn walks his way, her arms crossed over her chest as she watches him bust a move. After a minute, when she's close enough, she shoves him into the pool behind him, then she turns her attention to me.

'You sure you wanna do that?' I ask, doing the sprinkler enthusiastically.

'Pretty sure,' she says. 'You're goin' in.' She runs at me, prepped to shove my ass into the pool, fully clothed.

What she didn't expect was me wrapping an arm around her and pulling her in with me. The squeal as we hit the water makes it all worth it.

'Ha!' River yells as I pop out of the water. He raises

a hand for a high five. I meet his hand with mine as Hollyn watches, brushing her hair from her face.

'You two will kill me,' she says, bobbing in the water a few feet from me.

Penny's now dancing around the pool, singing her lyrics, the only one still dry, a glass of wine in her hand that I'm sure isn't her first of the day.

'I miss being on tour,' she says. 'Hols, you shook your three-year-old booty on stage in front of thousands of people once. Don't you remember how fun it was to break out into a dance party when you were kids? You loved it!'

'I'm still fun,' Hollyn says defensively, a bit unsure of her answer. 'You think so, right?' There's that missing self-confidence I want to help her find again.

'You keep me smiling.'

She flashes me an unsure grin.

'Come on,' River interrupts. 'The funnest thing you've done since you got here was throw bigfoot here into the pool. Otherwise, it's been all tears and whining. I vote for more of the pool thing. Who's with me?' Both River and Penny raise their hands.

Hollyn's eyes widen as she looks at me, waiting for my vote. Slowly, I raise my hand, and she splashes water my way as though she's trying to drown me. I swim over, as if I'm going to climb out but dunking her under as I pass. She flails around as I hold her under for a second before releasing her and swimming to the side.

'Funny!' she says when she emerges, glaring my way.

'My wallet votes for no more of the pool thing.' I pull it from my pants as I stand at the edge of the pool, removing everything and lying it all in the sun to dry. I've had to do this many times over the years as throwing one another into the pool was each of our missions when we were younger. The less the other person expected it, the better.

'Sorry,' Hols says as she swims over to me. 'Did I ruin anything?'

'No need to be sorry; it was all in good fun. Water dries. I may have even liked it.' I wink as she holds onto the pool's edge next to me. 'I almost saw the Hollyn I remember there.'

'I'm still the same Hollyn,' she insists.

'Nah. Just like I'm not the same Dax. But it's cool. I kind of like you as you are now.'

'Kind of?' She laughs, attempting to shove me into the water again but failing.

I push her back, sending her two feet farther from me and she splashes around, finding her footing again with a laugh.

Watching her have fun makes me feel good and something about her smile hits me in a place nothing else does. I'll gladly make a fool out of myself if it means seeing her happy. I need to remind her of who she was and make her see that she really is the goofy girl currently standing on a pool step in front of me, trying to pound water out of her ear.

'Maybe I've become a little uptight but I'm working on it,' she admits, now dragging her soaked self up the stairs and out of the pool.

Her pastel pink T-shirt clings to her, revealing her black bra through the now soaking fabric. She lifts the bottom of the shirt and wrings the water out of it, exposing her stomach as she does so.

And she's activated the launch sequence. Shit. Thank god water distorts things because she's creating a situation River would surely disapprove of.

'Let's get you some dry clothes,' her mom says, throwing an arm over Hollyn's shoulder, directing her into the house.

Thank god. All I have to do now is think about sushi, River, my grandmother, barking dogs, and anything that can annoy a hard-on back to its relaxed state.

'You managed to cheer her up,' River says, now

doing fully clothed backstrokes across the pool. 'Good job pulling her in with you. She didn't expect that.'

'I sometimes feel like I'm walking on eggshells around her. She's burst into tears more than once and I've hit her boyfriend right in front of her. Seeing her have fun for once was nice.'

'She'll come around,' River says as he swims to the pool's edge and lifts himself out. He grabs two towels from a cabinet on the patio, tossing one to me as I get out.

I hope he's right. I want to see her laugh like she did before Tristan. And *I* want to be the one to make that happen.

12

HOLLYN

The Next Afternoon...

'You're doing outstandingly, Hols,' Dax says, the two of us working as quickly as possible.

All the prep the show allowed us to do yesterday, we did. After the pool incident, I tried to loosen up a bit, even singing along to a song at one point. That surprised Dax. I figured if they all think I'm uptight, I must be. I'm here for change, and the only way to change is to do the opposite of what I'd usually do.

Now we're putting together the ceiling full of flowers. Before we started, Dax showed me some photos of his previous designs and I was blown away. I had no idea he was this skilled at his job and it's clear he's surpassed his father by miles already.

It's not just the flowers he's great at. He happily talks to everyone who approaches him. When he dropped off the wedding party bouquets and bouton-nieres, the mother of the bride requested one small addition, and he did it no problem, there and then, with a smile on his face, as they chit-chatted about life.

Now I'm standing on a stepladder, holding a two-by-four in place over my head while Dax secures it to the post next to him for the structure that will support the suspended flower arrangement. He's standing on another ladder, towering over me, a drill in his hand, screws in his lips, and looking far too much like some kind of construction worker women ogle on viral photos that travel around Instagram. Mercy's joke about this exact scene keeps playing through my head.

He walked in wearing blue jeans, white and black Adidas shoes, a black San Francisco Giants ball cap worn backward, and a white T-shirt that says *Iris my life to save you* across the front, which sent me into laughter when I saw him. He claimed I was the inspi-ration for the shirt choice. Flower pun shirts are his jam and it's so adorable it's sending my head all over the place.

'How do you work with this view?' I stare out of the entrance of the tent into the tulip fields.

'With fifty grand and my reputation on my mind?' Nervous laughter leaves his lips. 'Trust me; it's a challenge right now,' he says from above me. 'A real challenge.'

I glance up at him looming over me. His eyes are on me until our gaze meets, then he looks away. Why does it seem like we're not having the same conversation?

'Almost done,' he says. 'Think you can hold one more?'

'Absolutely. I haven't spent an hour a day lounging in a spa at the gym for the last eight years for nothing.'

He laughs. 'Thank god for gym memberships, right?'

'Exactly.'

When he's done, the two of us admire his creation. It's nothing special right now, just a wooden structure, but once the flowers are hung and the lights are strung, I'm sure it'll be incredible.

'It's beautiful,' I say with a smirk.

'Just wait,' he says. 'I'll be back with flowers.'

'How ya doin', Hollyn?' Ian, our camera guy, asks as Dax leaves the tent.

Ian's an older guy, easily late forties or early fifties. He's got a head full of graying hair, yet he's wearing skinny jeans. A middle-aged hipster.

I've been put in charge of winding five billion twinkle lights around the corner posts to disguise them. I never thought I'd hate twinkle lights, but after three splinters in one hand and hardly being done with post one after ten minutes, I already despise them.

'I'm doing,' I respond with a shrug, not looking up from my work.

'How'd you feel helping with the arrangements yesterday? Did it take long?'

I burst out a laugh. 'It took forever. Mostly because I was so slow, but Dax was incredibly patient and the perfect teacher, so imagine my surprise when we delivered them to the wedding party and got a brilliant response. Even about the ones I made.' I glance over at the camera. 'Dax's vision is gorgeous.'

I wind lights tightly against the strand below, continuing my way around the post.

'I think he's nervous, though.'

'About losing? Or something else?'

'Um...' I glance outside at Dax, who's pulling two

buckets of tulips at a time from the back of his delivery truck, setting them on the ground like he actually uses the gym. Those buckets full of water were so heavy I could hardly lift one at a time this morning when I helped him load them.

'I think he feels like his life purpose is on the line. He wants to use this money to buy back his late father's florist shop. He was just a kid when his dad passed and I watched his whole world collapse that day.'

It's a day I haven't thought about in years, partly because it still hurts to relive it.

When the police came to Dax's mom Rebecca's door, she immediately ran to our house because that's where Dax was. I remember her collapsing in the living room, my mom lying on the floor with her. The two of them sobbed as Dad shooed us kids from the room. We had no idea what was going on, and ten-year-old Dax was scared.

I sat with him in the family room while River took off outside. When they finally told him a couple of hours later, I watched from the stairwell. I was supposed to be in my room, but I knew how scared he was that he'd done something wrong and was in trouble. I couldn't leave him. I cried as I watched him cry. It's still the saddest day of my life.

There are moments of being with Dax now that I'm surprised at how much he turned out like Robert, considering he was so young when his father died. Robert was amazing. Tall with dark hair, soft-spoken and gentle, generous, always making jokes, and incredibly protective of his family and friends. All those qualities now exist in Dax and I don't even think he realizes it.

'I was too young to really understand it myself,' I continue. 'But seeing Dax grieving was tough to watch. I know his dad's old storefront means everything to him. I also know he's put his whole heart into becoming a florist. It's his passion, and he's truly amazing at it. I'm not worried about the talent part at all. The thing is, who's he competing against? And what do they have on the line driving them?'

Ian drops the camera momentarily. 'That was excellent, Hollyn. Pull at them heartstrings, girl.'

'Did that sound like a sob story?'

Crap. Why'd I go and say all that? Dax's gonna be mad I just told the whole world about the moment his life changed forever. God. Why don't I have a stop button on my mouth? He's never liked to talk about it, and here I go, letting it fly to the whole freaking world.

* * *

A Couple of Hours Later...

'This is gorgeous.' I step down the ladder and stare up at the flowers above me. 'I want to live here.' I walk to the center of the arrangement and lie down, gazing up at the sky of suspended flowers.

'Yeah?' Dax asks, taking the few steps down his ladder and lying next to me. 'Wow,' he says, 'this is even better than I'd imagined. Maybe we can convince everyone to lie underneath it?'

I roll my head his way. 'You're going to win.'

'If I do it will only be because of you,' he says. 'Had you not been here, I'd have never finished this in three hours.'

'You did most of it, Dax. I know I did *something* because I'm exhausted and will probably need a massage or a hot tub soon because my neck, back, and shoulders are killing me. Not to mention I've got a dozen splinters in my hands. None of that matters though, because this turned out beautiful.'

'I could make that happen for you.'

I sit up, turning to him. 'Make what happen? Winning? Cause yeah, like I said, you've got this in the bag, friend.'

He gets to his feet, walking under the arrangement as he inspects it. 'I meant the massage.'

I stand, wiping off my backside. 'You're going to give me a massage?' I ask. 'That's a little dangerous, don't you think?'

Maybe I haven't been in the dating world for a long time, but I know men don't usually hand out massages without expecting something else.

'Like a steep grade hill without brakes.' He laughs, his cheeks glowing a deep pink color. 'I wouldn't do it personally unless, of course, you wanted that.' He winks. 'But I know a place. I could set something up. As a thank you.'

'You'd do that?'

'Absolutely. I can help dig those splinters out too.' He whips a small knife from his pocket and grabs my hand playfully. 'This will only hurt a little.'

'Ah, no way!' I pull my hand from him, inspecting the tiny pieces of wood gleefully living just beneath the skin. They seem happy right where they are.

'You don't need to organize a massage either. You do enough for me. Trust me.'

'I don't do anything I don't want to do. Nobody's twisting my arm,' he says, lifting a shoulder. 'I like to see you smile, Hols.'

'You two ready to video chat with McKenzie?' Ian

interrupts our moment. 'She wants to check out your work, so I'll give her a tour, then she'll discuss her thoughts with the two of you. This part will be filmed, so be mindful of your language.'

'Sure,' Dax says. 'Let me just clean up real fast.'

The two of us pack the ladders and supplies back to his delivery truck, cleaning up anything we brought, so the wedding site is as pristine as it was when we got here.

'I'm nervous. Like' – he blows out a breath, running a hand over his beard – 'I kind of want to puke nervous.'

'Dax, the display is truly gorgeous.' I touch his shoulder. 'If this were my wedding, I'd be thrilled.'

'Yeah?' He glances at my hand, a hint of a smile on his face as he crosses his arms over his chest like he's not convinced.

'*Yeah*,' I say. 'You've got nothing to be nervous about.'

'Thanks, Hols.'

He closes the truck doors, motioning for me to follow him to the tent. I hear McKenzie's voice over the iPad Ian holds when we walk in.

'There they are,' Ian says, handing Dax the iPad.

'Hi,' he says to her, obviously nervous as he speaks.

'This. Is. Incredible. Ian laid the iPad under your arrangement, and I'm blown away. It's beautiful. The contrast between the look the wedding will have outside and then inside the tent is magical!'

Dax smiles. 'Thank you.'

'How do you feel you two did?'

I'm surprised when he grabs my hand, squeezing it tightly as he speaks. I can't even comprehend what he's saying with all the lights and sirens going off in my head, signaling a red flag where I'm sure there isn't meant to be one. I knew my red flag beacon was broken. This is proof.

Why is it suddenly hard to breathe? And why does my hand in his feel so wonderful?

No, Hols. Don't do this. Your feelings are liars. They make all the wrong choices. Tristan is proof.

'How about you, Hollyn?'

'Hollyn,' Dax says, squeezing my hand again.

'What?' I ask, glancing at the screen.

McKenzie grins. 'Welcome to the show,' she says with a smirk. 'How do you feel Dax did?'

Man alive, Hollyn. Pull yourself together and stop trying to figure out what him holding your hand means. It's nothing!

'I uh – he's beautiful.'

McKenzie raises an eyebrow, an awkward smile on her face as Dax glances at me, clearly confused.

'He is quite handsome, isn't he?' McKenzie says with a laugh. 'But I meant the flowers.'

'*Holy. Hell,*' I say, Dax now laughing nervously next to me. 'I *meant* the flowers. The arrangements are beautiful. *Not* Dax.'

Ugh, don't say that either!

'Er, well, I uh—' I need to stop talking.

Dax squeezes my hand tightly again and there's no misreading this message. He needs absolutely no support right now, just please, for the love of God, woman: *Shut. The. Hell. Up.* Message received, big fella. My lips are sealed.

McKenzie laughs. 'I love you two. You did amazing. Now, go. Relax and get ready for the filming tomorrow.'

I nod my head, biting my bottom lip to keep me from saying anything else stupid. How embarrassing was that? It'll add itself to my nightmares; that's how much.

When McKenzie clicks out of the call, Dax hands the iPad back to Ian and he laughs to himself.

'What, uh – what was that?'

'I...' I glance down at my hand, now free from his. There's nothing I can say but the truth. I drop my head towards the ground. If only the power of invisibility was a thing already. You led me on, Harry Potter.

'Well... would you rather know the truth or something similar to the truth?'

He chuckles. 'Let's see what the truth gets us.'

'OK.' I shove my hands into the pockets of my jeans. 'I seem to have lost all the power to my brain when you held my hand. I don't understand why either.'

An adorable bashful grin hangs at his lips. 'My fault, and I'm sorry. I got nervous; it felt right. Now that I know it affects you physically for reasons you don't understand, I promise, it won't happen again.'

My heart slows. Don't promise that. Wait, *what*?

'I wouldn't want to melt your brain or anything,' he says, a cocky grin on his pretty face. 'What do you say we get the hell out of here and grab something to eat?'

He's just going to pretend it never happened? That I didn't just ramble on like a braindead dummy and embarrass us both in front of God and the entire YouTube world? *Who* is this man?

13

DAX

The Next Day...

We flew into California this morning and we're now standing at a restaurant in Ocean Beach. We didn't exactly get a tour, but from what we did see, it's a very southern California surfer town.

Hols fell in love with the place immediately and has requested we not leave until she's put her feet in the ocean and now I'm looking forward to seeing that more than anything else we do today.

'Hi.' A tall woman with waist-length strawberry blonde hair approaches us. 'Where are you two from?'

'Suburb outside Portland, Oregon,' I say. 'You?'

'I live here. Ocean Beach. Born and raised. Isn't it just the cutest town?'

'I'm ready to pack my bags and move,' Hollyn says.

The woman standing in front of us looks like she belongs here. She's probably a few years younger than me, if I had to guess. Nearly six feet tall, pretty, and the type I'd typically go for. She's got a single lavender aster stem tucked behind her right ear that matches her dress perfectly. As a guy who studies flowers and what they mean, I know a flower behind a woman's right ear represents her being single. Sneaky.

She's wearing a short boho-style dress and strappy heeled sandals covered in fringe. Her wrists are stacked with bracelets of every color and design and I'd bet money her name is probably something like Luna or Rain. And I say that with the utmost respect having a best friend named River.

Her eyes are on Hollyn, looking her over, clearly judging her at first sight. Hols look great. She was worried she'd over or under-dressed, but I think she looks fantastic. Gorgeous. She's a thousand times prettier than the woman in front of us.

'Was your flight good?' the nameless woman asks. 'I hate flying. I'm dreading visiting other contestants.'

'I hate flying too,' Hollyn says. 'You know what helps? Booze.'

I laugh out loud. She had a couple of drinks on the plane and now she's got a permanent grin on her face. She's a touch drunk and it's partially my fault too. The moment we boarded the plane, she started in on how much she hates flying and I'd never seen someone white knuckle an armrest the way she did.

To help, I put her out of her misery with a couple of drinks and she was laughing at old stories in no time.

'Driving has a higher chance of death than flying.' A young woman stops at boho girl's side.

'You and your statistics.' Boho girl rolls her eyes. 'This is my little sister, Genevieve. I'm Celeste.'

I wasn't far off on the name.

'Dax.' I motion to myself. 'This is Hollyn.'

'So, what's the deal with you two? You're the only man and woman pair. Are you a couple?'

'A couple?' Hollyn asks, her voice higher than usual.

'Just old friends,' I say, taking the lead, so she doesn't spew out some nonsense about how beautiful I am again. Not that I didn't enjoy it.

I glance around the room and everyone looks pretty normal. Most of the other contestants are older than me, which probably means they've got more experience, but experience doesn't always mean anything. My gaze settles on an older man in a floral print suit. His bow tie even has a silk flower in the center. I can't compete with that, even with my flower pun T-shirts.

'Hello!' a woman says, clapping her hands together as she walks onto the restaurant patio. 'If everyone can take their spots.'

McKenzie went over how the filming will work the second we walked in and it seems as if she knows every contestant and is the go-to person for everyone.

'Dax,' Celeste says as our partners walk to our spots ahead of us. She touches my arm as I slow to a stop. 'Your tattoos are beautiful. I've got a few too.' She raises her left arm to display a watercolor sunflower on her inner arm. Her hand moves to my bicep as she steps closer, her breath now on my neck. 'Maybe I'll get a chance to show you the others some time,' she whispers into my ear, winking as she backs away from me.

What the—? My brain stalls out momentarily as I stand glued to my spot, only coming back to earth when someone claps their hands again.

I walk to Hollyn, who's now staring at me wide-eyed like she just heard the whole thing. Why do I suddenly feel guilty? Probably because Hollyn seems to own my heart again, and I never want to hurt her. She just doesn't know it yet.

'Welcome,' the mystery woman standing at the front of the room says softly. 'I'm Jillian. Before we get started, we'd like for each of you to introduce yourself to the others. Who you are, where you're from, the name of your shop, and who you're here with. Leo, let's start with you.' She motions to the guy in the floral suit.

He beams. How did I notice this guy's suit yet miss a handlebar mustache like that? A look I can*not* pull off. I'd look like a washed-up porn star from the eighteen hundreds.

'My name's Leonard Elliott. Leo for short. Born and raised in San Francisco. My shop's called Rainbow Bouquets, and I'm here with my oldest son, Bradley.' He motions to the younger guy standing next to him, who sadly isn't sporting a matching floral suit.

'We're thrilled to have you, Leo.'

'Thank you,' he says. 'Being here is taking my mind off the fact that my partner was recently diagnosed with leukemia.' He chokes up momentarily. That's rough.

'Oh no.' Boho Celeste lets out a concerned groan.

'We wish him the best in his battle,' Jillian says.

Leo dabs at his eyes with a floral print handker-
chief he's pulled from his pocket. I glance at Hollyn,
now a little panicked. Were we supposed to have
something tragic in the wings to help win over fans?
Cause I've got nothing. My motives for being here are
purely selfish.

'Celeste, go ahead. Tell us about yourself.'

'Hi,' she chirps, waving her open hand, her concern for Leo's partner suddenly non-existent. Her
voice is sweet like honey. Nothing like the way she just
whispered into my ear about unseen tattoos.

'I'm Celeste Graham. My closest friends call me
CeCe. I'm from right here in Ocean Beach, Cali. I run
The Flower Patch, a cute little organic floral farm outside town. If you have time, I'd love for you to check it
out.' Her gaze lands on mine momentarily as if she's
inviting me and me alone.

Never gonna happen, sweetheart. I glance at Hollyn, who's intently listening to Celeste speak.

'This is my little sister, Genevieve. I'm so excited to
be here amongst so much talent.' She applauds herself, her hands close to her chest.

'Celeste's flower farm is adorable,' Jillian says. 'I
had the pleasure of visiting yesterday when I flew in.
Just darling.'

'I appreciate that,' Celeste says, beaming with

pride as if it's the first time she's heard it from a mouth not her own.

'Onto you, Dax.'

My insides flop over, reminding me I was too nervous to eat this morning. Hell, I was practically too nervous to sleep. Now I'm starving, exhausted, and nervous.

'I'm Dax Hartley.' I raise a single hand. 'I'm from a small suburb outside Portland, Oregon. I run The Flower Boy out of a delivery truck for now. This is my childhood friend Hollyn who is acting as my assistant.'

'Childhood friends,' Jillian says with a coy smile. 'That's fun! Do I sense a rekindling of something?'

Hols' eyes go wide. I know if I don't speak now and clear this up, she'll ramble on about whatever half sentences are running through her head, and we'll probably both regret it later.

'We're just reconnecting as friends after a time apart. We grew up next door to one another. Her brother is my best friend.'

'Ah...' Jillian's face is very much the face the woman at the airport had when she heard the brother's best friend thing.

My eyes land on Celeste, who winks my way. She's

a little ballsy. I have a feeling that's going to be a problem.

'Marley. Tell us about you,' Jillian moves on.

The woman to our left takes a step forward. 'I'm Marley Sterling. I live in Eugene, Oregon. I run The Plant Shed. I do both florals and houseplants. I've been focusing more on the houseplant side lately and running a social media account dedicated to them as hashtag houseplant life. Got to grab ahold of those trends while they're happening.'

'Hashtag excellent idea,' Jillian says. 'Who's with you today?'

'Oh!' She laughs, glancing back at her partner still standing in her place. 'This is my best friend, Emily.'

'Nice to have you both with us. Onto Allie,' Jillian says to the last contestant.

'Hello!' Allie says in a bubbly voice. 'I'm Allie Rhodes, from the rainy city of Seattle. My shop is called Happy Petals. Flowers are just happy! Aren't they?' She lets out a giggle. 'With me today is my ex-coworker, Nina. We're former lawyers turned florist and novelist.' Allie says everything like it's brand new, supremely exciting news.

'Wonderful!' Jillian says, matching her excitement. 'Such talent standing before me. Did you all have fun with your first challenge?'

Hollyn and I stand silently as our competitors chatter about how much fun they had. I'm really out of my element here. I like to talk at times, don't get me wrong, but mostly I save it for the folks in my tiny circle of loved ones or clientele. Thank god Hols is here with me because if she wasn't, I'm not sure I'd be able to do this.

'I won't make you wait any longer,' Jillian says. 'We're going to give you rankings on the website. Viewers can either bump you up or eliminate you based on what they see while we've filmed and I'll announce the results on YouTube live every Friday. Ready?'

'Let's do it!' Celeste claps her hands with a wide grin.

'Two of you stood out to me this week.' Jillian pauses dramatically, looking at each of us. 'Celeste and Allie, would you take a step forward.'

Celeste's sister lets out a little squeal, the two of them embracing before she does as she's told.

'Unfortunately, your teams are in my bottom two this week.'

Damn, that was brutal. I didn't expect that. Their faces drop as though they've just watched someone kill a puppy. But the massive knot in my gut loosens a bit. We're not in the bottom two. Hallelujah. Hollyn glances up at me, a nervous yet adorable smile on her face. I can barely push away the nerves to even grin back, but I manage.

'Allie,' Jillian says, her tone now serious, 'I felt like you played it too safe. Your centerpiece didn't blow us away. To tell you the truth, I found it kind of generic.'

Allie nods as if she understands, words now apparently not her friend. You could almost see her previous excitement hitting the ground like a plane in a nosedive.

'You haven't yet lost; viewers could decide to keep you so don't let my thoughts bring you down. Your wedding was beautiful just not what *I'd* hoped for.'

I glance at Celeste. She's spinning a ring on her forefinger and staring at the ground. I didn't expect this to be so savage.

'Celeste.'

She lets out a heavy sigh as she waits for Jillian's words.

'You had the exact opposite problem. Your arrangements were a bit much. Nothing matched, and I feel you overdid the variety of flowers on display. Sometimes less is more.'

Celeste's gaze stays locked on the ground below her feet, and she says nothing, but the look of absolute humiliation on her face speaks for her. Ouch.

'I won't say who I think should go home. That's for the viewers to decide. Perhaps they'll see something in the two of you I didn't. Go ahead and step back to your places.'

The two of them step back, their assistants consoling them as they do.

'Now for our top two pairs.' Jillian paces in front of the five of us. Back and forth, playing on our nerves until finally stopping in front of Leo. 'Leo, and' – she continues past him, stopping in front of me – 'Dax.' She grins. 'Step forward, you two.'

Hollyn's hand on my forearm stops me. 'You did it,' she whispers with a grin.

I step forward, unable to knock the grin she just created off my face as I do. We made Jillian's top two. That's something.

'Leo,' Jillian says. 'Your rainbow display for the brides you worked with was outstanding. Beautifully done and on-brand for the ladies in charge. I understand this was their request?'

'It was. They were a peach to work with,' he says, smiling ear to ear. 'It was a lot of fun to put together.'

Beside Jillian is a massive television, playing clips of each of our weddings yesterday. I'm impressed. A flower arrangement rainbow. It's a damn good idea.

'Dax.'

Jillian stands a few feet from me, her hands folded in front of her, her smile as wide as possible. 'Your venue was my favorite. A field of tulips at sunset. It doesn't get more romantic than that, does it? Breathtaking. When I saw the white tent reception, I panicked for you a little. But your design left that tent anything but colorless and boring.'

My design plays on the TV next to her.

'Wow,' Celeste says under her breath, her and Genevieve whispering back and forth.

'Are you sure you've only been at this a couple years?'

'Two years, yeah.'

'Impressive,' she says. 'Very impressive.' She's now walking between Leo and me while she talks. 'I might be wrong about this, but if I had to choose a winner today.' She pauses dramatically, clearly more for the show than for us. 'Dax, it'd be you.'

Hollyn squeals as she jumps off the ground in my direction. 'I told you!' she says, wrapping her arms around my neck.

I momentarily rest my hand on her back with a laugh, Jillian laughing along with us.

'Sorry!' Hols says, suddenly realizing what she's done and stepping away from me slowly. She's touched me twice today, and yesterday she was afraid her brain would melt with our holding hands. I don't hate this change of heart.

'Don't be sorry,' Jillian says. 'It's well deserved. You two did outstanding work.'

All eyes are on us, but our eyes are on each other.

'We did it,' I say softly, holding out my closed fist. Hols fist bumps it with a grin, then moves back to her spot, her fingers now laced through each other in front of her chest as though she's praying.

'Whatever you two are, old friends, new friends, you're adorable,' Jillian says. 'Congratulations to you all. I'm as excited as you are to see who comes back to us next week.'

Jillian's words finally sink in as she stops talking.

Holy shit. Did I just *win* week one? Not technically, because the viewers will decide that but close enough.

As soon as they announce the cameras are no longer running, I turn to Hollyn. She's holding a single finger in the air.

'You did it!' She beams. 'Number one. I knew you would be.'

'We'll find out for sure Friday,' I say, mostly to remind myself that one possible win doesn't equal fifty grand. But I now feel better about my chances.

* * *

Moments Later...

'Our flight is in three hours,' Hols says as we walk from the restaurant towards the beach. 'Three hours to do anything we want.'

'Guys!' A voice stops us in our tracks and we both turn to see Celeste running our way. 'Hang on!'

Hollyn frowns, lifting a shoulder and looking pretty uninterested in anything to do with Celeste.

'Going to the beach? Mind if I join you?'

I want to say no. I'd rather just hang out with Hollyn, but that would be rude.

'Sure?' I say, flashing Hols an I'm sorry look. She forces a hesitant grin.

'The more, the merrier,' Hollyn says in a voice I know is fake.

Is she upset because she doesn't like Celeste or because she wants to hang out with just me?

The three of us walk across the street towards the beach, Hollyn pulling her flip-flops off as we get to the sand.

'I gotta say, Dax, I kinda want to know everything about you,' Celeste says.

Hollyn's face drops, and she takes Celeste's words

as a cue to walk ahead of us. She wastes no time heading straight to the ocean, glancing back at one point and flashing me an unsure smile before wading shin-deep into the surf, her long hair blowing in the breeze.

'It's cute you chose your best friend's sister as your assistant. Have you two always been close?' Celeste asks as we stop not far from where Hols is currently stepping into the ocean.

'We were,' I say, sitting in the dry sand. 'But it's been a long time.'

Celeste sits next to me, her long legs crossed over one another at the ankle. I lean forward, my elbows resting on my knees as I watch Hollyn stand in the surf, her arms out at her sides like she's on the *Titanic* with Leo himself. DiCaprio, not handlebar mustache dude.

She used to love that stupid movie. She'd bawl through the last hour and yell that Rose *did* have room for Jack. *Two people could fit on that, even someone your size*, she'd say to me, irritated as all get-out that someone as lovely as Jack had to die in the end.

I stare at Hollyn, pretending Celeste isn't here. I'm really not sure how much longer I can hold in telling her how I feel. But if I do it now, after only being around her a couple weeks, it'll just scare her off and that's the last thing I want.

'She's cute,' Celeste says.

I shake my head slowly. 'She's beautiful,' I correct her.

Celeste is quiet for a moment. 'You know who else is pretty beautiful?'

I glance over.

'You.' She runs a finger down my arm in a way that makes my skin crawl.

She tries to get close to me; I'm not sure I've ever met a woman this brazen. I think I prefer doing the chasing. How do I respond to this?

'Congratulations on having that early lead,' she continues, saving me from having to decide what to say to her earlier comment. 'Your display was gorgeous. What got you into flowers?'

If she's not going away any time soon, I might as well make conversation, so it's not completely awkward.

'My dad. He was a florist. Used to bring my mom flowers daily. I dunno, it stuck with me.'

'How sweet is that?' Celeste says with a swoony sigh. 'Did he retire?'

'Died,' I say matter-of-factly, knowing how much that response can shut down a conversation.

She pulls a hand to her chest, planting the other on my shoulder. 'I'm so sorry. Was it recent?'

'Nah...' I lean back, hoping to dislodge her hand from any part of me. 'I was ten.'

'Well, that's even more heartbreaking.' She leans back with me, now resting a hand over mine.

I immediately change positions, pulling my hand from under hers and focus back on Hollyn. She's still got her back to me, but when she glances around, she looks right at Celeste sitting way too close and her smile fades.

'Celeste, I'm only here for the money. I'm not looking for any kind of relationship.'

'Me either,' she says quickly. 'Had my heart broken once. Same for you?'

I look back out at Hollyn. 'Absolutely crushed.'

'I get it,' Celeste says. 'Well should you ever get lonely, I'm open to casual.'

Damn, she's even more ballsy than I usually am. I shake my head.

'No worries. I've got to get, anyway. I have a wedding this afternoon, and I don't want to be late. I couldn't help but spend a few extra minutes with you.' She grins sweetly as she stands from the sand, brushing herself off. 'I'll email you. The show gave us everyone's emails.' She ruffles my hair. 'See ya next time, Daxy.'

Daxy? I run a hand through my hair, undoing whatever she did.

Usually, I'd have taken the bait Celeste was throwing and probably be on my way to her place right now but I just can't do it this time.

I look back out at Hollyn. She's turning away from me, probably having seen that whole thing. After a few minutes, she walks back over to me, one hand holding her skirt above her knees.

'So,' she says, sitting down, 'you and CeCe had a little moment, did ya?' The way she says her name, the one only her closest friends call her, makes me laugh. She doesn't like CeCe, and she's not even attempting to hide it.

'It was nothing. Besides being florists, the only thing we have in common is tattoos.' I lift an arm Hollyn's way as if she hasn't already noticed them.

'They're nice tattoos.' She runs her fingers over my skin above the ink, sending sparks through my entire body. 'But I'm sure she was admiring the man they're on more.'

'Nah,' I lie. 'If so...' I lift a shoulder.

'You don't want to sleep with her? She's pretty.'

I glance over at Hols. 'So are you. But no, not feeling it today.'

Her brow furrows. 'Aren't you happy you won?' she asks, leaning back on her hands and staring out at the ocean.

'I'm thrilled.'

'This is *thrilled*, Dax? I'd have expected you to be dancing in the surf then Ubering yourself straight to The Flower Patch to sleep off some stress.'

I laugh out loud. 'You don't really see me as a guy who's out boning every woman in town, do you?'

She lifts her shoulders. 'I mean, I've heard rumors, but I haven't witnessed that in you, so I don't know. *Is that you?*'

I sigh, blowing out a breath and lacing my fingers together, stretching my arms out in front of me. Looks like it's time to clear my reputation if I want anything to ever happen between us.

'Honestly' – I side-eye her – 'it *has* been me. Lately, though, I'm just not into it.'

'What changed?' she asks, leaning back on her hands, her face lifted to the sun.

You. That's what I want to say. I haven't slept with anyone since the moment Hollyn came back into my life. Like my loins went on strike the second I saw her at the airport. I want exactly one woman, and she doesn't even know it.

'I dunno.'

'Is it me?' she asks, her voice small and hesitant.

Her reading my mind shouldn't be this scary.

'No,' I blurt out. 'You've been the bright spot in my days, Hols. I even enjoyed kicking Tristan's ass.'

She laughs. 'I'm sorry I got you caught up in my drama. Sometimes, I wonder if you're only this nice to me because I'm such a mess.'

'That's only 99 percent of it.' I wink, leaning forward, my elbows on my knees again. 'Haven't I always been nice to you?'

'Mostly,' she says. 'When you and River weren't doing annoying things like egging my car.'

I laugh. 'Pretty sure I went along with River because it forced you to notice me. I liked when you noticed me.'

If she wasn't wearing these sunglasses, maybe I could see her reaction to those words.

A slight smile turns the corners of her lips. 'I *always* noticed you, Dax. How could I not? You're seven feet tall and were at my house twenty-four-seven. We even spent holidays together. You're practically a part of the family. Truthfully, besides Mercy, you and River were my only friends.'

Is she saying I'm like a brother to her? Shit.

'Are you stressed?' she asks, probably noticing the sigh I thought I'd barely released.

'Very. The show is a lot of pressure. I've got money going out I don't normally have because I haven't had the time to do everything myself lately. I had to hire Jake to help unload orders at my mom's. I'm paying him in beer, but still.'

'I can always help.'

'You're doing plenty.'

Suddenly she gasps as though she's got a great idea. 'You know what you should do?'

'What?'

'Blow off some steam. *Not* with Celeste. I don't love her. But I'm going out with Mercy tonight, and the apartment will be all yours. You should call Sydney. I feel bad about almost poking her with a lightsaber. Not to mention interrupting your booty call.'

I drop my head momentarily before lifting it and looking out at the ocean. I haven't even thought about Sydney since that night. My mind is all Hollyn.

'I promise I won't come home and assault her,' she says. 'I could even stay at Mercy's for a night if you want. I'm sure her brother wouldn't mind.'

'No,' I say quickly, startling her.

The last thing I want is for her to find another

place to stay. Eventually, I'll *have* to face my feelings head-on, but the timing just isn't right yet.

'Text Sydney!' she insists. 'I hate seeing you so stressed. Don't stop being yourself on account of me suddenly infiltrating your life. I'm cool with it.'

'Can I be honest?'

I have to at least hint at what's going on inside. If I don't, my heart might explode. I need to know I'm not just another annoying little brother to her before these feelings become so huge that I crash like I did when she left.

'Yeah.'

'Us talking on the roof the other night, hanging out at your mom's, then all this; it reminds me of when we were close as teens. We always had fun together, even without your brother, and I want to spend more time with you. That's why I haven't been lady hunting lately.'

'You want to spend more time with *me*?'

I nod, looking back out at the ocean nervously. 'I want to be...' I stop, glancing back at her and seeing the nervousness on her face. I can't tell her yet. She's not ready. 'Friends again. I want to be friends again, Hols.'

God, I am a fucking coward.

'I want that too. You don't want the old me back,

though, trust me. I was a total jerk, only ever focused on my own feelings. I didn't see it then, but I do now.'

If only she saw *all* of it. All of me.

'I like you,' she says, touching the gemstone on the necklace around her neck. 'Maybe even differently than I did before? I don't know. Spending more time with you wouldn't make me sad, Dax. You're probably the nicest guy I've ever met.'

'I beat up your boyfriend. That's *not* nice.'

'It was for me. The girl he was hurting. You took care of a guy threatening me, and then you made sure I felt safe even though my request was completely unreasonable. Is it weird I've thought of that night more than once since it happened?'

My heart speeds up. I didn't realize she saw it like that. 'The fight?'

She shakes her head. 'The sleeping part.'

OK, so she either noticed my nerves, or she felt what I felt. Either way, it's a step closer to her realizing how I feel about her.

'Not weird. I have too.'

'You've thought about it?'

'Yeah. A lot, actually.'

I like you, Hollyn. I love you. Go on a date with me. I'm not just your brother's best friend. *Say anything here, Dax. Anything to finally get this off your chest.*

Instead, my mouth goes with: 'I'm sorry Celeste interrupted us. I could tell you weren't thrilled but I felt like I couldn't say no.'

'You can read me like a book, can't ya? That's a little scary.'

'It's all coming back to me the longer you're here.'

'We can always hang out. I live with you, for god's sake. Don't ignore Sydney because I'm back. I want you to be happy. Text her.'

Damn. She's not going to let this go. 'OK.' I pull my phone from my pocket, sending Sydney a text while she watches. But only because if I don't, she'll ask questions I'm clearly not ready to answer.

'See. The ball is in motion. Or maybe the *balls*.' She laughs at her own joke, nudging my shoulder with hers. 'You'll be de-stressed in no time.'

Doubtful, Hols. Seriously, doubtful.

14

HOLLYN

The Flight Home...

I sit down in the window seat, pulling my seatbelt on before doing anything else. Not that a seatbelt will save me if this giant air rocket goes down, but it gives me a little peace of mind.

I'm already regretting telling Dax to text Sydney. I feel like he was trying to tell me something he couldn't quite find the words for. He wants to be friends again? I thought we *were* friends. He wants to spend more time with me? We have been together lit-erally twenty-four-seven lately. I mean, he said I was pretty. I don't know what to do with that. Was he flirting with me? Trying to ask me out? What?

'You think you can do another week?' he asks, sitting next to me.

'I'm in it till you win it.'

He laughs.

'Seriously,' I say, glancing over at him as the plane boards. 'I'm proud of you.'

'Yeah?'

The woman shoving her bag into the overhead compartment heads to a seat in front of us. She looks back at me, her eyebrows raised before finally turning away and sitting down.

'Yeah. I liked the old you, but I completely respect who you've become. You've made something of yourself, found your passion, and you'll inspire others through this show. That's amazing. I think *you're* amazing.'

The slight smile on one side of his face is cute. 'I don't know what to say to that,' he says. 'Other than I feel the same about you.'

'You shouldn't.' I roll my eyes, staring out the tiny window to my left. 'I'm not that good of a person. You're so much better.'

'Hols, you're worth more than you give yourself credit for. I've thought about you often over the years.

Maybe you've changed; we all do as we grow up. I still like you.'

I look away down at my hands. This feels like a slippery slope. One that could slide out of control like an avalanche.

'Can you believe that Celeste?' he asks, changing the subject.

'That she wants you in her bed? Uh, yes,' I say through a laugh. 'Look at you! You're sexy as hell.' I freeze, stopping about three words too late, wishing I could take them back the moment they'd left my lips.

I did not just call him sexy, did I? I glance over at him. Crap. Based on the smile now growing on his beautifully bearded face, I'd say yes. *Yes*, I did.

'Hollyn Matthews. Did you just say I'm sexy as hell?'

I shake my head wildly. '*No*.' I pause, searching for the right word combo to turn back time. 'I can't even imagine a world where those words would leave my lips.'

He bursts out with a laugh so loud that the passenger on the other side of him looks over at us.

'I think that ya *did*.'

And I think he liked it based on his reaction. I raise my hand like I'm in third grade, searching for a flight attendant. When one looks my way, I sigh in relief.

'Can I get a drink? Preferably something alcoholic and strong? Anything really. Vodka? Mouthwash? Hand sanitizer?'

Dax is still laughing next to me. Finally, he pulls himself together. 'Trust me when I say you can't drink words away. They're out there now.' He leans into me. 'I didn't hate them either.'

My heart seizes in my chest. *He didn't hate them?* So, he *was* flirting back on the beach. We *are* flirting. Awkwardly, in a way I can't figure out the rules to.

'Listen,' he says. 'Don't get your panties in too much of a twist when I tell you that your stress relief plan worked, and Sydney accepted my invite. The invite I *only* sent because you insisted,' he reminds me. 'In my defense, I had no idea you were hot for me.'

I roll my eyes playfully, but truthfully, I can barely breathe through the buzzing now filling my insides. What is happening between us?

'I am not *hot* for you, Dax Hartley. More like lukewarm leaning towards cold. Have I noticed you're not as nerdy as you once were? Who wouldn't? Have I fantasized about you in the room next to mine? Eh – not *exactly*.'

'Whatever you say, boss.' He laughs. 'I just didn't want you to be jealous, that's all.'

'Pfft... *me*, jealous of *you*? No. Way. I could get laid if I wanted.'

'I don't doubt that you could,' he says, suddenly straight-faced. 'But I meant jealous of Sydney.'

'I am not jealous of Sydney,' I say hoping he buys it considering it's a lie. I am a little jealous. Dax seems to be a real catch. I can't understand why he's only in a friends-with-benefits situation. How does she not want to tie him down as her boyfriend?

'We could go out to my delivery van. Wouldn't want to tempt you with the thin wall between our rooms or anything.' He winks, my heart doing a tiny dance.

Stop. It. Heart.

'You have sex with women in your delivery van?' I scrunch my face as though I'm disgusted by this.

Maybe Mercy was right about him. He's probably been on his best behavior with me staying in his apartment. Why does him seeing Sydney at all suddenly piss me off?

The plane pulls away from the boarding gate, picking up speed as it preps for lift-off. I shove Dax's hand from the armrest and hold on for dear life. His hand unexpectedly on mine is the perfect distraction.

I glance down, then up at him. My heart races as I allow him to lace his fingers through mine. He smiles shyly, like he's as nervous as I am. I hold his hand tightly, closing my eyes and trying not to think about what's happening right now, but the only other things swirling through my head are this plane crashing and him boning Sydney.

As soon as we're in the air, I blow out the breath I've been holding and open my eyes. I side-eye him, meeting his gaze. His face is probably a mirror of my own, confused, but not enough for us to pull our hand from the other's.

'I can cancel the Sydney thing if you want.'

'Why would you do that?'

'Because it bothers you.' His voice is gentle and sincere as though he'd really do this for me.

How does he know it bothers me?

'Like I said, I'm totally cool. I've got plans anyway. Mercy and I are going out.' I'm now trying to save face and lying my ass off so I don't have to acknowledge whatever this is. 'I'm not a total loser. It's not like you're my *only* friend.'

He lets out a sigh, looking a little disappointed. 'I've never seen you as a loser. If anything, I've spent too much of my life wishing I was more like you.'

'What?'

'Don't act surprised,' he says with a smirk. 'You were always cooler than me although that wasn't exactly hard. Truthfully, I was shocked to hear you mention you felt like you had no friends earlier.'

'I wasn't cool,' I protest. 'Maybe by default, but that was *only* because of my mom. *Mom* was cool. Nobody but Mercy ever wanted to hang out with me. They wanted to hang out with Penny Candy.'

He shakes his head, clearly disagreeing. '*I* wanted to hang with you. Still do. Thought I made that clear on the beach earlier.'

The flight attendant I begged to bring me a drink stops at our aisle and hands me a glass. Dax pulls his hand from mine to pass it to me.

With one swallow, I down the contents which I'm pretty sure is straight vodka. Yuk. Gross.

'Seriously, Dax, have at it if you want to knock boots with some chick in your delivery truck.'

He raises an eyebrow, now flipping through the *SkyMall* magazine. 'Doesn't your mom have a song about knocking boots?'

I glare. 'You know as well as I do it was Candyman with a knocking boots song. Not Penny Candy.'

Suddenly the woman in front of us stands from her seat, turning to face me. '*That's* how I know you! Your mom is Penny Candy! The singer?'

I shake my head, pretending I've never heard of her, ignoring the fact that I've just said her name at least twice.

'Gawd,' she says. 'You look just like her. Think I could get a photo?'

I glance at Dax almost frantically. This is what I didn't want to happen when I came home. I don't want photos or questions or people asking for my autograph. I'm not famous. And I don't want to be recognized.

'She's not who you think she is. Sorry,' Dax says to the random woman after he picks up on my silent plea.

'Oh.' Her face drops. 'I thought I heard you say—'

'Nope,' he cuts her off, shaking his head.

'Sorry. You should look her up. You look just like her.' She finally turns around, leaving Dax and me in awkward silence.

'Thank you,' I say quietly.

He lifts a single shoulder, tapping the screen of his phone before turning it to me, the volume very low but the notes of 'Knockin' Boots' by Candyman now playing as he grooves in his seat like a total goofball. He's mouthing the lyrics. How the hell does he still remember them?

I laugh. 'Sometimes, I wish I *didn't* like you so much.'

'Good to know.' He winks, still mouthing every word.

It's like a superpower he has. He has always somehow just known the words to every ridiculous song from my mother's time on stage, and he wasn't even born until 1994.

Finally, I give in and dance with him in my seat until the guy next to us gives us a dirty look. Dax stops the song.

'Party pooper,' he whispers in my ear.

* * *

Later That Night...

I waited until I heard multiple doors closing before I bolted from the apartment to the Uber I had ordered on the way home from the airport. I'm meeting Mercy at The Rosewood, the drag club her brother owns. The music from within blasts through the door before the bouncer even opens it for me.

Sunday nights are more popular than I expected

and the place is packed. I glance at the stage. I don't know that guy, so I haven't missed Edie yet. I scan the tables as I walk, looking for Mercy's head of dark hair.

Then I see her holding two drinks in the air. I laugh. Anything to distract me from the scene playing through my head of Dax and Sydney. In his room. Alone. Nope. I can't do it. I should have taken his offer of canceling the whole thing but had I done that, he'd have *known* I'm starting to feel something for him and I can't risk that. He's made it clear we should never cross that line.

'Hola!' she says, pulling her drink from her lips. 'You took forever to get here, so you gotta play catch up.' She motions to the two martinis sitting on the table.

'No complaints from me.' I grab one and down it without taking a breath.

'Whoa,' she says. 'That went down easy. Did he lose?'

I shrug. If only that's what this was about.

'He asked Sydney over. To be fair, I suggested he do it.'

'That was big of you. Though I'm not sure he should be fucking her with you in the next room. The boy's got some nerve.'

'Why do you think I'm here?'

She shakes her head in irritation. 'You know what? Two can play. We can totally get you laid. I'm sure there's someone here who plays for our team...' She scans the room.

'No.' I touch her shoulder, halting the search. 'I'm not ready. I'm also not ready to hear my friend and new roommate getting absolutely railed in the next room. But I'm picking my battles here. He had a life before I got here and Sydney was a part of it. I'm cool with it.'

Mostly.

'Hello, folks!' A man's voice interrupts us. 'Put your hands together for Mz. Edee!'

The crowd around us erupts in cheers as the room goes dark. Mz. Edee has some fans. Music blasts through the room, making me immediately laugh to myself.

'Is this... Beyoncé?' I half yell over music so loud it feels like it's forcing my heart to beat in time with it.

'Ed's on a real Beyoncé kick right now. I could do this routine in my sleep.'

He struts onto the stage, and I mean struts Victoria's Secret supermodel style, wearing thigh-high platform-heeled boots and a tiny red dress more revealing than anything I've worn in all my life. I haven't seen Edie in years, and he looks fantastic.

Edie is Mercy's half-brother and her only family. He's handsome as a man and gorgeous as a woman. You can't help but smile when you watch him. Both him and Mercy got that performance gene, and they're good at it.

For a moment, all the worries in my head fade away as I watch the stage full of drag queens, dropping it like it's hot. God, I missed this.

Midway through his set, my phone buzzes in my pocket. River. I answer with a half-whispered hello.

'I need a favor,' he says, wasting no time informing me he didn't call to talk about me.

'What?'

'Wait.' He pauses. 'Where are you?'

'The Rosewood.'

'Drag place, eh? Seeing Edie?'

'Yep.'

'Dax with you?'

'Uh, no. He's home, with Sydney.'

He lets out a weird yelp. 'That girl's dirty as fuck. Probably best you left.'

I scrunch my face and Mercy looks at me confused. *River*, I mouth. She grabs the phone from my hand before I can protest.

'What do you want?' she asks in not quite the whisper I was trying to use.

She and River have a like-hate relationship. They're very similar, and he's for sure the little brother she never wanted.

'Hols is busy right now, and your buddy bringing women home to bang with her in the next room is not cool. You're gonna let that shit fly in her fragile state?'

She has one elbow on the table while the phone is to her ear. Her face is pinched, and I know her well enough to know she's not impressed with whatever River is saying.

'Rein that boy in, would ya? He's going to traumatize our recently dumped girl.' She rolls her eyes at whatever he says then hands the phone back. 'He's maddening.'

I nod. It's not like I can disagree.

'Are you seriously bothered by him sleeping with her?' he asks as I pull the phone to my head. 'Don't tell me you like him?'

'I don't *like* him,' I lie. 'At least not *like* like.'

'Good. Cause that can never happen. Bro code, Hols. Bro code.'

'What do you want?' I ask, hoping to steer him back to why he called instead of annoying me while I'm having a little bit of fun.

'I need you to work Mom's shop tomorrow. She's got a gig. The first in her comeback series.'

'Work at the shop? I haven't worked there in years. I'd have no idea what to do.'

'Cause it's real hard to ring up shit on a till and make sure no one loots the place. Trust me when I say even you can handle it. Nothing's changed. Mom's not big on upgrading. She peaked in the late eighties, remember?'

I laugh to myself; I know exactly what he's saying. At the pool the other day, she was wearing a pair of hot pink spandex under her skirt that I'm sure made an appearance when she toured decades ago. She's not always been one to keep up with the times.

After Mom stopped touring, she still had the music bug so she opened a small music store that still, to this day, sells mostly records, tapes, and CDs. The store's become one of those nostalgia-type mom-and-pop shops that calls in teens and music lovers from miles around.

I spent a lot of time there as a kid, as did River, Dax, and Mercy. We all worked there. I even had my sixteenth birthday party there. Mom set it up like an underage dance club. She even hired a DJ.

'What time?' I ask River.

'Meet me there at eight. I'll show you the ropes.'

'Bring coffee.'

'Food is how I bribe people to do shit. If you were around more you'd know this.'

'Well, I'm around now, so it better be a big coffee.'

'Fine, ya pain in my ass. See ya tomorrow.'

'Later.'

'Hols!' he yells into the phone before I can hang up. 'Wait!'

'What?'

'What time did Syd come over?'

'I don't know. An hour ago?'

He mumbles to himself. 'It's nine now. Last time it went on for an hour and thirty-two minutes, that puts us at—'

Ew. Riv. You time them? Good Lord.

'—Uh, don't go home until about ten. They drag this shit out and utilize the entire apartment. Also, word to the wise, *knock*. You'll know she's gone because he'll be wearing hot pink dishwashing gloves while he cleans. All I can say is thank god that boy's a clean freak cause no one wants to eat on a counter where someone else was getting—'

'You two are disgusting.' I cut him off, not wanting to hear the end of that sentence even a little bit.

'Don't I know it.' He laughs. 'Later.' He ends the call abruptly.

'What'd he want?' Mercy asks.

'For me to cover the shop tomorrow.'

'Blast. From. The. Past,' she says with a laugh. 'Maybe I'll stop in and "borrow" some CDs.' She waggles her eyebrows. That was her thing when we were teens. She's obsessed with music; obviously, she's a musician. Back in the days of our youth, she'd 'borrow' CDs, burn a copy, then bring them back unnoticed. Really, she should be in jail right now.

'Come by. I'll let you build the playlist for the day.'

One of Mom's requirements is a brand-new playlist every day. God forbid a regular customer come in two days in a row and hear the same song. I realize she hates change, but she loves music more, so River set her up on Apple Music a few years back. That day he called me to yell the things he wanted to yell at her while teaching her how to use it. It wasn't pleasant.

'I'm up for some nostalgia. What time?'

'I'll be there eight to five.'

I guess you *can* turn back time. Tomorrow will be interesting.

15

DAX

The Next Day...

'It just... *wouldn't work*?' Jake looks horrified as he says the words.

Maybe I overshared?

'That's right. Everywhere I looked were pieces of her. A sweater thrown over a barstool. Her make-up spread across the bathroom counter. That damn Snuggy was on my couch, Jake. I couldn't get her out of my head.'

'Or your pants,' he says with a laugh. 'Was Syd mad?'

I chuckle, but not because it's funny. Impotence is never amusing. I found that out last night. My head and groin were on two different planets, and nothing I tried aligned them.

'She uh' – I laugh – 'she yelled at it at one point. Eye to eye. If anything, it just scared it more.'

Jake belly laughs, making me feel like the biggest loser on the planet. I stand at the back of my delivery truck, dropping my head back.

'Yeah, yeah, get it all out.'

'I'm sorry,' Jake bellows. 'It's funny.'

'Just wait; your turn's coming.'

He shakes his head as if it's impossible. 'Maybe the magic is gone?' He grabs an arrangement from the makeshift floral shop I've got set up in my mom's garage and walks it over to me. 'Honestly, not sure how you've ever felt magic with Sydney. Girl's hot as fire but cold as stone. Brynn says she's the Patricia to your Joe Fox.'

I roll my eyes. 'Brynn watches too many romance movies.'

'I'm not arguing with that,' he says. 'Let me ask ya something. Do you even actually *like* Sydney?'

Jake agreed to help me with deliveries today because I've gotten double the orders I usually would ever since the show started doing promotions. It might only be on YouTube, but word has somehow spread.

I step into my truck to arrange things so everything will fit.

'Of course I like her. I wouldn't spend time with her if I didn't. Would we make a terrible couple in real life? Without question. She's way too business for me. But for a couple hours a week, she's exactly my type.'

'That was almost romantic,' he says. 'Though, I think you meant she *was* exactly your type. Your penis protested last night because the cute hot blonde you've crushed on your entire life moved into the bedroom next to yours a few weeks ago.'

I drop my head, rubbing the back of my neck. 'This is kind of a mess. I tried to tell her yesterday, and it came out all weird, so I abandoned ship. Then she slipped up on the plane and called me sexy? So, I took a chance and held her hand on take-off because she was nervous. And she let me.'

'Oh...' Jake is suddenly at the back of the truck, interested in my every word. 'Gossip I *want* to hear. Was your penis working at that moment?'

I lower my chin. 'We were on a plane.'

'So? You never heard of the mile-high club?'

'No. Not with Hollyn. She deserves better than that.'

A smirk grows on Jake's face. 'You're suddenly worried about what she deserves, not what *you* deserve? Are your thoughts for Hollyn as unmagical as the ones for Sydney?'

Are they? Or am I just letting Hollyn creep into places I don't usually open up for others? I can't quit thinking about her. When she touches me, my insides light up like a lightning storm. My sex drive for anyone else seems to have left the building. I'm standing here telling my friend about her.

Fuck, dude, you've got it worse than you thought.

'What I feel for Hollyn isn't anything I've felt for anyone else. I can't explain it.'

'You got it bad,' he says, walking back into the garage to grab another arrangement.

'Let's just stop talking about it,' I suggest.

'I'd agree to that, but' – he turns the card on the arrangement he's carrying out to me, raising both eyebrows – 'this one has her name on it.'

Caught. I was hoping he wouldn't notice that one.

'I don't know what I'm doing,' I admit.

He sighs heavily, handing me the flowers. 'OK,' he says, his tone serious now. 'You have no father, so let me give you some fatherly advice.' He tilts his head back and forth as he decides on his words. 'Many moons ago, you told me the key to escaping relationships and keeping things strictly physical was being able to separate feelings from sex. *Be as hot as ya want*, you said, *but don't bring in romance*. Remember?'

I nod. I don't completely remember, but it sounds like something I'd say.

'Like the dork you are, you compared it to flowers. Casual relationships weren't flower-worthy. That was your invisible line. Flowers lead to romance, romance leads to feelings, and feelings lead to more than sex. Once you crossed that flower line, you were on your way to a relationship. You didn't want that. All your words.'

He wags his finger my way. 'You're bringing her flowers. More than once, I believe. Doesn't that mean you're feeling romantic about Hollyn and hoping it leads to you becoming a taken man?'

I stare at him blankly.

'You got feelings for her, man!' he half yells.

'Big ones,' I finally admit. 'But she's not ready. River's forbidden it anyway.'

'Pfft... River.' He rolls his eyes. He and River get along; they do. They share a similar immaturity. But Riv sometimes annoys Jake who is the oldest of the three of us by five years. 'You can get around that.'

'Timing's off.'

'In life, timings are never on. You think I was ready

to have a kid? Hell no. We planned it, sure, but I wasn't ready. You're never ready for the big things, even when you think you are. You'll just make your move if she's worth it and hope you got a shot. What's hiding it from her all these years done for ya?'

He's right. Hiding it has made me miserable.

'Fellas.' River suddenly appears at the back of my truck.

Jake's eyes go wide as he returns to the garage for another arrangement.

'I thought you were filming today?' I ask, hoping he didn't hear much.

'Picking up the folks and all the crap they think they need, then heading to the Hawthorne to shoot a set for local fan club members.'

'Sounds fun, but we gotta get,' I say, stepping out of the truck. 'Let me just run these to Mom.' I grab the bundle of irises I saved for her and take them into the house.

When I was a kid, I'd pick Penny's irises and give them to my mom like I'd hunted them out. I was so proud. Eventually, once Penny figured out it was me, she put up a sign in her iris bed that said 'Dax's Garden' (it's still there now). I could pick them anytime I wanted to cheer up my mom, who never remarried after my dad passed. I was her entire world. Everything she did, she did for me. The least I could do was make her smile and flowers did that.

One of my favorite memories of my dad is him bringing home flowers after work every night. Sometimes it was just a single stem, other times, it was a more elaborate arrangement, but every time she swooned. They had the magic Jake was referring to earlier. Right until some irresponsible woman ripped his life away after drinking too much to be driving. Killed him instantly. She lived. That last part pissed me off for a long time.

Scattered amongst the wreckage were the roses Dad was bringing home for Mom that night. We saw that part on the local paper's front page in the grocery store a couple of days later. *Local businessman killed on way home* was the headline. I've never been able to forget it. When Mom saw it, she collapsed in the aisle, and for a moment, I thought I was going to lose both parents. It crushed her in a way I didn't know was possible.

I've never brought her roses because of that, but I got roses tattooed on each arm – one with his initials and one with hers. Star-crossed lovers separated far too soon, memorialized on my skin to remind me what love is supposed to look like.

'Hey, sweetie,' she says, scrubbing a dish in the sink. 'You get it all loaded?'

'We did,' I say, pulling the flowers from behind my back, just like I used to.

She beams.

'My first smile of the day,' I say, handing her the flowers. 'It's what makes this job worth it.'

'You are a good man, Dax.' She pats my chest. 'Your father would be so proud of you.'

She turns from me, pulling a crystal vase from under her sink, filling it with water, and arranging the flowers to her liking.

'Brynn's got a watch party planned at Bible Club Friday night. She rented the whole place. You coming?'

Bible Club is a local bar, not a church group.

'If I didn't, she'd have my head.'

Mom nods, setting the vase of flowers on the counter beside her, admiring them before turning back to me.

'I'm proud of you too, Dax. I never thought you'd end up so much like him when you had so little time with him. But you're the spitting image of him. It both hurts and heals my heart.'

'So far, it's done me well. Can't imagine having it any other way.'

She smiles. 'Now, go, make some other people happy.'

I kiss her cheek. Without her, I wouldn't be as grounded as I am. Growing up with one parent is hard, and I know it's been even harder for her. The more I grew up, the more I looked like him. I know that's exactly what she means when she says it hurts and heals her heart.

* * *

Later That Day...

I dropped Jake off at his apartment before heading back. I figured the last person I need with me when I drop these flowers to Hollyn is a guy who now knows too much.

I pull up to the curb in front of Penny Candy Records and park. As I grab the flowers I glance across the street at my dad's old shop. The windows are covered in brown paper, a for-sale sign secured front and center between the glass and paper. A vision of what it once was flashes through my head. I can't lose this place.

'*What* are you doing here?'

I turn towards the voice slowly, facing Mercy timidly. Of course she's here. If Hollyn left a note on my fridge telling me where she'd be today, I should have known she'd tell Mercy too. Those two know everything about one another.

She stares at the flowers in my hand before looking up at me. 'Trying pretty hard to get into her panties, aren't ya?'

'That's not what this is,' I say. 'Despite what you think, I don't sleep with every woman I meet.'

'Oh, really?' She crosses her arms over her chest, clearly not planning on leaving soon. 'Then you didn't scare her off last night when you invited Sydney over for a good old-fashioned game of jamming the clam?'

I laugh out loud, shaking my head at her ridiculous words.

'That was Hollyn's idea. Yes, Sydney came over,' I say. 'But there was no clam jamming as I couldn't get it u—' I stop mid-word, horrified I've even talked this long.

Why the hell would I tell her this? She's the one person who will tell Hollyn anything I say.

Her eyes grow wide and her smile wider. 'You couldn't get it up?'

'*Mercy*,' I say her name sternly. 'Pretend I didn't say it.'

'Are you *serious*?' She steps closer as if trying to keep the subject just between us.

This is just what I needed. To explain all this to her now.

'Listen.' I walk over, leading her away from the storefront before Hollyn notices us, if she hasn't already. 'I like Hols. It's true. I always have, you know this. That said, I'd never sleep with her then walk away. I couldn't do it. Not to her.'

'There's no way I'm allowing you to break her heart. She's been through enough.'

'Who says I'd break her heart? Do you remember what I went through to get over her? I could never hurt her.'

She holds her glare.

'Come on, Merc. You gotta give me a break here. I haven't hurt her yet. I'm bringing her flowers, cheering her up, making her smile.' I pause. 'I beat up Tristan.'

This gets her, and she drops her arms, cocking her head. 'Fine,' she says. 'Unadulterated friendship, Dax. That's what she needs right now. Until she pulls you from the friend zone, that's where you'll stay. Keep making her smile, and we don't have a problem.'

I grin. 'I promise, Merc. I'll behave. Hollyn's calling the shots here. Am I cleared to bring these in?'

'Don't mention this conversation or the whole world will know your penis has retired. Got it?'

I laugh under my breath. 'Cross my heart and hope to die.'

Mercy rolls her eyes. 'Careful what you wish for there, pretty boy.'

I know where I went wrong with Mercy, and in my defense, I was a different man back then. Just a horny kid, really. I've grown. It's what we're put on the earth to do. Despite what she and Brynn think, I'm no longer prowling town looking for women. After last night, I think I may be over that lifestyle permanently. Humiliation isn't even a strong enough word.

16

HOLLYN

Moments Later...

The door dings open, and in walks Dax. *What* is he doing here? I successfully avoided him when I got home last night. His bedroom door was closed, so I went straight to my room, put on headphones, turned up the music so I wouldn't overhear anything, and went to bed. When I got up this morning, he was already gone.

'Hi,' he says with a grin. 'Brought you something. I swear they aren't tulips.'

'If I never see another tulip for the rest of my life, it'll be too soon.'

'By next Sunday, you'll wish you'd never seen these either, I'm afraid. Bride's choice.'

I take the bouquet of dark pink flowers he's handing me, lifting them to my nose to see if they smell better than the daisies did. Slightly powdery, like a perfume my grandma wore when I was little.

'What are these called?'

'Anemones.'

I repeat his word slowly. 'I love them. Thank you.'

'It's my pleasure.' He turns to wander through the shop as I stand behind the front counter, his fingertips grazing along the tops of the albums. 'This place brings back some memories, doesn't it?'

'You don't still come in here?'

He shakes his head, a slight frown on his face. 'I haven't been here in years. Now that I am, I feel a little bad about that.'

'Not much has changed. Except this.' I walk over to the stereo system that has had more than a simple upgrade like River claimed, turning up the volume as loud as Mercy had earlier. The *shake-the-front-windows* level, as she called it.

Dax walks through the store, glancing back with a

grin as I blast the music. This reminded me of my child-hood when Mercy and I did it earlier. My house was known for loud music, famous musicians stopping by unannounced while they blew through Portland on tour, random dance parties, and laughter. Sure, the paparazzi were always trying to grab our photos when we walked to and from school or played in the front driveway, but looking back, it wasn't that bad. I was absolutely loved.

'Maybe your life's calling is to be a DJ?' Dax asks with a laugh.

'No,' I say, turning the volume down to a manage-able level. 'Mercy built this playlist. You'd be ashamed to know I've avoided getting too into music the last eight or so years.'

'*You?* The daughter of a pop star has avoided mu-sic?' He laughs like it's unbelievable. 'No wonder you're such a terrible dancer.'

'Hey,' I protest.

He walks around the end of the counter, before hopping up onto it. 'Can I ask you something serious?'

'I'm sure we can make things more awkward if we really try.'

He shakes his head, laughing to himself. 'Why did you leave and never look back? All your friends were left behind.'

I sit on the employee stool a few feet from him, my

feet propped onto the counter next to him. I lift my shoulders.

'I needed a new life? I dunno,' I say. 'Cause I'm an idiot?'

'No. You're not. Try again.'

'Truthfully, I never felt like I could live up to my mom. Everything she did, she did better than me. She's a bit of an attention whore if you've never noticed.'

'Not sure how anybody could not notice that,' he says, glancing at the life-size cardboard cutout of her that lives in the corner of the shop.

'I always had this internal voice telling me I wasn't good enough to be her daughter. I mean, come on, when she was sixteen, she was playing malls across the country. When she was eighteen, she was on her first international tour. When she was twenty-one, she won a freaking MTV music award that still graces her fireplace mantel.'

'That's a lot of pressure for a teen girl.'

'Right?' I feel genuinely heard for once. 'When I was twenty-one, I dropped out of college and moved in with a guy I barely knew that was practically her age. She nearly had a nervous breakdown. And it almost killed my dad.' I frown, now picking at my nail polish.

'She made me feel like the best I'd ever be was disappointing to her, so I turned to what I thought was love and never looked back. It felt easier than watching her be frustrated with every decision I made.'

'I'd have probably done the same if my mom was Penny.'

'Your mom is amazing,' I say. 'I was always jealous of you.'

'You were?'

'She was normal, Dax. No one knew her, and no one expected you to be her. She was so proud of everything you did. She wasn't drawing attention to herself when she went to your baseball games. No photographers followed her around; no one asked her for autographs and photos. You have no idea how badly I wanted normal.'

'That's why you froze on the plane yesterday when that woman asked who your mom was?'

I nod. 'I haven't had that happen in years. It brought back every feeling of self-loathing I'd ever had. Like that.' I snap my fingers.

Dax frowns. 'If I'd known, I'd have gone a little easier on the teenage torment.'

'You couldn't possibly have understood because *I* didn't understand.'

'I'd have tried.'

He makes me feel like a better person than I am. 'I know you would have,' I say. 'Can I ask *you* something serious now?' I have to know. 'Were you disappointed I left?'

For a moment, he struggles for words as he hops off the counter and wanders towards my mom's office before turning back to me.

'Yeah,' he finally says, his face stone-cold sober. 'I thought you'd come back for holidays and summers, but you just disappeared. I texted you a few times but never got a response. Then I heard River and Mercy mention they still talked to you. Honestly, that hurt. I thought we were closer than that.'

My heart slows. I hurt him. Damn it. And yet here he is, the one doing the most for me right now. Always with a smile on his face too, as if he enjoys my company or something.

I drop my head towards the ground then glance up at him. 'Dax, I'm sorry. I didn't mean to leave you out. We *were* closer than that. What I did, it was a jerk move.'

He shrugs, flashing me a smile. 'Hollyn, I think you're...' His gaze is on mine. 'You went out on your own, made mistakes, and now you're facing them head-on. You got lost in life and have a second chance.

Yet you're spending it helping me. I know you think you're this selfish asshole who doesn't deserve to be forgiven but to me, you're selfless. I forgave you a long time ago.'

I blink back unexpected tears, standing from the stool I'm sitting on, and take a few steps to him. 'Promise me you'll never stop lying to me.'

He chuckles. 'I already promised others I'd be on my best behavior around you, so consider that done.' He winks, my heart doing a little spin.

He steps aside when a customer carries an INXS album to the counter, handing me a fifty-dollar bill. I ring him up, give him his change, and slide the record into a brown album bag.

'Thanks for shopping with Penny Candy Records,' I say, side-eying Dax and his obnoxiously goofy grin plastered on his face.

'I feel like I've gone back in time, and I don't hate it,' he says as the customer leaves. 'You need a ride home? I'm done with my deliveries, and we're going the same way. We could pick up take-out?'

'Yeah, I'd like that,' I say with a nod. 'Want to help me close?'

'Absolutely,' he says. 'But first' – he walks to the store stereo, scrolling through the iPad attached, looking for a song – 'let me introduce you to a little band I like to call *not* Penny Candy.'

Once he's chosen a song, he grabs the floor sweeper and dances it into the shop. How is he this charming? It's like nothing has changed and he somehow makes me happier than I've ever been.

17

DAX

Wednesday Afternoon...

I don't want to jump the gun, but after being deemed potential week one winner, I'm throwing common sense to the wind and looking at my dad's shop again.

'Now listen,' Brynn says. 'This guy's kind of a twat. We can't piss him off, or he'll bail.'

We're standing on the sidewalk outside the shop, waiting for Kevin, the aforementioned twat owner. I brought Brynn with me because she's somehow convinced me she's got the magic touch. We're hoping she can tickle his fancy enough and sweet talk him by reminiscing about the couple of dates they went on in high school. Tip the tables in my direction, if it's possible.

'Don't think this guy could hide the twat thing if he wanted to,' I say, half under my breath in case he's walking up behind me.

'This place is a pile of garbage. He'd be lucky to give it away.' She motions at the storefront.

It is run down. The people who leased it previously obviously didn't believe in maintenance. It's a single-story building on the corner with floor-to-ceiling paned vintage (aka out of date) windows along three sides. Perfect for displays. It's not big, but big enough. It needs a good clean, paint, curb appeal, and the inside is even worse.

'There he is.' She nods towards the end of the block, where the middle-aged man with little hair and a beer gut meanders towards us. 'Follow my lead.'

'*Follow your lead?*' I ask. 'Last time I followed your lead, I ended up as someone's flower boy, and now I'm in the midst of a floral competition I *have* to win to even make this happen.'

'You should be thanking me. Now shush. I have a plan that I'm sure will work, so let me do the talking and just' – she glances at me, her lips pressed into a straight line, the same face she has when she lies –

'don't ask questions, and go with whatever might happen.'

I blow out a nervous breath. Whatever might happen? Great.

'Kevin!' she says enthusiastically as he approaches. 'I haven't seen you in so long. Geez, you haven't aged at all!' She turns to me with a grimace.

'And you are?' he asks, stopping in front of her, void of all emotion.

'Brynn Thomas! Or you'll probably remember me as Brynn Hartley. We went to school together.'

Kevin looks her over, his gaze lingering at her breasts. Finally, he scratches his head. 'Not ringing any bells.'

Well, that's great, Brynn. He doesn't even know who you are. Big help. Kevin glances my way, his brow furrowed. I flash a smile, but he turns away, shoving the key into the front lock.

'Did we sleep together after junior prom?' he asks suddenly.

Brynn almost loses her nerve with that one. Her face goes from offended to suddenly remembering why we're here. 'Um... maybe we did, big boy.'

Big boy? I just lost some respect for her.

'I got another guy interested, so what are you thinking?'

'Someone else is interested?' I ask as Brynn moves behind Kevin's back, shaking her head frantically and mouthing words I can't make out.

Kevin glances back at her, following my line of sight. She goes still as a statue, plastering on a grin.

'He called a few days ago; we've been discussing things via email, and last night he offered me ten grand over asking.'

Brynn motions a phone with her hand, holding it to her head while pointing at herself.

OK. I'm not reading her cues. 'What is the asking price?'

'One eighty.'

One *eighty*? A few weeks ago, it was one sixty-five. What a prick. I shove my hands in my pockets. How the hell can I come up with that much?

'Tell ya the truth, Kevin, I'm still about two months from where I'd need to be financially. Not sure the place is worth—'

'What if he gave you ten grand cash right now?' Brynn cuts me off, blurting out the one card I had to play. Smooth.

The shop's front doors bang open, and Jake walks in wearing a beret and a fake mustache. *What. In. The. Hell?* Please, God, tell me this is not her grand plan.

'You Kevin?' Jake asks loudly, looking me up and

down like he's not impressed. He winks as he gets closer as though I haven't recognized him yet.

Did they forget we're all grown-ups here? They're going to blow this.

'Jeremy?' Kevin asks, extending a hand his way.

He gets a greeting, but I'm somehow invisible? This guy's a super douche. Every time we talk, he acts like I'm nothing but a pain in his ass, but Jake walks in wearing an obvious bad disguise, and he *buys* it? Maybe I've been trying too hard?

Jeremy? I mouth.

Jake shrugs.

'The place ain't in great shape,' Jake says to Kevin. 'I'm not seeing one sixty-five worth of building here, if I'm honest. What's it appraised at?'

He told *him* one sixty-five? This guy's a real piece of work.

Kevin rocks back on his heels, his hands shoved in his pockets. 'It's appraised low, needs some work, but has potential. Right on Main Street and windows for days.' He waggles his finger around the room, towards the windows. 'Those windows are good for business.'

Jake shrugs, not giving Kevin a smidgen of approval. 'Let's be straight, Kev. Single paned windows aren't good for anyone. It'll cost a fortune to heat the place and even more to replace them. The shop hasn't been updated since the seventies. You realize how long ago that was? Nearly fifty years, Kevin. Count 'em.' He uses his fingers to count by tens until he reaches fifty.

'I guess it's been a while,' Kevin says with a nod.

'When's the last time an electrician was in here? These outlets are all two prongs. How do you expect me to run a business with four two-prong outlets?' Jake's now wandering the room, pointing out the things that are wrong.

'And what are those?' He glances to the ceiling. 'Water stains? Probably needs a new roof.' He shakes his head, clearly disappointed. 'The stairs out front are crumbling. It needs paint, desperately, and not only exterior.'

'Just the mortar needs repairing with the stairs is all. I'm pretty certain these ceiling stains are old.'

'Are they fifty years old, Kev?' Jake bellows. 'You seriously trying to sell a place being just "pretty certain"?'

Kevin doesn't answer, but his face grows harder if that's possible. Brynn waves my way to get my attention, giving me two thumbs as if this is going well. I'll give her the fact that it's entertaining, but that's it.

'What's with the bars on the windows? Looks like a damn jail cell in here. We're in the burbs, Kev, not

New York City. Removing them will cost a pretty penny. Then what the hell do I do with them? I mean, come on, Kevin. There's not any curb appeal. You ain't selling a house here.'

'I – uh,' Kevin mumbles to himself.

Sweet Jesus. Is this actually working? I can almost see Kevin's head spinning.

'I'm gonna say it,' Jake says, stopping in front of Kevin and pulling a pipe out of his pocket. 'The place is a piece of shit, Kev.' He lights up the pipe, coughing with the first hit. 'It's not worth anything near your asking price.' He stands head-to-head with Kevin, smoking a pipe as though he's Sherlock Holmes. Even I'm starting to sweat.

'What do you think it's worth?' Brynn asks Jake.

'One twenty. Tops.'

Brynn's jaw drops open slowly as she walks around to face Kevin.

'Kev, sweetie...' She runs a finger down his left arm.

Gross. How Jake is staying in character right now is beyond me.

'You told Dax your price was one eighty. You weren't trying to con the nice guy, were you?'

Kevin scowls.

'Well,' Brynn scoffs. 'I never expected you to turn

into this guy. You were such a sweetheart in school. I'll never forget that night we had after junior prom.' She sighs as if she's swooning all over again. 'I think you were possibly the best quarterback Cleveland High ever had.'

She remembers his football position? Jeez. She's really digging deep here.

'If only I'd pulled through on that last championship game,' Kevin says, suddenly pumping a fist. Ah, the guy who still regrets his last big game. Now it's making sense.

'Don't let her sweet talk ya, Kev. I think I might be interested in this place after all,' Jake says, attempting to pull back the reins from his wife.

Kevin lifts a hand towards Jake. 'Let's hear what the lady has to say,' he says, suddenly interested in the attention Brynn is throwing his way.

She's going to need to go home and take a boiling hot shower after this. We all are.

'One twenty is my last offer, Kev. The place is a dump,' Jake says in a last-ditch effort.

'I put more into it than that!' Kevin growls.

Shit. Don't piss him off, you idiot! I glare at Jake.

'What would you say if Dax here offered you one fifty?' Brynn asks.

'Fifty thousand down today,' I say, upping my ten

grand offer. 'I could commit to July first to pay the remaining. *Cash*.'

What am I doing? Risking everything.

'Pfft,' Jake says. 'It ain't worth all that.'

'Shut it,' Kevin says to him.

I have to force away a laugh.

'One fifty-five and a night out with you,' Kevin suggests, now blowing Brynn a kiss.

We must all look horrified, but Kevin doesn't notice.

'Well,' Brynn says, pulling a hand to her chest. 'I'm flattered, but I don't think my husband would approve.' She blows him back a kiss anyway.

'It was my dad's store,' I remind Kevin, hoping that pushes things in my direction.

He nods his head slowly, looking between the three of us, finally extending a hand my way. 'It's yours for one sixty-five. As is.'

I hardly think Brynn is worth ten thousand dollars, and all this did for me was keep the price at his original one, but I've got no choice. I reach over and shake the man's hand.

Kevin pulls a business card from his wallet. 'Drop the deposit here by the end of the day, and I'll have the paperwork drawn up while I wait. No keys until the last payment is made. I won't be ripped off. You fuck around; you lose fifty big ones.'

'Understood,' I say, my heart racing in my chest. 'I'll head to the bank right now.'

'Let's go.' He herds the three of us towards the door. 'I got other places to be.'

Before he exits, he reaches behind the brown paper and yanks down the for-sale sign. Holy shit, we did it. I know it's not a done deal *exactly*, but we're way closer than we were.

The three of us watch as Kevin disappears around the end of the block before all breaking into laughter.

'You freaking goofballs,' I say. 'I almost had multiple heart attacks back there. When did you two come up with this?'

'After the Altman wedding. We did some roleplaying, and it just came to us.'

'Gross.' I direct that at Jake, who's still doing the talking.

'We got you a shop!' he says, lifting a hand for a high five. It takes me a minute, but I high five him like the dorks we are.

'Looks like you owe me. *Again*,' Brynn says.

Jake peels the mustache off his upper lip and presses it to the center of my T-shirt.

'Top-notch cover, by the way.' I motion a chef's kiss. 'I hardly knew it was you.'

He bows dramatically. 'My mom always said I could have been an actor.'

'She might have lied to you.' I laugh. 'Brynn, though, you went the distance, and I'm thoroughly disgusted by what I've witnessed. I'm going to need to go home and scrub my eyeballs. Excellent investigative work on a guy you went to school with nearly twenty years ago.'

She laughs. 'Oh, honey. You act like this was my first investigation. Not even close.'

I should have known. I don't even care what she had to do. Their doing this was huge and I'm not sure how I'll ever pay them back.

18

HOLLYN

Friday Night – At Dax's Apartment...

I'm sorry, Hols. We'll talk. I'm just not ready yet. -V

She's not ready yet? I stare at the text. I freaking knew it. Maybe she hasn't said the actual words 'I stole your boyfriend', but I know it was her. She's waited weeks to send this text.

'Everything OK?' Dax knocks at the bedroom door again.

We were supposed to leave ten minutes ago, and here I am, still half-dressed and now preoccupied with a text I never thought I'd get. I don't care that she's stolen my boyfriend. Day by day, I think about him less and less. But she and I were friends, or so I thought. The least she can do is be honest with me.

I click out of the text. 'Yeah,' I lie, standing in my bra and panties in front of suitcases on the floor piled high with every piece of clothing I own.

'The show's gonna start without us if you don't hurry up, Hols.'

'I know, Dax. I'm almost ready.'

I want to tell Victoria off. But if I piss her off, I probably piss off Tristan even more than he already is, and then I've got no leverage to get my money back. If I stay on her good side, maybe I can somehow sweet talk her into convincing him to do the right thing. I won't hold my breath, but if there's even a hint of possibility to do this without involving my parents, I have to at least try. They're disappointed in me enough.

'You sure you're OK?' Dax yells through the door again.

'Yes!' I grab a dress from a suitcase and slip it over my shoulders. Shoes, shoes, I need shoes. I step into a pair of hot pink strappy heels, lacing them around my ankles twice. One final check in the mirror to make sure I don't look like a troll in heels, and I open the bedroom door to Dax.

He steps back, his eyes moving over me slowly. 'Wow.' He shakes his head as if he can't believe it. 'You look gorgeous,' he says, a shy grin on his face. 'I suddenly feel underdressed.'

It's just a dress. Nothing fancy. No frills or ruffles or lace: just a plain black dress. But by the look on his face, I'd say it's not entirely boring.

'Seriously, Hols. You're beautiful.'

I laugh to myself. 'There you go lying again.' I wink. 'Dare I say, you're pretty too.'

His grin grows. 'Might you even say, sexy as hell?'

'Funny,' I say, turning to look him over better.

He's wearing jeans and a T-shirt with a single dandelion flower, the text reading *If you were a flower, you'd be a* damn*delion.*

'I love the shirt.'

He glances down at himself. 'Too much? I've been saving it for the right occasion. You think this is it?'

'I think it's perfect. You're truly the flower boy in every way.'

We ride to the bar silently, staring out of the windows with our own thoughts. He smells good. Some light, clean scent I can't place but I like it.

'You guys!' My mom greets us as we walk into the bar. 'This is so exciting!'

Dax is pulled away by his friends, glancing at me

as he disappears into the bar and flashing me a grin that makes my heart do a little spin.

'You need a drink?' Mom asks, pulling me towards the bar by my hand.

'Yes, yep, I need a drink. Possibly, a few.'

'I knew you got a least *some* of my genes,' she says enthusiastically. 'Drinks on me,' she says.

As we walk towards the bar she begins talking. 'I want to thank you for doing such a good job at the shop earlier this week. A couple of my regulars called me, and they raved on and on about you and your sunny self. I haven't heard that about you in years.'

'Really?'

Who could have called her? The place wasn't even that busy. There was an hour where it was just me, and I worried that maybe the shop wasn't doing well and how Mom would take that. Leave it to me to create a problem that doesn't exist.

'I'm proud of you, Hols. You're doing things out of your comfort zone, and you seem... *happy*?'

Am I happy? Besides the Tristan and Victoria thing, I think I am.

'I missed happy, bubbly Hollyn.'

'You did?' I've been gone for eight years, and not once has she ever uttered the words, I miss you.

'Of course I did.' She wraps an arm around me,

pulling me against her. 'You're my only daughter, and I was a bit of an attention whore of a mom. That couldn't have been easy. Parents make mistakes too, and I now see that I was always trying to be your friend more than your mother, but that's not what you needed. I'm sorry. Maybe we could be friends now?'

What is happening? Did she just apologize?

'Wow,' I say, flustered enough to have all other words escape me. 'You saying that means a lot, Mom. Thank you.'

'Four shots of tequila!' she says to the bartender.

There's the mom I know. I should probably apologize in return, considering Dax made me realize I've hurt people more than I thought when we talked about me leaving everyone behind the other day. The look on his face broke my heart, and I've been thinking about it ever since.

The bartender sets the four shot glasses on the bar, filling them to the top, spilling some on the counter.

'Mom,' I say before she can get started on the shots she's ordered. 'I'm sorry too. I've been a terrible daughter. Self-centered and secretive. It wasn't fair of me to cut you out. Maybe you guys can forgive me?'

She cocks her head with a sweet grin. The same

one she'd use when she'd have these kinds of heart-to-heart talks with us as kids.

'Of course I forgive you. Your dad might take some more convincing, but *we're* good. I'm even willing to overlook the money you lost.'

'You *know*?'

She laughs. 'River can't keep a secret for the life of him,' she says. 'I say, what's done is done. You made a mistake. If you can get it back, invest it into something you believe in. That's my advice.' She lifts a shot, handing me one and clinking her glass against it.

Ugh. Tequila. I down it fast. Who created this and thought *we should put a worm in it then drink it*? Mom downs shot number two like the pro she is and glances around the room, her face lighting up at the sight of my dad, who's now standing across the room chatting with Dax.

'I'm off. Best of luck, girl. I'm sure you two nailed it.'

I nod, unsure of what to say to her new we're-gonna-be-friends attitude.

'What was that?' Mercy asks, approaching the bar as I sit in a cloud of disbelief.

I point to the leftover shot I thought I needed until I had the first one and she wastes no time in downing it.

'She said she was proud of me.'

Mercy's jaw drops as she sets the now empty shot glass onto the bar.

'Then she apologized for being an attention whore of a mom. Said she'd like to be friends now.'

'*What?*' Mercy asks in a high-pitched voice. 'Is she already drunk?' She scans the room to witness it.

I lift my shoulders, as confused as she is. 'She didn't slur even one word, so I'm guessing, no? She meant it?'

'Wow. Tonight really is special then, isn't it?'

Across the room Dax laughs at something my dad says and they chat before he looks my way, flashing me that same heart-twirling smile.

'I saw he brought you flowers,' Mercy says.

'You saw?'

She nods.

Besides Dax recently, I've never had a guy bring me flowers for fun. There's always been an ulterior motive. Tristan refused; thought they were a waste of money. River brought me flowers once when he accidentally let my cat out and it never came home. My dad would bring me flowers when I'd lose a softball game to cheer me up. A prom date brought me flowers the day *after* prom because when I refused to sleep with him that night, he went out and got it from

Ashley Christopher and told all his friends I was a prude.

I want to believe Dax brings them to me for fun, but I can't help thinking he has to be saying something. I just haven't completely cracked the code yet.

'He's nice, Mercy. Even said I was beautiful earlier. He's starting to remind me who I could have been had I not fallen in love with the wrong guy.'

'Love, blech,' Mercy says. 'It's an awful emotion, isn't it?'

'Confusing too.'

The room quiets down as the episode starts and Mercy and I sit at a table near the back of the room.

'This seat taken?' Dax asks, pulling out the chair next to mine.

'It is now,' I say with a smile.

Tonight's show is just a quick recap of Monday's hour long show before Jillian announces who got voted winner and who's going home. We watch in silence, listening as the rest of the room reacts to everything. Somehow, they even have a video of Dax and me sitting on the beach together after leaving the restaurant in Ocean Beach that day. Of course, the show played up the Dax and Celeste angle first. They would; it's drama. People are drawn to drama. I glance at Dax, watching him watch the recap show, grinning as they flash images of the two of us. He even laughs with the room when I call him beautiful. God.

When it's time for the big moment, he grabs my hand, holding it against his chest, cupping it with both hands.

'Hey.' River pokes my shoulder, leaning across Mercy. 'What's this?'

'He's nervous. It's what he does. It's nothing,' I whisper back.

I wish it felt like nothing, but it doesn't.

'Don't do something stupid,' River warns me. 'He's my best friend. This' – he motions between the two of us – 'is a no go.'

Mercy intentionally jabs him in the ribs with her elbow. 'Oh, sorry,' she says with a sly grin. 'Did I get ya?'

River glares at her. She's a master of distraction.

'The count is in, folks!' Jillian says with a wide grin. 'I had a feeling too. Dax and Hollyn! You're our winners overwhelmingly this week!'

Our friends and family cheer. Dax and I glance at each other wide eyed. 'We did it,' he says, setting my hand back on my knee with a squeeze.

'*You* did it.'

'Now for the bad news.' Jillian's voice interrupts us. 'Marley, despite the fact you weren't in my predicted bottom two, the voters weren't convinced and unfortunately you won't be joining us next week.'

'Sorry, Marley,' I say with a guilty grin, 'Dax deserves this.'

He beams, shaking his head as though I've embarrassed him. Seeing him so thrilled with winning makes it all worth it.

* * *

Later That Night...

When we get home, I go straight to River's room and drop face-first onto his bed. My phone is filled with texts from Tristan, who somehow heard about the show and texted me while he watched the live results tonight. I didn't realize it until we were on the way home.

'What is up with you?' Dax asks, stopping in the doorway. 'Did I do something wrong? Say something I shouldn't have? Was it the hand-holding thing again?' He sounds worried.

I roll over with a sigh, now staring at the ceiling.

'Truthfully, that was my favorite part.' I sit up. 'It's nothing you did.'

'Then what? You haven't said a word in forty-five minutes, and you hardly talked back at the bar. I'm sensing something's up.'

I plaster a fake grin on my face. 'I'm fine.'

'Stop lying and dish it out, girl,' he says, walking into River's room and sitting on the edge of the bed next to me.

'Tristan saw the show and has been texting me. And Victoria.'

'Who's Victoria?'

'Victoria was my college roommate and best friend in Seattle.'

'Alright,' Dax says. 'What did Professor Douch-wagon have to say now?'

'No,' I say. 'We should be celebrating you. You won week one! That's huge.' I stand from the bed, throwing my arms out looking as excited as I can. Because I am. Unfortunately, Tristan and Victoria in my head are beating away the reaction I'd like to have.

He cocks his head, lifting his eyebrows in a way that says he's not going anywhere until I've told him everything.

I sit back down next to him with a huff. 'You don't have to listen to my problems.'

'I know I don't *have* to. I want to.'

'*Why?*'

'We're friends. Try me; maybe I can help?'

'It's humiliating.'

'I once held your hair while you yakked under a tree at a high school party. I can handle it.'

He remembers that? Don't drink on an empty stomach was what I learned that night.

'Tristan used to cheat on me. A lot. I don't know why but I always gave him another chance. He was really good at saying the right things to make that happen.'

Dax drops his gaze towards the ground. 'Why did you stay with him, Hols?'

I shrug my shoulders. 'After a while, I thought it was all I was worth. He had a way with words that meant he could charm me into doing what he wanted.'

'That's called manipulation.'

'I know. I see it now, but then I didn't. The day Tristan and I broke up, Victoria went radio silent. Wouldn't respond to texts, calls, emails, nothing. Once I got here, she blocked me on all social media, and I don't know if River told you this part, but I'd found an engagement ring a month or so before we split up. The night he dumped me, I actually thought he was going to propose. But uh – the ring wasn't for me.'

'God,' he says, gently touching my back. 'River said something like that, but I was hoping he was wrong. I'm sorry. You didn't deserve that, you know that, right?'

I lift my shoulders like I'm not sure. Because I'm not.

'Victoria texted me earlier today and kind of confirmed it was for her, but isn't ready to talk about it.' I roll my eyes. 'Like she gets to make the rules when I'm the one they broke.'

This gets Dax's full attention. 'You feel broken?'

'Yeah,' I admit.

'I kind of want to kill him now.'

'You and me both.'

'Hols, Tristan is a narcissist who gave up control by letting you go, and he's now regretting it. Don't let him do it via text. Whatever he's saying, I'm *sure* he's lying.'

'He called you a fuck-boy chump,' I tell him, thinking back on the texts I've already deleted.

Dax bursts out a laugh. 'I'd rather be that than *Professor* Fuck-boy Chump.'

'You're *not* that,' I say. 'You're the complete opposite.'

19

DAX

Moments Later...

'If you know I'm not those things, you should know that whatever he says about you isn't true either.'

She's now picking nail polish off her freshly manicured nails. I have to say something to make her feel better. Something to remind her she's worth more than this.

'Do you, uh, remember that time you got dumped at prom? What was that asshole's name?'

I swear I have a point here. I'm not just bringing up guys breaking her heart to hurt her.

'Justin McCarthy,' she says. 'I actually just thought about him.'

'What reminded you of him?'

She bites her bottom lip. 'You, actually.'

'*Me?*' Shit. I don't want to remind her of that turd.

'When you brought me flowers earlier this week, it got me thinking about all the times men have brought me flowers. Every time, besides you, it was always someone getting ready to let me down. Justin was one of them. Why do you remember that?'

'I think I remember that night differently than you do. I saw a girl who felt like her universe fell out from underneath her and all I wanted to do was fix it for you. But I was barely sixteen, and fixing women's problems wasn't my specialty. I gave it a hell of a shot, though.'

'You *did?*' Confusion fills her face. She honestly doesn't remember?

'Storytime,' I say with a shy grin. 'Picture it.' I motion my hands like an invisible movie screen is in front of us. 'I was staying the night with your brother, as usual. He always fell asleep first, and I could never sleep. I don't know why.'

I know why. We're getting there.

'That night was warm. We rarely had warm nights in May. I couldn't sleep, so I decided to have a little night swim. I loved that your parents were the first to get their pool going every year. I adored that pool. I don't know if you've noticed, but I'm a total romantic, and night swimming seemed romantic to me.'

'You were romancing yourself?' she asks with a laugh.

I chuckle, now a tad embarrassed. No way am I admitting that. '*Anyway*, I was in the pool when you got home.'

'Oh my god,' she says suddenly. 'You were. I remember. Mom and Dad always left the back door unlocked when we were out late because River and I lost house keys like it was our job. When I turned the corner into the backyard that night, you scared the crap out of me.'

I nod. 'It didn't help that I was naked,' I say, feeling the heat rise to my cheeks. That's great, now I'm blushing. *Blow by it, Dax. Just focus on the story.*

'Once I'd finally convinced you to stop laughing and throw my boxers in, you settled down.'

'I saw nothing,' she says, a coy grin growing on her pretty face.

'Your loss.' I wink. 'We talked that night. Do you remember?'

She shrugs. 'A little?'

'Lucky for you, I remember. We were sitting poolside in the dark; the only light was from the water and the moon. Our feet were dangling in the pool, and we were talking about everything our teenage selves were going through. I don't remember every word I said, but one thing I do. It still stands today. Well, two things stand then and now.'

A hesitant curious grin hangs at the edge of her lips.

'I said you were beautiful that night. I'd never said that to a girl before. You were then, and you are now. Even more so if possible.'

'You'd never said that before me?'

'You were my first.'

She drops her head, attempting to hide the embarrassment plastered on her face.

'You were always too good for Justin McCarthy, Hols. That's what I said that night. Almost twelve years later, I think the same thing about Tristan. I always have. He never deserved you.'

Her gaze meets mine, her eyes glazed over with tears that slide down her face before she can wipe them away.

'I don't understand. I've been nothing but a pain in your ass since I got here, and yet you've never once hesitated to pull me from whatever pit of depression or self-doubt I've had. I don't deserve *you*.'

'Not true. I told you this story to prove I've always had your best interests at heart. You trusted me with your problems as a teen, and I promise you can trust me with them now, too. Tell me what happened with you and Tristan, and I can help. We're not kids anymore; please let me try.'

She takes a moment, but finally, she relaxes, breathing deeply, then blowing the air out dramatically.

'When I started college, my roommate was a girl from southern California. Victoria Kelly. A woman with a trust fund ten times the size of my own. She was very Celeste.'

Maybe that's why she doesn't like her? Here I thought she may have been jealous, but in reality, Celeste just reminds her of someone else.

'We were pretty much a couple of spoiled brats living college life like it was an all-inclusive paid vacation. Victoria was sophisticated and beautiful and had so many friends. Everyone liked her. As you know, I'm not exactly the most adventurous spirit, so she was always convincing me to do things I normally wouldn't. Things like sleeping with my college professor.' She sighs. 'Every girl in school had a crush on him. He was very George Clooney. A gazillion signs were trying to warn me. Honestly, if a red flag exists,

I've probably ignored it.' She rolls her eyes. 'When I gave Tristan my heart, I gave him way too much of myself too.'

'We all learn that life lesson.'

'Did *you*?'

'Yeah,' I answer honestly. 'At a young age.'

She looks genuinely surprised by this.

'Who?'

I shake my head. 'A crush took over my world.'

I'm going to tell her. Just not yet.

'Is this...' She motions a hand over me. 'New Dax, a result of that crush?'

I pretend to clear my throat and nod. 'Maybe a little.' YES.

'I didn't know.'

'After your story, I'll tell you all about it,' I say, coaxing her along.

'The worst part of all this...' She swallows hard. 'Tristan and I bought a condo seven years ago. It was in an up-and-coming neighborhood outside the city, so we got a good deal. We paid cash, both agreeing to go half. A hundred and fifty thousand each.'

'Don't say it, Hols.'

'Yup, you guessed it. He only gave me back fifty-nine grand as my share.'

'He stole ninety grand?'

I should have fucking killed him that night.

'I didn't want to believe it at first. I mean, who steals from their girlfriend? But the more time that goes by, the more I realize it's true. I'm still entertaining texts from him and Victoria because if I ghost them, I'll never see that money again.'

'Do your parents know?'

She nods. 'Mom mentioned it tonight. She's coming around, even apologized earlier. Dad isn't. He's hardly said two words to me since I got here. Truthfully, he's hardly said two words to me in eight years.'

My heart hurts for her. I remember how close she was to her dad. River never told me things were this bad.

'You can't let him get away with this, Hols. Ninety grand is jail time, probably. You know Sydney?' I ask, feeling dumb the second I do. Of course, she remembers Sydney. 'She's a lawyer. She can help.'

'No.' She shakes her head. 'This isn't your problem. It's mine. River and I agreed we'd give him a month to come to his senses.'

I know she's right. Me getting involved besides being here for her isn't my job right now.

'Did you really love him?'

She bites her lips together, shaking her head as if she's unsure.

'I don't think I even know what love is, Dax. I thought about leaving him a couple times. But *every* time, he'd say the right thing and drag me back. Always some version of one of two things,' she continues. 'You'll never be able to take care of yourself, which, come on, we can both see that's true. When all this went down, the first thing I did was call River to save me. Not to mention shacking up with you.'

'It's not true.'

She rolls her eyes. 'Then there was his favorite, the ever-famous, overly used: no one will ever love you the way I have.' She repeats his words with the same condescending tone I'm sure he used, a tear rolling down her face. She glances over at me, her face sad in a way I've never witnessed before.

'Maybe he was right all along?' She chokes out the words through a sob she's desperately trying to hold in as she stands from the bed, then walks to the couch and grabs her stupid Snuggy. She dabs at her eyes before draping it over her shoulders and walking back into River's room, now leaning against the open door behind her.

Fucking hell. I can't believe that asshat has done

this to her. I stand, walk to her and rest my hands on her shoulders.

'None of those things were ever true, Hols.'

'How do you know?'

I've got to do this now. She can't feel like he's right because if anyone knows he's not, it's me.

'This is quite possibly the wrong time to tell you this, but I think you need to hear it, and I need to finally tell you before your brother or Mercy do.'

She stares at me as I search for the words. How do you tell someone you've spent your entire life in love with them and never told them because you were a complete coward?

'You need to tell me what?'

'I know Tristan was wrong because...' I hesitate, staring into her eyes, suddenly more nervous than I've ever been. 'Because he could have never loved you as much as I did.'

She wipes an escaped tear from her cheek, staring at me wordlessly for longer than feels comfortable.

'I don't understand.'

'*You* were the crush, Hollyn. The one that ruled my world. You changed everything about me. All I ever wanted to do was be good enough for you to notice me, not just as River's best friend.'

Her eyes grow wide.

'I was about twelve when I realized it. What do you do with that kind of emotion when you're twelve, and the girl you've fallen for is older *and* your best friend's sister?' I laugh under my breath.

'Nothing. So, I worked hard to be your friend and admired you from afar. I'd fall a little harder when you'd allow me in a little. I would have done anything for you. Then one day, you were just gone.'

'That's why it hurt when I left,' she says to herself. 'You've been trying to tell me this all week, haven't you?'

I laugh. 'I've been trying to tell you this for fifteen years.'

She's got the look of someone who's not quite understanding what I'm saying. I can see her processing it.

'I was going to tell you that night by the pool. At that point, you were pretty much all I thought about. I could never fall asleep at your place because River knew, and I was afraid he'd do something while I slept to embarrass me in front of you. Turns out I was pretty good at doing that part on my own.' I laugh, but she just stares at me, wide-eyed, mesmerized by my words.

'We were lying in the grass near the pool later that night, looking for shooting stars. I was pointing out constellations like the nerd I was, er – *am* – and we saw one. You'd never seen one before and—'

'And you made me close my eyes and make a wish.' She finishes my sentence with half a crooked grin.

I nod, hesitantly touching her hand. 'I planned to kiss you once you closed your eyes, but I panicked you wouldn't return it. So, instead—'

She drops the Snuggy to the ground, laces her fingers through mine, and squeezes my hand tight.

'Instead,' she says, 'you cannonballed into the pool. I squealed when you splashed me, and that's when my dad caught us.'

'Yep,' I say nervously, stroking her hand with my thumb.

I've never seen the look on her face before, and I've no idea if what I've just admitted has made things better or much worse.

'Dax,' she says, stepping closer, her voice hardly more than a whisper as she closes her eyes. 'Do it now. Kiss me now.'

And like a total fool in love, I do. Sliding my hand to the side of her neck, I press my lips to hers. A tidal wave of butterflies settles over me. It's better than I'd ever imagined. She kisses me back and it's slow and sweet, and she tastes like the green appletini she was drinking earlier.

Her hand slides up my chest, her fingers brushing my neck, and as her tongue meets mine it practically knocks the wind out of me. If this never ends, I swear I'll never sleep with another woman as long I live.

It's the key in the front door that stops me. River.

Since I'm utterly wordless at this moment and not exactly in the condition to answer the door, I glance around the room. How can I save this before River walks in on us?

'What's wro—'

'River,' I say as the front door opens.

I shove her onto the bed, probably scaring the hell out of her. 'I'm sorry, Hols.' I grab the remote from the dresser, flip on SportsCenter, and drop onto River's bed next to her, the stupid Snuggy draped over my midsection.

'Act normal. I'll talk to him later.'

She nods, touching her lips, looking at me with those big blue eyes. Good god, woman. I don't know if I'm thankful for River or not right this second. Had he not just walked in, things may have moved too quickly.

'Hello?' River hollers as he walks through the

living room. 'What up, dorks?' he says when he sees us. 'Why are you watching TV in here?'

'Hols, uh – she wanted company while she cleaned,' I lie, glancing around the room at the obviously untouched mess.

River looks around the room, his brow furrowed in confusion.

'I was going to ask, what's with the shoes?' He points at the pile of shoes I hadn't even noticed. The two of us look over at her.

She's now unlacing her heels, tossing each one onto the floor before crossing her legs beneath her and sitting next to me on the bed.

'I stole all his left shoes when I left.' The lift of a single shoulder and the smirk on her face tells me she's proud of this little detail.

I want to kiss the hell out of her, but all I can do is laugh. *That* is the girl I used to know. With one kiss, I just fell completely head over heels in love with her. Again.

20

HOLLYN

The Next Morning...

The knock on my bedroom door sends me flying out of bed. Oh. My. God. It's happening. My thoughts have been swirling somewhere between my heart and groin all night. I like him, and it's too soon. He kissed me last night. Like *kissed* kissed me, with tongue and everything. I did what I felt was right in the moment, and had he not kissed me, I was ready to make a move. That story and the way he told it, I'm having feelings I am not familiar with now.

River interrupted before I could do something

stupid like lasso my panties around his neck and have my way with him which is probably best at this point.

My brother stayed *for-ever,* too, insisting on watching hours of sports coverage with Dax. The nerve of him, making himself at home in his own apartment. Eventually, they moved into the living room, and I went to bed, but not without pining for hours on end, wishing Dax would storm through the bedroom door and finish what he started. Now, it's happening.

I glance in the mirror, smoothing my hair down and frantically pulling a make-up remover wipe from the package, wiping away my raccoon's eyes before he worries I've slumbered into full-on depression. I slide my glasses on to see him and walk towards the door, glimpsing my pajamas in the mirrors of the closet.

'Crap!' I hiss to myself. I was wearing these the last time he saw me in pajamas. I can't have him thinking I only change them a couple of times a week.

I dig through the unpacked suitcases all over the room, finally pulling out a pair of fleece pajama bottoms covered in penguins wearing scarves – my Christmas pajamas. Tristan always hated them, but they'll have to do considering I'm running low on clean laundry.

'Hols? You alright?'

I tear off the shorts, pulling on the pants as he knocks again.

'Yeah, yeah!' I call back. 'Just a sec!'

Jesus. I glance around the room. He told Riv I was cleaning this mess last night. Perhaps I should actually do that at some point. I'll just leave the lights off and the blinds closed. That way, he can't see it. But... is leaving the room dark a good idea?

He knocks again, a slow knock that says he's growing tired of me standing here wondering what reaction to have when opening the door.

'On my way!' I say sweetly as if I've got an entire house to get through.

I flip off the lamp, realizing how dark that leaves the room. 'Way too dark.'

Dark is mysterious. Maybe even romantic. Very rarely have I had sex with the lights on. What if he thinks I'm inviting him into my lair to have my way with him? It wouldn't be the worst idea I'd ever had.

Wait. What if he's *not* here for sex? If I make this all about that possibility, and that's not what this is leading to, I'll feel like a bigger idiot than I already do. Blinds open. Final decision. I race to the windows, twisting open the blinds.

'Come on, Hols!'

'Hollyn,' I say to myself. 'Relax. He most definitely is not here for sex. Calm your horny ass down.'

Finally, I stop at the door. 'It's Dax. It's just Dax.' Breathe, girl. 'Dorky, constellation, flower-loving, hotter than hell, Dax, for crying out loud!'

I open the door, his million-dollar smile greeting me as he leans into the door frame.

'Dorky?' he asks, a single eyebrow raised.

'*What?*'

'Hotter than hell, Dax?' He repeats my words, the smirk on his face doing things to my insides I've never experienced. 'So, you *are* hot for me...?'

'Uh...' Words escape me as I try to remember what I just said to myself *out loud*.

He laughs, his gaze moving over my body slowly before meeting mine again.

'The rooms aren't soundproof, Hols, remember? I heard Roger Dodger over there getting it on with what I can only hope was a consenting woman just last night. Grossed me out like nothing ever has.'

I stare, my jaw agape. The day I eavesdropped on him and River's conversation plays in my mind. He *heard* me? No, no, no, no, *no*. I called myself horny! I was talking about having sex with him! *Out. Loud.*

'Relax,' he says, reaching up and closing my mouth with one finger on my chin. 'I'm not here to have sex with you.' His grin tells me he finds this more than amusing.

'Don't get me wrong,' he continues. 'I don't know if I'd be able to say no should you try it.'

I'm lost for words, and he probably sees that all over my face. He glances around the room, his gaze landing on Tristan's shoes. 'Did you really steal all his left shoes?'

'Yeah.' I nod as though I'm half brain dead.

'Evil.'

'Take that as a warning,' I say, walking past him out of the bedroom. Staying in there feels too dangerous.

'Note to self: don't piss off Hollyn,' he says, jotting the note down on an imaginary notepad.

He follows me into the kitchen, where I don't know what I'm looking for, but I have to find something to look busy.

'I wanted to talk to you about something.'

'OK,' I say, pulling the toaster from the cabinet where he keeps it, sliding four slices of bread into it.

'About last night.'

My heart sinks. He regrets it. I knew it.

'Don't make that face,' he says, making me suddenly aware of what my face is doing.

'I'm not making a face,' I say, popping a k-cup into

his Keurig machine. I tap the button that creates the dark magic coffee I so love. 'What about last night?' I ask innocently, as I lean on the island countertop, facing him.

He raises a single eyebrow.

'Oh, you mean when you kissed me?'

He grins, his eyes boring a hole into my heart. 'You mean kissed you because you *asked* me to. "Do it now. Kiss me now."' He mimics my words.

'Ah,' I groan. 'I was trying to be romantic. Was it not?'

'It was,' he says, laughing. 'Swept me off my damn feet.'

I smile. 'I swept you off your feet?' I can sense the same giddy feeling I had while kissing him, building in my chest like I'm about to explode.

'Nearly.' His eyes move to the coffee maker next to me. 'You gonna put a cup under that?'

I glance over at the Keurig machine, coffee splattering off the tray where my cup should have gone. I grab one, sliding it underneath the stream. Not soon enough to prevent a mess, and definitely not soon enough to play this off like I meant to.

'OK, fine.' I lift my hands into the air, surrendering all sanity. 'I asked you to kiss me, but in my defense, you said you loved me.'

His smile makes me weak in the knees.

'I did say that.' He nods, now making himself comfortable on one of the barstools opposite the island from me. 'It wasn't a lie.'

'Do you – uh, *still*?' I ask. 'Love me?'

He drops his head, glancing up with only his eyes. Oh, sweet smoldering sex appeal. Don't do that.

'I don't know,' he says. 'That's kind of what I knocked on your door to talk to you about.'

'Go on then,' I say, growing impatient.

'Well,' he says with a slight chuckle. 'I feel something. For you.' He lifts a shoulder. 'But—'

Crap. There's a but. Of *course* there's a but! I wouldn't be me if *something* didn't go awry.

'But you regret it,' I say for him. 'OK.' I sigh heavily. 'I get it. I'm fresh out of a terrible relationship that has so many unresolved loose ends I hardly know where to start. And I'm a terrible person, but I'm *really* trying to change that. That said, nobody – *nobody* – has *ever* kissed me like that. *Ever*. I've spent most of the night doing more fantasizing than thinking, so I have no idea what to do.'

He grins as he listens to me speak, nodding his head when he decides I'm done. 'I can tell by the incessant talking that you're going to read extra meaning into every word I say, so I'll choose my words wisely.' He pauses, gazing into my eyes in a way he shouldn't if he wants me present during this conversation. 'Maybe we shouldn't take that next step. Not right now anyway.'

My face drops. I've never been able to hide disappointment.

'You're upset,' he says nervously. 'I didn't say *never*, Hols. I just said right now. You have no idea how hard this boundary is for me to make. I want this. You. It's all I've ever wanted. But I have to focus on *Battle of the Blossoms* right now, and me diving into a romance with you won't help me do that.'

'I know,' I mumble. I'd say something else to prove it's not a big deal, but it feels like a big deal for my heart.

'What can I say to help you not overthink this?'

Why is he so perfect?! I scream the words in my head. He's way more grown-up than I am. A real old soul while I feel brand new at life every day. I lower my chin, my bottom lip firmly gripped between my teeth.

'Besides *that*—'

'All I'm saying is that we clearly have chemistry, and if you need to get it out of your system or clear your head or whatever, I'm game.'

'I can't just get you out of my system, as romantic

as that sounds. I *want* to, so please, don't misread this. But I – I just...'

I've embarrassed him. He's tripping over his words, his cheeks growing pinker by the second. *Fix it, Hols!*

'Pretend I didn't just say that,' I say suddenly, trying desperately to save whatever this is. 'I do have a few questions that may ease my overloaded head. And probably my overheating loins.'

'Go.'

'Did *you* think it was a good kiss? Like, you've had a crush on me a long time. I imagine you've thought of it. Did it live up? Or was it just blah compared to your many lady friends?'

'Surpassed any daydream I've ever had.'

That's not terrible. 'But did you *feel* anything?'

'I felt a lot of things. Yes.'

'Good things?'

'Very, *very* good things, Hols,' he says. 'Anything else?'

'How far do you think it may have gone had Riv not showed up?'

'I think we'd be having a very different conversation right now.' He gazes at me with those smoldering eyes again. 'Let me ask *you* a question,' he says, suddenly turning the tables on me. 'Do you really think you're in a place where us taking this' – he motions between us – 'to the next level wouldn't add to your current problems?'

He just had to go and ask *that* question? 'It would make me crazy. I'm not gonna lie.'

'That's what I thought.'

'*But...*' I drag out the word, trying to save face, 'last night triggered something in me that I didn't even know existed, and I don't know if I can turn it off.'

He smiles as though he's relieved. 'That makes two of us. But, considering where we are right now, maybe we should take this slower than we have. I haven't been in an actual relationship in' – he thinks about it – 'in a *very* long time. I haven't talked to your brother yet, we've got the show, and you've got Professor Douchecanoe troubles. Maybe—'

Is it wrong that I like the fact that he hates Tristan? 'Maybe we could keep getting to know one another and make out in secret?' I suggest. Not my worst idea ever.

'I dunno, Hols. Maybe?'

I grin, a massive grin that won't disappear and probably makes me look certifiable, so I bite my lip to rein it in.

'I'm also going to need you to stop doing that.'

'What?'

'Biting your lip. It makes me want to buy a dead-bolt for my bedroom door and do dirty things to you. Things I know neither of us is ready for. Maybe dial back the sex appeal, could ya?' His eyes move down me, his smile growing.

I laugh like a schoolgirl with a crush. 'I can try to stop with the raw sex appeal I clearly ooze, but I hardly even know I'm doing it.'

He laughs. 'Well, I notice from across the room. So, unless you want things to get *really* complicated *really* fast...'

I kind of do. But I can tell by his seriousness that he needs things to move slower. 'Less sex appeal. Got it.'

'Hols,' he says, reaching across the island and shyly touching my hand. 'I like you a lot. I don't doubt I'll say some stupid shit and try to flirt with you. I can't possibly pretend this isn't happening. I just need to move slower. OK?'

Again, words evade me. I nod.

'Never in a million years did I picture finally telling you how I felt, kissing you, and then asking you to slow things down.' He laughs to himself, shaking his head. 'This isn't me turning you down. I want this. Just know that, alright?'

'I like you too. And I think I want to know what this is,' I say truthfully, but nervously.

'So do I.'

'But I can wait till the show is over. It's not like you're saying we can't hang out anymore.'

'Exactly. We're *living* together, Hols.'

My god, we are. My mind wanders back to kissing him again.

'We should, uh, get ready for our gig today.' He stands, pulling his hand from mine.

'Yeah,' I say, handing him the half cup of coffee I flawlessly brewed.

He takes it with a laugh.

This is gonna be complicated.

* * *

Hours Later – At the Wedding...

So, we've acknowledged we like one another, but we can't go there. That only means we'll be pining away for something just out of reach while still spending every second of our days together. Seems a tad impossible. It also means we can now openly flirt and say things we've probably been holding back because we know the other wants the same thing. We've peeked behind the curtain and didn't hate what we saw.

'Hollyn,' Ian says my name, camera pointed my way.

'Yeah?'

'That was the third time I'd said your name. Distracted today?'

Third time? I guess I am. 'A little.'

'Dax seems distracted, too. Did something happen?'

'What?'

'You two fight?'

'No,' I say, shaking my head quickly.

Ian cocks his head. 'Was it the opposite of a fight?'

I stop what I'm doing, thinking about his question. Yes. It was exactly the opposite of a fight.

'No. He's probably just nervous.'

'Hey, girl!' Mercy says in a singsong voice as she approaches, violin case in her hand. 'How's my winner this morning?'

'You know me. Just following orders like a good little girl.'

She pinches her eyebrows together. 'Good little girl? Blech. That's boring.' Her eyes are on the arrangements I'm working on. 'These are pretty. But where's Dax?'

I shrug my shoulders. He kind of bolted when we got here.

'How don't you know? Aren't you his assistant?'

'Yep. I'm his assistant and his assistant only,' I say, shoving a flower into an arrangement so hard the stem snaps. 'Crap.'

'Only his assistant, eh? Does that mean something else was a possibility?'

I glance at her, my face probably doing all sorts of things I don't want it to. I forgot who I was talking to. She can read between the lines of anything. I could tell her about last night, especially since I have a feeling she knew about the crush thing all along. Dax said something about needing to tell me before River or Mercy did. She had to have known. Why else would he say that?

'Fuck. Fuck. *Fuck.*' Dax walks into the awning I'm working under, mumbling swear words under his breath into his shirt pulled to his mouth as though that will hide them.

I stare in a way I shouldn't, forgetting entirely that Mercy is standing next to me.

'What's wrong with you two?' she asks.

Dax practically growls as he drops his shirt. 'I

fucked up an order, and now I have to start over. How long do we have?' He looks at me, his jaw clenched, a hand on the back of his neck.

I glance down at my phone, tapping it to life. 'An hour and a half.'

'I need your help,' he says, pleading with his eyes. 'We can throw these together at the end.'

Because of River showing up last night – yes, that's what I'm going with – we didn't quite finish the arrangements for the reception, so I've been working on those.

'Whatever you need,' I say, dropping the flower stems in my hand to the table. I glance at Mercy. 'Sorry, assisting calls.'

'Don't mind me,' she says, backing away with a clenched-teeth smile. 'I just came to chit-chat because Dylan won't shut up.' She walks away slowly. 'Not sure why I thought working with my ex was a great idea…' Finally, she exits the awning, disappearing inside the ceremony space.

I follow Dax to where the ceremony is taking place. 'What happened?'

'I know we agreed to slow things down hours ago, but I can't quit thinking about it, and you, and instead of a C in the center of this flower wall, I was halfway through an H.' His eyes finally meet mine, the corners of his lips turning as if he's almost amused.

'An H? Like for—'

'Don't say it,' he says with an irritated laugh. 'I've never made a mistake on something like this, but my head's all over the place. The bride caught it. She wasn't thrilled.'

Stop smiling, Hollyn. That would be easier if he didn't have the same guilty grin on his face.

'We can fix it. Just tell me what to do.'

Over the next hour, we dismantle part of an H (for Hollyn, I assume; how freaking cute is that?) and redo the floral wall. A C sits happily in the center when we're done. The bride seems happy, and we still have time to finish the reception centerpieces. I've already done most of them, so Dax has no problem knocking out the small ones much faster than I could. Only minor damage is done internally, mostly to my heart. I'm feeling big things for Dax and noticing everything. He's right, none of those feelings will make this easier, but how do we avoid them now that they're out there?

21

DAX

The Next Day – At Battle of the Blossom's *Filming...*

'Dax and Allie,' Jillian says, now standing in front of the two of us.

She's already talked with Celeste and Leo, so I know what she's about to say. Having to stand here for ten minutes, in front of Hollyn, knowing that we both probably know my fuck-up may land us in Jillian's predicted bottom two might have been the most torment I've felt in all my life if it wasn't for the situation I've now gotten myself into with her.

I can't quit thinking about her. Last night I found

myself staring at her while we watched TV, half tempted to go back on everything I'd said earlier. Instead, we came up with a compromise. We'd sit close on the couch, but no kissing. When it got too tempting, we disappeared to our own rooms for the night and spent hours texting instead.

'I'm sorry to say that the two of you are in our bottom two this week,' Jillian continues.

I drop my head towards the ground. Allie lets out a squeak. The bottom two. It sounds so much worse than I expected. This is precisely what Hollyn was afraid of when she signed up for this gig. Way to go me. I just had to go and tell her I loved her.

'Allie, you were in our bottom two last week as well. Unfortunately, I'm not sure you'll make it through this week. Of course, the fans could get those votes in and surprise me again.'

I glance over at her, giving her a sympathetic look. It's either her or me. I don't want it to be me. Sorry, Allie.

'I'm most surprised to see you here, Dax.' Jillian stops in front of me. 'You won the first challenge by a long way. I really thought you'd float through this competition like you'd done it before. Walk me through what happened yesterday?'

I glance at Hollyn, completely ashamed of myself.

She looks as upset as I am. Like it's her fault. That makes it even worse.

We're in San Francisco today. We talked about what I would say if this came up on the plane ride over. I knew I'd probably have to address my mistake since they have it on film, but I haven't even tried to tell River what's up with me and his sister, and the last thing I need is him figuring it out via a YouTube show with the rest of the world. He won't take that well.

'My personal life kind of took over my head yesterday. It tripped me up before I even began.'

This is precisely why I decided early on not to let anything happen with Hollyn. I need to win this to buy the shop, and getting into a relationship will definitely not help me do that.

'You made a mistake?' Jillian asks.

'Many,' I say with a laugh. 'But one giant one nearly sunk me. I didn't double-check an order; my head was on another planet and I realized partway through that I'd created the wrong initial on my flower wall.'

Celeste gasps. 'Oh no,' she whispers, not entirely under her breath.

'Thank you, Celeste. It was exactly that humiliating.' I attempt to lighten the mood by laughing at myself. 'I never expected to be standing here at all. When

I found out my cousin had applied for the show, I was dealing with another unexpected event in my personal life.'

Don't look at Hollyn. There's no way she doesn't know you're talking about her.

'I should have been able to separate the two and be the professional I am, but I couldn't do that yesterday.'

'You think maybe you're being a little hard on yourself?' Jillian asks.

'Yes,' Hollyn says in a near whisper.

'We all make mistakes, Dax,' Jillian continues, ignoring Hollyn altogether. 'The fact that you learned a lesson from it will serve you well in the future.'

'Maybe.'

'The viewers love you two, so who knows what might happen,' Jillian says, giving me a bit of hope.

Being in the bottom two wouldn't be so bad if I didn't want so badly to make sure Hollyn sees me in the best light possible. Like a kid in love, I want to impress her but I feel like I've just let us both down.

* * *

Moments Later...

'It's OK,' Hollyn says as we leave the building. 'It was bad timing on our part. Like you said.'

'Dax!' Celeste says my name, her heels tapping on the floor behind me. I drop my head. Speaking of bad timing. 'I'm so sorry, Daxy.' She gives me an awkward hug.

'I'll just wait outside,' Hollyn says, walking away from us.

I hope she doesn't think this Celeste thing is anything to worry about because besides her emailing me daily, it's not. I never even respond. The girl can*not* take a hint.

'Your final product was gorgeous,' Celeste says once Hollyn has disappeared out the front door. 'The bottom two sucks, though. Going through it on week one was humiliating, so I feel you.'

'Thanks, Celeste.'

'Wanna hang out? My flight doesn't leave for a few hours.' She seems hopeful as she asks, batting her eyes at me as she waits on my answer.

'I've actually got something planned with Hollyn, so...'

'Oh,' Celeste says, defeat now in her voice. 'No worries.' She waves a hand my way. 'Call me later. I sent you my number; we'll talk. You can tell me all about the problems you're facing. I'm a great listener.' She touches my chest, planting her lips on my cheek before walking away, turning once to flash me a smile that makes me cringe.

'Looks like someone wants a piece of Daxy,' Hollyn says as I join her on the sidewalk.

'She's persistent. I'll give her that.'

She reaches up to wipe Celeste's lipstick from my cheek. 'This is really all my fault,' she says.

'*How?*' I ask. 'It's not like I had to break out the secret crush thing when I did.'

'True,' she says with a nod. 'It's all *your* fault.'

'You, uh...' I reach down, taking her hand in mine. 'You think holding hands is too risky?'

She glances down. 'I think it's pretty safe,' she says, lacing her fingers through mine.

My hand around hers makes my brain fizz. Maybe going slow was a bad idea. I can't get my head off her. Off us.

'This is our car.' Saved by the Uber I ordered pulling up. 'We're doing something fun.'

'What about our flight?'

'I had McKenzie move it to this evening.' I open the car door. 'I made plans,' I say, coaxing her into the car.

'Plans?' she asks, sliding into the back seat. 'Like a date?'

I cock my head. We hadn't talked about dating.

'Do you *want* it to be a date?'

'Maybe,' she says with a nod, lifting a shoulder.

If I wasn't nearly six five, I'd slide into that back seat next to her. But considering this is a compact car, I get into the front, greeting the Uber driver before glancing back at Hols.

'Alright,' I say. 'Let's say it's a date.'

We pull up to a local florist thirty minutes later. It was the only place I could find open on a Sunday.

'You really can't get enough flowers, can you?' she asks, stepping onto the curb, flipping her sunglasses to the top of her head.

'When I first started my business, I'd go to the Saturday market on Sundays and hand out single stem flowers for free. I can't count how many people would gush that they needed it at that moment. There were a lot of tears those days, and not all from me.' I wink, although that's truer than I want it to be.

'Really?'

I nod. 'I doubt you remember this, but today is the anniversary of my dad's death.'

'*Today?*' she asks, her hand moving to her chest.

'Dax. I'm sorry. I didn't remember, or I'd have said something earlier.'

'How would you remember that?' I grab her hand again. 'The last few years, I've thought of him a lot. I've been trying to do things to honor him however I can. He was really into helping people. Be it with flowers or whatever he had in his pockets. Did you know he delivered free arrangements for every funeral in town? I didn't know until a few years ago when an old client of his told me.'

'Robert was a good guy, Dax. You remind me of him.'

'Yeah?'

She nods and I like the sound of that. Especially coming from someone who knew him. I want to be like him.

'This afternoon, we're teaming up with Earth Angel Homeless Mission and handing out flowers and cash to people in need.'

Her jaw drops open. 'Dax Hartley. You make *me* want to be a better person.'

I pull open the door of the shop. 'I'm not *all* good, Hols. If you could read my mind lately, you'd know that.'

She laughs shyly, her cheeks turning rosy. 'You arranged all this?'

'Yeah.'

I withdrew two thousand dollars from my account that I probably shouldn't have to do this. Not to impress her; I had no idea I'd have told her I loved her when I planned this. It just felt like something I needed to do for my dad.

We chose red chrysanthemums as they symbolize hope and love, the two things I hope to bring to these people today, and two words that completely sum up my father.

The folks from the charity, Bret and Carroll, help put together a hundred flower stems the florist, Rita, has donated to the cause because my story touched her heart. I guess I have a story after all.

Cards in envelopes are attached to each flower stem, and inside is a note that reads: *Never Stop Looking Forward – Courtesy of the late Robert Hartley.* Along with a twenty-dollar bill and info for local shelters and homeless support. It takes the five of us an hour to put everything together.

'You two ready to make some days?' Bret asks.

I'm excited about this. Hollyn holds my hand tightly on the ride there, glancing over at me periodically as though somehow, I've suddenly turned into someone I wasn't before. She finally sees me as more than River's friend. It's all over her face, and I can't get enough of it.

'We'll stay together,' Bret says as he pulls into the chosen neighborhood. 'Don't be afraid to chat with these people. Most of them are just down on their luck. Most days, they give *me* hope.'

'Stay close,' I say to Hols, handing her a bundle of flowers. 'I'll be right behind you.'

The road is full of tents and makeshift homeless camps. A fire burns down the way, and a child filling a Tonka truck full of rocks sits near a grouping of old lawn chairs. People are hesitant, but they slowly emerge when they hear Bret's voice. He's obviously well known down here.

My eyes keep being drawn back to Hollyn even while I talk to folks. She's so gorgeous, and the sincerity in her tone, while she talks to some of the women in this camp, reminds me what a fantastic person she really is. She doesn't even realize it.

A woman approaches her, her eyes fixed on the flowers in Hollyn's hand.

'Hi!' Hols says. 'We're honoring my friend's father today. Would you like one?' She extends a flower to the woman as a child joins her. Hollyn grins at the little girl, kneeling to her level, balancing on her heels. 'I'm Hollyn,' she says. 'What's your name?'

'Sadie,' the little girl says.

'You're so pretty, Sadie, just like these flowers. You'll give the envelopes to your mommy?' Hollyn asks, pulling two flowers from the bundle and handing them to the little girl.

Once Sadie's run off after her mother, Hollyn turns to me, her hand over her heart. 'This is gonna make me cry more than doing deliveries with you. I see why you wanted to do this.'

My heart practically bursts in my chest. What I feel for Hollyn is getting overwhelming to the point I don't know how slow I can go. Even as a dorky cowardly teenager, what I felt for her didn't consume me like it is right now. Maybe I just got terrible news being tossed into the bottom two of the show, but I don't care because something I've wanted for way longer is standing in front of me, looking at me the way I've always imagined.

22

HOLLYN

Friday Night...

When Dax pulls up to his mom's house, we're surprised to see the street lined with cars. Music wafts from the backyard to the street.

'That's the sound of our childhood,' Dax says, getting out and shimmying his way to me in front of his car.

'You're nuts.'

'It's all your parents' fault.'

'I know,' I say, shaking my head. 'It's kind of scary.'

We follow the path alongside my parents' driveway to the backyard, stopping in our tracks at the sea of people mingling.

'I thought this was a small backyard barbecue watch party?' Dax asks.

'This *is* a small Matthews' barbecue.'

'My favorite kind.' He waggles his eyebrows, now doing the running man backward in front of me.

'There's that weirdo neighbor kid again.'

'You know, he still likes you, even with the stick up your ass.'

'Hey!' He's obviously kidding but I know how much he likes getting reactions from me.

Nothing else has happened between Dax and me. Well, not *nothing*, but not *that* either. There have been a few rules broken. We sit way too close on the couch while we watch TV. He holds my hand in the car. We've been on a few harmless dates. Dinner. A movie. One night when things almost got away from us, he nearly floored me by running his thumb over my lips, kissing my forehead sweetly and walking away. It was romantic as hell. The way he looks at me makes my heart flutter. Tristan never looked at me that way.

'Dax!' River's voice interrupts his teasing.

We glance his way as he waves us towards the house.

'I thought this was a small barbecue?'

River bursts out in a laugh. 'You know Mom. She's got five hundred close friends.' He rolls his eyes. 'Want to do an interview for the documentary?' he asks me. 'I got everything set up inside.'

'Sure. But no questions about things they don't know about.'

'Drama sells, Hols. I ain't making that promise.' He finishes the drink in his hand, holding up a finger. 'Let me get a refill, and we'll get started. Join me, Dax.' The two of them meander through the party towards the bar my parents had built when we were kids where I see Mom's even hired a bartender for the occasion.

I wander through my parents' house as I wait for River. His camera faces the wall full of family photos and they draw me in. Pictures of my parents in their glory days. Mom on the stage at the MTV Music Awards. River and me on the stage of a concert when we were tiny. Graduations. Birthdays. Even Dax appears in some of these photos. The memories make me smile.

'What're ya doin'?' River asks, sipping his new drink when I turn his way.

'I haven't seen these in forever. Our life was fun, right?'

'Most of the time,' he says, standing next to me,

looking at the photos that fill the family room wall practically floor to ceiling. 'You ready?'

'Yeah.' I pull myself away from the photos, sitting in the chair he's directing me to.

'We're just having a casual conversation, OK?' he says, fidgeting with his camera before sitting next to it. 'What's your favorite memory of growing up the daughter of Penny Candy?'

Favorite memory? Hmm. I glance around the room, then out the windows overlooking the pool and patio. Mom's done a lot of crazy things for us over the years.

Once, she made us dress up as Penny Candy for Halloween. We were young, early grade school years. Mom dressed like her friend Staci, who played guitar. Dad was her drummer, Rico. River was her bass guitarist, Sammy. And I was Mom. It was a colossal hit with people who recognized her but I hated dressing up as her. Can't use that memory then.

I stare into the yard some more, racking my brain for a favorite. Suddenly the song drifting through the screen door triggers something.

'My thirteenth birthday.'

'I knew it,' River says with a laugh.

'I wanted Maroon 5 or Jonas Brothers or Gwen Stefani. What thirteen-year-old kid back then didn't?

Obviously, she couldn't get them. But she didn't disappoint me.'

'It's burned into my brain,' River says. '"Hollaback Girl" will never be the same.'

I laugh. No, it won't. 'Mom performed the hell out of it. I'd never been so cool in all my life. It may as well have been Gwen on the stage to my friends. She even dressed up like her.'

'A memory I'd love to forget, considering I crushed hard on Gwen and not so much on Mom.' River scrunches his face as if he's disgusted just picturing it. 'Do you remember anything about being on tour with her as a kid? I don't.'

Mom toured for a long time, even throughout part of our childhood. While she was gone, Dad took care of us, and when he wasn't around, her mom, my grandmother, moved in to pick up the slack. She lived in an apartment over our garage until the day she died.

River and I went on tour with Mom until I was old enough for kindergarten. Dad was putting himself through medical school at the time and came when he could; otherwise, we were taken care of by nannies and security guards.

'I remember being on stage a couple of times. Mostly it's the screaming I remember. When you're three or four, that's terrifying. Mom likes to tell the story about the times I met people like Madonna and Mariah Carey, but besides the photos to prove it, I don't remember.'

As a tween, I wished I'd have remembered meeting them and would talk about it like I did, but nope, no memories of it.

'One thing I do remember is my nanny, Justine. She wasn't very old, probably just out of high school? She traveled around with us, and I spent most of my time with her and a security guy. I don't remember his name, something with a P, maybe Paul? Phil? I don't know, but he always drove, and he was huge. Like bigger than Dax. I remember him letting me ride on his shoulders a few times. Felt like I was on top of a mountain.'

I haven't thought about any of this in so long. It's weird to have people be a part of your life, then one day, they're gone. Maybe that's where I learned to run away from my problems. I thought that's what you did when you were over something or when the world felt too big to handle. You disappeared. Created your own peaceful world. Only the world I created wasn't peaceful. I realize now my own choices over the years mixed with my childhood insecurities traumatized me in ways I didn't expect. Ways I'm struggling to get past.

'There isn't much I could say for sure happened when I was that young, just bits and pieces of a chaotic life in unfamiliar hotel rooms every night. I remember it was loud, like all the time, loud. Probably why I prefer quiet now.'

'I never got a bodyguard,' River says with a huff.

'I keep telling you; you were never as important as me,' I joke.

We do a few more questions about life as Penny Candy's daughter, then he tosses out the one I was hoping he wouldn't ask.

'What was the worst thing about being Penny Candy's daughter?'

I blow out a breath. 'You sure you want to do this one? I might hurt her feelings.'

'Wanna know my answer first?'

'That might help.'

River sips his drink. 'I always felt like I'd never be what they were, what they *are*. I still feel that way. I mean, Mom was famous. And Dad is a fucking gynecologist. The jokes from my friends were endless. Instead of doctors and musicians, they got a guy struggling to break into the film industry and a self-absorbed you.' He scrunches his face again, eyes on me as if *I'm* the real disappointment. I know he's kidding, but I also know he's right. 'Sometimes, I think they'd rather have had Mercy and Dax as their kids. They expected too much from us, and we both disappointed them.'

'I felt like she wanted me to become the next Penny Candy, and we've all heard me sing.'

'Like swinging a bag of cats against a wall.'

'Exactly,' I say, feeling like River and I are genuinely bonding. 'I've felt like a disappointment for a long time, Riv. Dad hasn't talked to me in years. I mean, he'll chit-chat here and there but not *really* talk. Until recently, Mom was the same. Our lives were so public. As a kid, especially a teen, that was humiliating.' I sigh, lifting my shoulders. 'Did you know my first kiss was reported in a celebrity magazine? Penny Candy's daughter all grown up.' I groan. 'I was fourteen. Hardly grown up at all. Mom got mad at me for that. Like I should have known better and not the adult photographer taking the photo and sending it into the world.'

The article wouldn't have been so bad if my classmates hadn't found it. Imagine kissing a boy for the first time on your porch as he dropped you off from your first actual date and having a photo of it printed for the entire world to witness. That boy never called me again and I can't blame him.

'Do you really think I'm self-absorbed?'

'Yes,' River says, not hesitating at all. 'But so am I.'

I guess that's something.

'I was a little worried what this whole Tristan thing would do to you. Seems like you're doing alright?'

'I think so? Dax is helping. He keeps me laughing. I hardly even think about Tristan anymore.'

'Then keep doing what you're doing. I have a feeling the money thing will work out.' He stands up from his chair, downing the rest of his drink. 'We're good here. If I need something else, I know where to find you.'

23

DAX

In Dax's Part of the Yard...

'Dax!' Penny waves, walking my way. She's always been happy to see me. Sometimes even more than River. 'Come get a drink with me.'

'Let's do it, Mrs Matthews,' I say, extending an elbow her way that she gladly takes.

Penny's been like a second mother my entire life. She's best friends with my mom and has been around for all my milestones. She and John have come to every important event I have with as much enthusiasm as they had for their own kids. I honestly feel lucky to have so many people on my side.

'Your mom's working this evening, but she'll be here for the results, so you're free to have a drink if you want,' Penny informs me.

My mom hasn't had a sip of drink since my dad was killed. For most of my life, she was the president of the local MADD (moms against drunk drivers) group. She questioned any friends who tried to pick me up, River included. Sometimes going as far as marching herself down to the police station to turn in the ones she'd discovered had drunk and drove. She even bought a breathalyzer test and if I missed a curfew or was with someone questionable, guess who got to check their blood alcohol level? Yep, me. She has settled down over the years, but I learned very young not to drink around her because her heart can't take it. I never want to be the one to test that. I'm all she has.

'Let me ask ya something, Daxy.' Penny's one of the very few people on earth I allow to call me Daxy, because the nickname came with the territory of growing up next door. It could be worse. I could be known as 'hot for my daughter' or 'too into space'.

'You doing OK?' she asks. 'The pressure getting to you? Shall we take Hollyn off your hands?'

This is where Hollyn gets her curious, over-talking self. It's rarely one question with either of them. It's more like the rapid-fire of a gun coming at you too quickly to answer. I've learned to listen and respond when they stop voluntarily.

'I'm good. Choked a little this last challenge, but I feel more focused now.'

'And Hollyn, how's she doing?'

'She's great, Penny. I'd even say she seems happy.'

Hollyn definitely smiles a lot more than she did when she first got here.

'You two getting along? Because I know how you boys liked to torment her when you were young. Spying on her, pushing her into the pool, listening in on her phone calls...'

'Good times,' I say to her with a laugh.

Penny laughs too. 'I think secretly, she liked it.'

'What do you think of the Tristan thing?'

It can't hurt to hear it from her. Hols has kept his name pretty quiet recently, and I wonder if that's because she's getting over him or is just distracted by whatever is going on between us. Or both?

'He's a real piece of work,' Penny says, her voice less than amused. 'Who steals money from their girlfriend? I knew he was trouble the moment I met him. John turned him in to the college, but somehow, he fooled them, ruining my girl's life in the process.'

'You think she's ruined?' Seems kind of harsh.

'I think she's pulling out of it. Let's just hope she's strong enough to not go back to him.'

God. My heart practically jumps from a cliff, free-falling in a way that makes me forget to breathe. I hadn't even thought of that. Her going back to him? It hurts just thinking about it.

Suddenly Penny stands up straighter, turning to me with a wide smile. 'Maybe you should take her out? Distract her. Show her how a man's supposed to treat a woman.'

'*What?*'

'Come on, Daxy. I've heard the stories. You're handsome, charming, and I know your mom raised you right. Show my girl a good time and make her forget all about Professor Buttknuckler.'

I burst into a laugh. Buttknuckler? That's a new one.

'Hols and I... we're just friends, Penny.'

She cocks her head. 'I didn't ask you to sleep with her. I said take her on a date.'

'Right,' I say, dumbfounded. Nobody has to ask to put that idea in my head. It's living rent-free without permission.

'Oh no!' she hisses, pulling me away from people mingling around us. 'You already slept with her, didn't you?'

'*What? No.*' I rub the back of my neck nervously. 'Why would you think that?' This isn't a conversation I want to have with her mother.

She gasps. 'You're rubbing your neck. I'd know that nervous Nellie move anywhere. You *did*!' she exclaims before lowering her voice, her tone changing. 'You *did*?'

'*No*,' I say firmly. 'I *didn't*.'

I can tell she doesn't believe me. She stares into my eyes, cocking her head slowly. 'Maybe you haven't. *Yet*. But something is going on, isn't it?'

'Yes,' I say. 'We're competing in a flower competition together.'

'That's not it,' Penny says with a wide smile.

'Seriously.' I hold up a hand. 'As much as I wish I were back home and *not* having this conversation, I can truthfully say Hollyn and I have never slept together.'

At least not without clothes. Yet. Something her mother needs to know exactly nothing about.

'Word to the wise: if you suspect it may happen, talk to River first. I've heard him talk about the bro code thing. He'd take it better if he heard it from you first.'

Or, I could pretend I'm not as close to her family as I am, do what I want, and ask for forgiveness later. That seems easier. Probably the way River would play his hand.

'I'll keep that in mind.'

Is it *that* obvious something is going on between us? There's no way. We're literally barely anything at this point. But if Penny suspects it, maybe River will too. I'd planned to talk to him tonight, then I convinced myself not to because my inner teenage coward has resurfaced.

Penny meanders away from me, heading onto the makeshift dance floor where John is currently busting a move.

'Finally,' Mercy says, approaching me. 'Someone I know. What the hell is this? I thought it was a small-ish friends and family watch party?'

'They duped us.'

'Well?' She looks up at me. 'Did you win? Or are you a big fat loser?'

'I find out with the rest of you with the live results.'

She rolls her eyes.

'You've been voting for me, right?' I ask, busting her balls a little.

'I'm voting for *Hollyn*,' she says with a glare.

'It counts.'

'Where is she anyway?' she asks, glancing around the yard. 'I have her phone; she left it in my car last night.'

Jake and I went golfing yesterday, then he convinced me to have a few drinks, which then turned into half a dozen, so I didn't get home until well after midnight. I'd forgotten Hollyn went out with Mercy.

I considered knocking on her door when I got home, but I was tipsy, and tipsy Dax is known for doing dumb shit. I couldn't chance it. Thankfully, Jake and I knew we'd probably drink, and we took an Uber there and back. Hollyn has no idea I spilled my guts to Jake – again – while drinking away my frustrations.

'Can I show you something?' Mercy asks, stepping closer to me and pulling Hollyn's phone from her pocket. She taps the screen, typing in a code so fast I couldn't crack it if I wanted to, pulling up her text messaging app.

She looked through Hollyn's phone? Thank god I didn't text her what Jake suggested I text her last night. That would have been biting me in the ass right now.

'Did she tell you about Victoria yet?'

'She did.'

'That bitch has been texting her. It's all so vague.' She scrolls through the texts. 'Tristan cheated, ya know? A lot.'

'Yeah,' I say, still pissed about it. 'Hollyn thinks Victoria is the other woman.'

'Well, I don't *think*,' she says. 'I *know*.'

'Hols said she hasn't admitted it yet.'

'Hollyn doesn't *want* to be sure because she's still convinced icky Vicki was *actually* her friend. She wasn't.' She scrolls through the text messages, stopping at a couple of photos. 'Look.' She points at one of the photos. 'Victoria heard Hollyn had found an engagement ring receipt, and she suggested the *two* of them go try on wedding dresses.'

'That seems pretty normal for a couple girlfriends. Does it not?'

'It does,' Mercy says. 'Except Victoria meant they'd *each* try on dresses. That's not normal. The bride to be tries on dresses, no one else.'

She flashes two photos my way. 'When Hols had picked her favorite, she labeled it as "The One!" Vic's photo is labeled as "The *real* One!"'

My heart sinks a little. She was trying to tell her, and Hollyn didn't see it. That's terrible.

'I bet poor Hols was floating through her days on a cloud. Never seeing the thunderstorm headed her way. She gave that guy way too many chances. Easily a dozen.'

'A *dozen*?' I ask, shock dripping from my voice. 'He cheated *that* much?'

'Probably.' Mercy shoves Hollyn's phone into her pocket, marching past me to the bar. 'Give me something strong,' she says to the bartender.

'All in, eh?'

She turns towards me. 'I'm about to tell my best friend I snooped through her phone like a jealous husband, followed by; icky fucking Vicki has stolen your boyfriend. Booze will help with that.'

Mercy squints as she downs the shot, slamming the glass onto the bar precisely how River does at times.

'Wish me luck!'

I mingle for a bit before I finally see River again.

'Dax!' he thunders, an empty glass in his hand as he walks my way.

'River,' I say as he blows by me towards the bar.

'Scotch on the rocks. Make it another triple.'

Another triple?

'Dax!' he says again as he spots me as though we didn't just have this conversation one minute ago.

'How drunk are ya?'

'Not gonna lie, buddy, this one got on top of me,'

he says with a drunken chuckle, throwing an arm over my shoulders. 'Rough day; Summer dumped me.'

Shit. I slink out of his half hug, his arm dropping to his side as I do. River is painfully honest when he's sober. Things you thought he'd buried away forever slowly start to surface when he's drunk. Loudly.

'What happened?'

'I fucked it up. *Again.*'

He's never had the best luck with women. He desperately searches for what he considers his one, but he is also the guy who tells the truth when asked a question like, 'Do you think I've gained a few pounds?' – a fatal flaw.

'How?'

'It's not important,' he says. 'You know what?' He takes a step closer, wrapping an arm around my waist and laying his head on my chest. 'I love you, man. I don't tell you that enough.'

'We're not doing this,' I say, pushing him an arm's length away.

'Why do we all avoid love?' he asks sincerely. 'It's the one emotion every person searches for, yet we pretend like it's too much to handle. We're scared of it. *Why?*' Suddenly he laughs to himself. 'You should tell Hols you've loved her since you got hair on your balls.'

'You're a little loud; you know that, right?'

I can't talk to him tonight. He's clearly in no shape. It might go over better, but I can't do that to him.

'Show her your wang, man.'

A few guests glance over now, looking River up and down judgmentally. Jesus. I grab his drink, setting it back on the bar. 'You're done,' I say, pushing him towards the side of the house. 'I'm bringing you home.'

'She called me a child. Said she felt smothered,' he says as he follows me to my car. 'I put my sister ahead of my girlfriend and moved too fast. I'm an idiot! You think I'm an idiot?'

'You're not an idiot,' I say, pulling open my passenger door and practically shoving him into it.

'It hurts so bad.' He grabs his chest, leaning forward and allowing his forehead to smack my dashboard. Now he's crying. Great.

I get him strapped in as he wavers between broken-hearted and giggly drunk. Looks like I'll have to watch these results from home tonight while 'babysitting'.

24

HOLLYN

Moments Later – Inside her Parents' House...

My phone beeps with an incoming text. I glance down at the notification. Dax.

Have Mercy drive you home? Riv is drunk. Taking him home.

He's *drunk*? God. I hope Dax didn't talk to him, and he took it *that* badly.

I notice Mercy's eyes meandering to my phone screen as she stands in front of me.

'Did you want to read this one too?' I snap with a glare, flashing my phone in front of her.

She just announced that she's snooped through my phone and has questions. How did I think keeping things from her wouldn't come back to me? I want to be mad, but truthfully, she brings up some valid points. I've been lying to her and she knows me well enough to know that and she's not afraid to call me out on it.

'I'm sorry, Hols. I wanted to help and you're not talking so when your phone started beeping with incoming texts, I had a look to see if there was anything I could do. I'm absolutely certain *Vicki* is the other girl. Look through your texts with her and you'll see it.'

The day Vic and I tried on wedding dresses is now playing in my head. I didn't see that one like Mercy did. Maybe I just didn't want to, like she says. Mercy and River saw right through Tristan, and I didn't believe them. *Why?* They're the two people I trust the most. What in the hell was wrong with me to not trust my brother and best friend?

I drop onto the couch, laying my head against the back cushion, letting out a long, exhausted sigh. I've been telling Mercy I've been avoiding Tristan and Vicki. If she knew about the money he's stolen, she'd see why I'm trying to stay in their good graces.

'I know she is, Merc! I've picked up all the clues. It's just... humiliating to admit.'

She walks over, sitting on the couch not far from me.

'Things happened so gradually with Tristan that I didn't see much of it. Next thing I knew, I'd lost myself and kept hoping the Tristan I knew would show up and save me from the one he'd become. He wasn't *all* bad, ya know.'

She pinches her lips, obviously not believing that for a second. It's my fault, really. Had I not disappeared and instead included her more in my life, maybe she'd have seen Tristan's good side too.

'You deserve a guy a million times better than Professor Assface, Hols. A Ryan Reynolds, Liam Hemsworth, Chris Evans...' She mentions every unattainable man on the planet.

Dax Hartley? I sigh.

'I feel like a loser. Living out of suitcases. No job. A pile of my ex's shoes on my bedroom floor. Sleeping in my brother's bed.' I shiver. 'How is everyone else so much better at life than me?'

'Uh, not one of us has anything figured out besides how not to starve to death and basic self-care. I'm not thriving. I work gig after gig, most of them with my ex. I bartend in the evenings and trust me when I say bartending is *not* my calling. I've got exactly 312 dollars in my account that's gotta stretch a week. Edie and Carlos are house hunting, and I haven't even attempted to find my own place, even though Ed thinks I'm on my way to being approved for an apartment I may or may not have made up.'

'You lied to Edie?'

She laughs under her breath. 'Many times. We're all a mess, Hols. Every one of us flies by the seat of our pants until something feels right, then we follow that path until it fucks us over. It's the circle of life.'

'Biblical.'

She nods. 'I'm sorry I looked through your phone. I wasn't trying to snoop into your life, I just wanted to help with the Tristan thing because something seems off and you never want to talk about it. When I did, I noticed some stuff. If I didn't say anything, what kind of best friend would I be?'

'Well I suppose I love you for that. But—'

'*But*,' she interrupts me, 'you can't keep entertaining this idea that eventually, Tristan will somehow turn into Prince Charming and beg to have you back. As for Vicki, well, she was never your friend to begin with. You gotta let them go.'

I know she's right about everything, especially that last part. Neither of them ever had my best interests at heart. It was always about what *they* wanted. I see it now. I need to tell Mercy everything. I'm no better a friend than Victoria if I don't.

'Ready for the truth?'

'Say it.'

'Tristan stole over ninety grand from me.'

'*What?*'

I nod, completely ashamed. 'That's why I'm keeping the lines of communication open. I'm trying to get it back without involving my parents.'

'Hols—'

'Come on,' I say. 'You know how fragile our relationship is. I can't bother them with this. I should be able to handle it. I'm twenty-nine.'

'So, what, you're just going to talk to him until he finally gives back the money? Cause I think that's a bit of a fantasy.'

'There's something else too,' I say, dropping my head. 'I know you warned me about this, but I don't see him how you see him.'

'See who?'

'Dax.' I glance up at her. 'He's not who you think he is. He's better, good in a way I've never experienced. The way he looks at me. We have fun together without even trying and he makes me feel safe. I think

I'm falling for him, Merc. And I can't stop it. I don't want to stop it.'

She's silent, her eyes as wide as I've ever seen them.

'We kissed,' I continue. 'He kissed me *real* good and I don't regret any of it.'

'You kissed *Dax*? *Why?*'

'*Why?*' I ask with a laugh. 'Besides the fact that he's the sweetest, funniest, smartest, best-looking man on the planet?'

She stares at me as if she doesn't understand.

'He told me, Merc.'

'Told you what?'

I can't believe she's going to play this off like she doesn't know. I know she does. Dax said so. 'How long have you known he had feelings for me?'

She rears her head back as though she's stunned by my question but I know her better than that.

'If you want the truth from me, you gotta give it in return, Mercy.'

Finally, she drops her head with a sigh. 'Fine,' she says. 'I suspected it all through high school but I found out for sure right after you left. He was in the beginning phase of his "glow-up".' She rolls her eyes. 'He'd been acting so weird. Broken-hearted. I didn't get it because he'd never even had a girlfriend.' She shrugs her shoulders. 'River blurted it out. Apparently, Dax was depressed for a long time. I think he even tried seeing a therapist. He was never the same. Went from the dorky Dax we all knew and loved to the bearded dreamboat he is now. I thought it was just a stupid childhood crush. Kind of figured he'd grow out of it, ya know? Obviously, he'd have a crush on the girl next door. You were always around. Once we were out in the real world, I thought it would fade. But it never did.'

'Mercy, I didn't know, not even when we were in high school. I thought we were just friends.'

'My god, you're bad at reading signals from people, Hols. I thought you just weren't interested. How could you not have seen it? The stupid star watching. You telling him about your anxiety late at night. He drove you to school every day during our senior year. You two were always paired up on shifts at the record store. I'd try to change the schedule, and it'd be changed back.'

How did I not know any of this?

'He'd bring you coffee and watch chick flick movies with you. He made you Rice Krispie treats in the shape of hearts one Valentine's Day. He'd bring you chicken noodle soup and your homework when you were sick. There's so much more, and you thought all that was just a teen boy being your *friend*?'

Oh my god. Until right now, I hadn't seen through any of this. I sincerely thought it was just him being a good friend.

'Don't even get me started on senior prom night; after Justin left you there to bone Ashley in his car. Sure, you left early, but Dax hunted him down the next morning, threatened his life, and made him apologize to you. Did you think *Justin* bought those flowers? No. That was all Dax.'

'What?'

She nods, verifying the words that just left her lips.

He made Justin apologize? We just talked about this, and yet no mention of this part. None of our past was him just being the nice guy. He liked me. Or, in his words, he loved me. I thought he was nice to me because I was his bestie's sister. But it was more than that the whole time?

I drop my head into my hands, tears quickly pushing through. I couldn't see him as anything other than River's best friend and the kid next door. That must have been so hard for him. Then I unexpectedly show up here, and River pawns me off on him. God, he was probably a nervous wreck. All the awkwardness I've sensed between us was him trying to hide all this.

My breathing speeds into impending anxiety. 'I have to make this up to him.'

'I'm sorry, Hols. I didn't know you didn't see it, or I'd have told you. I thought you just weren't interested.'

'Mercy, I could have had a completely different life.'

'I wouldn't go that far. You were just teenagers.'

Cheering outside muffles the music still playing and earns our attention. I glance out, confused.

'The show!' Mercy says suddenly, running to the patio door and stepping out. 'You guys got top spot again,' she says, a proud smile on her face as she looks back at me.

I forgot about the show. We won another week when Jillian put us in the bottom two? I have to talk to Dax. Like right now.

'Can you take me home?'

25

DAX

Fifteen Minutes Later – At Dax's Apartment...

'Dax.' Hollyn walks in suddenly, slamming the door behind her, her make-up smudged under her eyes.

I stand up from the couch, instantly worried about her. I take it she and Mercy had a fight?

'Firstly, you won,' she says, a hesitant grin on her face.

'I know. Even when they put us in the bottom two. I can't believe it.'

'Secondly, Tristan's not the first one of my boyfriends you've threatened, is he?'

I'm confused. 'What?'

'After what I told you by the pool that night, after prom, you threatened Justin too, didn't you? *You're* the reason he apologized? You bought those flowers he brought me?'

Shit. OK, no longer confused. 'Uh—'

'I already know the answer, Dax. I just want to hear it from you.'

I swallow down the lump growing in my throat, before finally nodding. 'Yeah,' I say. 'To all of it. I'm sorry. I just – I couldn't stand that he'd hurt you like he did. So, I gave him two choices. Apologize or die.' I shrug. 'He didn't choose death.'

Hollyn heaves a sigh as she walks across the room, stepping up onto the ottoman, kissing me hard. Her hands are in my hair, and I forget to even breathe for a second because I've never had someone kiss me like this.

Within seconds, I'm kissing her back, my arms around her, pulling her as close as possible. I don't even care if River walks out of his room and catches us. He can deal because this feels desperate in a way I can't stop. When she finally pulls away, she steps off the ottoman, grabs my hand, and leads me towards my room.

'What are you doing?'

'Something I should have done a long time ago,' she says, not even looking back at me as she leads the way.

'Hols, River is *here*.'

It's one thing to get caught making out; it's another to get caught having sex with her.

She turns around when she reaches my door. 'Then River is soon going to wish he wasn't.'

'Summer dumped him.'

I'm not shutting this down because I don't want it to happen. I do. God, I do. But I don't want it to happen because she thinks she owes me for something that happened nearly a decade ago. If she knew all the things I did for her back then, we'd be in that bedroom for days. I want this to happen because she feels what I feel.

'What happened between Summer and Riv?'

River suddenly bursts out of his room, racing to the bathroom with a groan.

'Listen.' I step closer to her, reaching up and touching her neck, my thumb on her cheek. 'We can talk about this, hell we can even *do* this, as soon as River is passed out. OK? I'm not rejecting you. I want this.'

Hols reaches up and touches my hand resting on

her neck. When the bathroom door opens, we drop our hands like nothing is going on.

'Taking back my bed,' River says as he exits.

'What happened?' Hollyn asks.

'*You* happened if you must know.'

Come on, Riv. Don't be a dick to her.

She grunts as if she's offended, now walking towards him. '*I'm* the reason you broke up?'

'Yep,' River continues. '*You*. Apparently, I'm too clingy. I'm invading her space. And I blame you.'

'I'm sorry. I uh...' She sighs, her head dropping as though she's embarrassed.

This is hard to watch. I want to go over there, wrap my arms around her, and tell her it's probably not her fault. River could have broken it to her differently.

'Can I do anything to make it up to you?' she asks.

'You can commandeer Dax's bed for a while.'

She snaps her head my way. '*What?*'

'He'll sleep on the couch,' River adds.

'No.' She shakes her head. 'I can't do that.'

'It was *his* idea, Hols.'

Oh, yeah, go announce that shit, would ya? Hollyn's eyes meet mine. I lift my shoulders, a clenched-teeth grimace on my face. Considering not even two minutes ago, she was ready to throw me onto that same bed and have her way with me, I don't think it was a terrible idea. Now she looks unsure.

'*Your* idea?'

I cock my head. 'Bad?'

She furrows her brow, rubbing her forehead with her fingers. 'No, I'm not taking your bed, and you're not sleeping on the couch in your own apartment. If anyone should sleep on the—'

River groans, interrupting her as he leans against the wall next to him. 'He's got a king-size bed. You're both adults. Just man the fuck up, put some pillows between you, share the damn bed, and let me suffer through my own choices in peace.' He pushes his nearly shoulder-length hair from his face.

'I gotta lay down.' He leans the top half of his body towards his room, the rest of him following awkwardly. 'No funny business either!' he yells as he slams his door shut.

Hols and I immediately look at one another. Then she walks my way, allowing me to grab her, kissing her desperately. When she slides her hands to my neck, I pick her up, her legs around my waist. I've imagined this exact scenario about a million times.

'I'm such a jerk, Dax. I'm sorry I never saw you for who you really are. If I'd have known, I'd have never left you the way I did.' She talks while I kiss down her neck, carrying her into my room, kicking the door closed behind us.

'You know *now*, Hols.' I shove her against the door, kissing her lips again when a moan from her makes my mind go blank.

'I liked you *then*, Dax. We spent so much time together I don't know how I didn't see this part of you. Now I see—'

I pull away. 'What *do* you see now?' I ask, staring into her eyes. I need to know. I set her on the ground, on her feet, in front of me.

Her hands are on the sides of my neck, sending sparks through me with her light touch. 'I see the most amazing man I've ever met. You're smart and funny, charming, honest, mind-numbingly handsome—'

I kiss her again, a gasp coming from her as I do. She starts tugging at the back of my shirt, silently asking me to pull it off for her.

'Holy hell,' she says, shyly touching my chest with only her fingertips after I toss my T-shirt onto the floor. 'You're not teenage Dax anymore.'

'He's long gone.'

Her hand glides up my chest to my neck, pulling me to her again. She's got the softest lips I've ever kissed, and somehow, she knows exactly how to do this like we've done it a thousand times before.

Nervously, despite standing here shirtless, I slide my hands underneath her shirt and up her back. She heaves a sigh, breaking the kiss as if she can't handle my fingertips on her bare skin and her lips on mine. She leans her forehead against mine.

'You're sure you want to do this, Hols?' I ask with a heavy breath. Please, don't say no.

She pushes me away from her, silently unbuttoning her blouse, answering my question without words as it drops to the floor, exposing that same black bra that nearly sent me over the edge at the pool the other day.

'Jesus,' I say to myself, grabbing her by the waist. 'Fuck the slow thing.'

'You took the words right out of my mouth,' she says, her voice breathy in a way that's melting my brain. She kisses my chest. 'I want this. With *you*, Dax.' Her bright blue intoxicating eyes are now fixated on me. 'Do you want this with me?'

God, she's more beautiful than she ever has been. I stroke her cheek with my thumb. 'More than you know.'

* * *

Later That Night...

'So... you're not just tall then,' she says with a breathless laugh.

'I'm way more than tall,' I say in a cocky flirtatious voice.

'That was – *wow*.'

I nod, as all the words I know seem to have escaped me. Did that *actually* just happen? I look over at her, lying next to me in my bed and she flashes me a smile. *Say something, Dax*. I roll onto my side, touching her face and softly pressing my lips to hers.

'Never,' I say. 'I *never* thought that would happen.'

'And now that it has?'

I run my fingers down her neck, over her collar bone and shoulder. 'Now that it has, I never want to let you go. I'm sure that probably scares the hell out of you, but I can't keep hiding how I feel about you, Hols.'

'Nothing about you scares me,' she says, wiggling around, making herself comfortable now pressed against me, her head on my bicep and her eyes on me. 'But how much I find myself liking you scares me.'

I can't pretend I haven't slept with a lot of women,

but what we just did was easily the most incredible, emotionally charged experience I've ever had. I said things I've never said to anyone else. She stared into my eyes in a moment so intimate I'll never forget it. She's lucky I can speak at all right now.

'Oh,' she says suddenly. 'Speaking of liking you, I almost forgot something.' She sits up, searching the room with her eyes before jumping out of my bed and grabbing her phone.

I like how she seems so comfortable with me now, being this intimate. The whole thing is blowing my mind. This seems right. As though it's not our first time. It's definitely not our last.

'I couldn't sleep one night, so I was thinking about Cassiopeia.'

'You were thinking about *Cassiopeia*?'

'Fine,' she says with a laugh. 'I was thinking about you, and Cassiopeia infiltrated my thoughts. So, I looked the constellation up.'

A smile slowly grows on my face.

'I found something,' she says, tapping the screen of her phone before turning it so I can see it.

In the middle of a starlit sky is a mass of red gas, vaguely in the shape of a heart. My eyes move back to her.

'It's a nebula known as the heart nebula. And right

here is another one called the soul nebula. The heart and soul nebulas live inside Cassiopeia's constellation. So, maybe she was as vain as they come, but deep down, the story is much more complicated and romantic than I thought. Did you know about it?'

I'm glad she can't hear the crashing in my chest right now cause the girl just swept me off my feet, and I fell *all* the way in.

'Yeah,' I say, trying to keep my cool, as if her learning about nebulas didn't just floor me. 'Wanna *really* see it?'

'How?'

I grab my T-shirt from the floor, tossing it her way. 'Put that on. The last thing I need is the entire apartment complex getting an eyeful of my girl.'

'Your girl?'

She pulls the shirt over her head as I throw on some sweats, grab a T-shirt from my dresser, and pull it over my head.

'Was that too far?'

She shakes her head. 'Do you want that?'

'I've always wanted that. God, Hols, I'd attempt to *move* the stars for you.'

She flashes me a smile. 'I think I want to be your girl.'

If my heart swells any more it'll explode.

'I have a private balcony and a high-powered tele-scope.' I pull open my blinds, sliding open the sliding door. 'Ladies first.'

'You got the good room; I should have known,' she says with a laugh, leading the way. 'This must be where you charm your ladies?'

'Only one woman's ever looked through my tele-scope,' I say, now looking through it to find the nebu-las. I've looked at these a thousand times and once I've found them, I move aside so she can see.

She leans down, peering through the telescope with one eye.

'*Wow!*' she says excitedly. She stares at the sky for a long time, finally turning to me with a grin. 'I always thought you knowing all this stuff was cool. I thought you were so smart, and I listened because of that. And now I know it was never your stories about stars that mesmerized me.' She takes a step towards me, touching my hand. 'It was you. I don't know how I didn't see it before.'

I laugh under my breath. 'You may not think it, but you're pretty damn charming yourself.'

'Am I sweeping you off your feet?'

'You have no idea, Hols.'

26

HOLLYN

The Next Morning...

'You two are being way too fucking loud out here. What's so funny about toast?' River says, shuffling into the kitchen. He grabs a bottle of water from the fridge. 'Guy with a hangover here,' he reminds us, before downing half the bottle.

'Sorry we made you get puking drunk last night,' I say, rolling my eyes when he glares over at me. I glance at Dax, whose eyes widen as he turns away from River, with half a guilty grin.

Many things happened last night; us being quiet

wasn't one of them. After living here for more than a month now, I know how thin these walls are. If River *doesn't* know what happened, we'll be lucky. Heck, if creepy Roger wasn't taking notes, I'd be shocked.

'What in the hell were you two watching last night? It was loud as fuck.'

'Um...' Dax chuckles to himself. 'Some show she likes. *New Kid*? *New Girl*?'

He almost remembers the name of my favorite show. That's pretty cute.

'Oh, yeah,' I say when I notice his look of panic. 'That Schmidt cracks me up.'

'Maybe next time, consider the guy in the next room with a raging fucking headache.'

'You're our top priority, sugar,' I say sarcastically sweet.

River glares my way.

'Here,' Dax says, buttering a piece of toast that resembles charcoal. 'It'll help with nausea.'

River grabs it from him, exits the kitchen and disappears to his room.

Oh my god, I mouth.

'I'll talk to him,' Dax says, carrying over two cups of coffee and setting one in front of me. 'He'll deal.'

'What if he's mad?'

'He won't be.' He leans into me, his hand on my

lower back. 'I promise. I'll take care of it. For now, let's get ready for the wedding we're working today and not worry about anything else. Sound like a plan?'

'Sure,' I say as he kisses me on the cheek.

He finishes his coffee, walking towards the bathroom, pulling his shirt off midway through the room, and glancing back at me.

I grin like a looney toon. I'm watching, honey, God, am I watching. I blow out a breath, carrying our cups to the sink. I feel like I'm in over my head in the best possible way.

Dax's phone pings on the counter where it's plugged in and unintentionally, I glance over at it before the notification disappears.

Syd: Wanna try again tonight?

My heart dives from its spot on cloud nine, landing in my gut like an anvil. Sydney. I forgot about her. There's no way he'd say yes to this. Is there?

Wait. I just looked at his text! This is how Mercy got caught up in my phone! *Why* did I do that? I shouldn't even know he got that text.

'What are you doing?'

I let out a tiny squeal, practically jumping at the sound of River's voice.

'You're looking at his phone?'

I spin towards him, his gaze moving from Dax's phone to me.

'No,' I lie.

'Why you so deer in the headlights then?' He suddenly points my way. 'You're hiding something. I'd never forget that look. Lying has never been your thing. What do you know?'

'Nothing, Riv.' I storm out of the kitchen, past him, and towards his room.

'Did something happen last night? You're being weird.'

'Besides *you* getting blackout drunk? No. Nothing happened. You created the awkwardness you're feeling there, big fella.' I drop onto my knees in front of one of my suitcases, digging for clothes.

'These can find a new place to live,' he suggests, pointing at my bags all over the room, then dropping onto his bed.

'Where am I supposed to put them?'

'I don't care, just get them out of here. Maybe you can go sweet talk Mom and Dad into letting you stay with them.'

My heart sinks. 'You want me to leave?'

'You really want to sleep on our couch? You've been here weeks. Do you have a job? Anything?'

'Stop,' Dax says from the door. 'She's helping me with the show. She's not leaving.'

We both glance back at him. He's fresh from the shower in only a towel. Hell's bells, he's beautiful. His face is filled with concern as he looks from me to River.

'What the hell do you care?'

'We need to talk,' Dax says, focusing on River. 'I don't have time right now, but tonight. Bible Club. Seven?'

'Sure?' River seems confused but isn't arguing.

'I'm just gonna go shower,' I say, grabbing my things.

Dax steps aside, allowing me out of the room before following me towards the bathroom. River's door closes behind us.

'If you want to stay with your parents, you can, I just – he was being an ass, and I went all protective. Again. I'm sorry. Old habits.'

'You'd protect me from *River*?'

He nods. 'Just like he'd protect you from me. But I'll back off. You're not exactly mine after one night.'

I grab his hand before he can back away from me. 'Maybe I want to be,' I tell him.

He stares at me for a long time, a grin growing on

his face. 'Mine?' he asks. 'You'd consider actually dating me?'

I laugh, confused by his perplexed tone. 'You thought this was a one-night stand?'

'No, I want it to be more. I just...' He lifts a shoulder, an adorable half-smile on his face as he slides his thumb over my palm. 'I thought suggesting an actual relationship was too soon after your break-up, and I didn't want to pressure you.'

'I do what I want to do, Dax. Right now, I want to see where this goes.'

He plants a kiss on me that takes my breath away. No tongue, just absolute adoration that makes me crave more of him. I am totally falling for him. Me, in love with Dax Hartley. Who'd have guessed it?

27

DAX

Later That Day...

Maybe she does want to be mine. I keep thinking about her responses to that idea this morning. She has no clue what those words have done to me.

We finished most of the flower arrangements for this wedding just before we had to leave for the venue and we're now halfway through the timed arrangements for the reception. Our show-stoppers this time are giant centerpieces made of roses, hydrangeas, and birch branches. They'll sit in the center of the ten reception tables and two extra-large pieces that'll bookend the bridal party table.

'Ah!' Hollyn hollers from a few feet away.

I glance over and bolt to her, grabbing the vase falling my way. She's on a ladder standing over the arrangement that's practically as tall as she is, and right this second, I'm our only hope to salvage the vase of flowers on its way to the floor. I somehow grab it, knocking a few chairs over in the process.

'Oh my god,' she says, with a sigh of relief once I've got both hands on it.

She's still holding a stem in the air where the arrangement was as I get it back to standing.

'I'm so sorry.'

'Accidents happen, Hols. Just uh – go easy. You're doing great. We're almost done.'

My phone rings in my pocket. Sydney's name is on the screen when I pull it out. I need to do this now.

'I'll be right back,' I say to Hols before half jogging out of the room to answer the call. 'Sydney,' I say into the phone quietly, hoping Hollyn doesn't overhear and worry about this.

'Did you get my text? I have an idea for tonight, and I'm absolutely certain you won't have the problem you did last time.'

'Um, *actually*... I can't.'

'You're busy? We can do tomorrow? I'm free all week. Doing a little staycation from work.'

'No, I uh – I'm gonna have to pull out.' Ugh. Why'd I use those words?

'Bareback rides are a no-go. You know this.'

'Unfortunate choice of words,' I say with a laugh. 'I mean, bail. I've met someone, and I can't do this anymore. I can't risk hurting her.' I stare into the room at Hollyn as I speak, grinning like a boy in love. I couldn't rein it in if I wanted to.

She's got a single flower stem between her teeth as she weaves one into the arrangement gently as if she's disarming a bomb. She's getting good at this.

Sydney sighs into the phone. 'It's lightsaber girl, isn't it?'

'Yeah, lightsaber girl swept me off my feet, and I went all in. Gonna have to cancel our arrangement.'

'Damn,' she says. 'I kind of guessed after the other night. I could tell your head was somewhere else.'

'Understatement of the year, but absolutely correct. I'm sorry.'

I don't know what else to say. She's a lawyer for crying out loud. When we first talked this out, she suggested signing an *actual* contract. After my balking at that for five minutes, she claimed she was kidding, and we moved on casually.

'You don't owe me an apology, Dax. I'm just wondering where I might find someone of your uh *–skill level.*' She half laughs, but I can tell she's serious, and I'm flattered.

'Can't say I've got any recommendations.'

'Not a problem. I hope things work out, but you know where to find me if they don't.'

'Pretty sure I'm off the market for good.'

She lets out a gasp. 'Dax Hartley. Did you fall in love?'

Hollyn glances out at me as though she's heard her, which I know is impossible. She flashes me a smile.

'I sure did,' I say, not even questioning it. 'Hard.'

'Wow!' She laughs. 'I'm truly happy for you. I guess I'll see ya around?'

'See ya, Syd.' I hang up, shoving my phone back into my pocket.

'Off the market for good?' Jake asks, walking up behind me. 'Is that what I just heard you say?'

I drop my head. Of course he'd be standing behind me.

'Maybe.'

'Hmm...' He circles me, stopping between me and the room Hollyn now stands in. 'I'd bet money you're not closing down your business. The only other thing that could possibly be off the market is maybe your sweet, sweet loins?'

I grunt a laugh, shaking my head like it's not true. As a guy who doesn't love getting too deep into his personal life, I'm doing far too much of that lately.

'Hollyn?' Jake asks, glancing into the other room.

'You need to keep your big mouth shut until I say you no longer have to. I haven't talked to River yet. Tonight.'

Jake rubs his hands together as if he's hatching an evil plan. 'He's going to punch you right in the mouth.'

'No, he's not.' I roll my eyes. 'He'll be fine. If he's not, he's going to learn real quick to deal with it because it's out of my control.'

'How's it out of your control?'

I look past him at her, now climbing down the ladder and inspecting her work from ground level. She adjusts a few stems as she walks around the arrangement. Her eye for this is getting better and better.

'I'm in love with her.'

'*Ho-ly. Shit*,' he says, way too loud, causing Hols to glance our way.

She cocks her head, a confused look on her face. After a moment, she turns back to her arrangement.

'Are you serious?' Jake lowers his voice. 'You *love* her? You've never loved any woman. Did you tell her?'

He's not wrong. I've never said those words to anyone. Anyone but her, now. 'Yes, yes, and yes.'

'Who's in love with whom?' Brynn asks.

Why didn't I just take out an ad in the newspaper or maybe announce it on Facebook this morning? *Hollyn and I had sex; leave your questions in the comments.*

'If it's you' – she points at Jake – 'you better be talking about me.'

He throws his hands in the air. 'It ain't me.'

'Well, well, *well*,' she says in a tone I know I don't want to deal with right now. 'You're the only other person here.' She raises a single eyebrow, suddenly leaning around me and glancing at Hollyn, flicking her line of sight back to me quickly. She waves a finger between Hollyn and I. 'You two?'

'He just dumped Sydney for her,' Jake says between fake coughs.

'You're as good as dead,' I threaten.

He rolls his eyes.

'You *did*?' Brynn looks from Jake to me, her curiosity to know everything about everyone growing into a vast grin. 'Are you serious?'

I nod, sighing deeply as I do. 'Firstly, Sydney and I

weren't an item, so I didn't *dump* her. Just called things off. Secondly, I didn't know I'd need to explain myself personally to every person I know one by one. That said, *yes*, I'm serious. Lines have been crossed.' I move a hand in front of me, drawing an imaginary line I now step over.

'Does *she* know?' Brynn asks.

'Seriously?' I ask, rolling my eyes. '*Yes*, she knows. But we haven't exactly announced it, so if you two could shut up before Mercy gets here, that'd be much appreciated. We've hardly had a chance to process it ourselves. All of it's against River's stupid bro code, so please, let me have a few days with her so we can figure things out.'

'Wow! Well, when you get married—'

I hold up a hand, shutting her up. 'We're far from there, so just keep it in your pants, ya wedding whore.'

She laughs, pinching her lips together tightly, pretending like what I said isn't true.

'We've got thirty minutes left to get these arrangements done before McKenzie calls to either praise or reprimand us, so please save all your ridiculously invasive questions until after my deadline. Keep your trap shut.' I point right at Jake. 'You especially. If River gets wind of this before I tell him, it's *you* who will receive a fist to the mouth. Got it?'

He crosses his arms over his chest with a huff. 'You know how often you've threatened that and never followed through?'

'Today might be your lucky day then.'

'Go!' Brynn says, pointing at the room behind me. 'If we make you lose the comp and the shop, I'd feel terrible. So, get back in there with your lady love and win this thing.'

If it weren't for Brynn, I wouldn't be doing any of this. I wouldn't have the shop simmering on the back burner. I don't know if Hollyn and I would have had as much time together as we have. I owe her a lot when I think about it.

'Everything OK?' Hols asks, brushing her hands off over a trash bucket as she cleans the table next to her.

I grab a flower from the table where I was working, walking past it to her. 'I can't show you *how* OK everything is, so' – I hand her the flower – 'a hint.'

'There's that charming thing again.'

'You bring it out in me.'

Her smile is intoxicating. I literally feel drunk in love around her.

'Wow!' Mercy's voice carries through the room. 'You two have outdone yourselves. This is beautiful! I think these arrangements are bigger than Hols.'

'Some are,' Hollyn says. 'Totally Dax's vision; flowers seem to be one of his *many* superpowers,' she jokes, biting her bottom lip, making damn sure I notice. She winks at me as I back away towards the arrangement I'm still working on. I like hearing her talk about me this way. 'But I agree, they're all gorgeous.'

'No way you're not in the top two this week. Just no way.' Mercy walks the room, looking at all the arrangements. 'I can't believe I'm about to say this, but maybe you two should consider being *actual* business partners. I think Hols here has a flower power of her own that she never knew about.'

The idea of that makes me smile. My head hasn't had the opportunity to think of anything beyond the show and where things are going with Hollyn. Maybe it's not a bad idea?

'I just wanted to come by and apologize for snooping through your phone. *Again*. We're good?' Mercy asks Hollyn.

'I could never stay mad at you.'

'Things went OK here?' Mercy asks under her breath, obviously not intending for me to hear it.

Luckily, my back is to them, so she can't see my face. That'd give me away.

'Yeah,' Hollyn says softly. 'More than OK.'

'McKenzie's calling in ten,' Ian announces.

Mercy takes that as her cue and cuts out, leaving Hollyn and me to quickly clean things up, prepping for her call.

'Beautiful!' she says through the iPad as Ian films near me. 'You're back on track, Dax. The arrangements are incredible.'

'What do you think, Hollyn? Is he still as beautiful as he was on day one?'

She laughs, nodding her head. 'More, if that's possible?' Her eyes meet mine, a sly smile on her face. Her calling me beautiful has been something McKenzie has enjoyed. She brings it up practically every time they talk and I don't hate it.

'Dax, how do you think Hollyn has improved?'

I reach down and envelop her hand with mine. 'It's like she's done floristry her whole life.'

Mercy's right: Hollyn has a talent neither of us knew she had. She's picked up on this so fast. She even gives me ideas now. We seem to make a good team in more ways than one.

'That's the sign of a good teacher,' McKenzie says. 'Would you agree, Hollyn?'

'Absolutely.'

'You two have grown. The first time we did this, you were stumbling over your words. Something's changed.' She stares at us through the camera as though she's trying to figure it out. 'Well, I'll see you two tomorrow. I'm excited to visit Portland!' As soon as the words leave her lips, she taps out of the call.

This competition is anyone's to win at this point. Bring it on.

*　*　*

Later That Night – At Bible Club...

I'm so nervous I almost just dropped my drink as I tried to take it from the bartender. I wipe my sweating hands on my jeans and try again.

'Thanks,' I say, feeling like a dumbass as I walk away.

River's harmless, really, but he's very protective of Hollyn. I get it. I am too. Surely he'll see we're on the same side here.

He walks through the front door, glances at me, holds up a hand, then points to the bar. I lift my chin, acknowledging his arrival and plan.

I'll just say the words. As soon as he sits down, I'll

blurt it out. Waste no time, beat around no bushes. Just get it out there.

The front door dings open. I glance up, practically falling from my chair when I see Dr John walk in, Penny right behind him. You have *got* to be kidding me.

'Sorry,' River says, now approaching my table. Once we're away from anyone else he whispers, 'Parents saw me driving through town and followed me here.'

'It's cool.' I wave a hand casually.

River cocks his head in confusion. 'What's wrong with you?'

'What? Nothing. Nothing's wrong.'

I pull my shirt away from my chest a few times, hoping for the air I need to survive this.

'Something *bad*?' he asks, sitting across from me knowing full well something's up. 'You're not dying, are ya?'

'*Dying*? From what?' Guilt, probably.

'I dunno. You find a lump in your stones? Brain tumor? The clap?'

'*What?*' I laugh. 'No. Can you die from the clap?'

He lifts both shoulders, now sipping his beer. 'I don't wanna find out.'

'OK, we're way off track here. *No*, I don't have the clap or a tumor *or* lumps.'

'Just say it then.'

'Well.' I glance up at John and Penny, both still at the bar. Here goes nothing. 'I'm in love with Hollyn.'

River glances around the room, bellowing with laughter as if I've told him a joke. 'Did we just go back in time?'

'Riv. I'm serious. Something happened.'

His face finally sobers, and he stares across the table at me. 'What do you mean something happened? *What?*'

'I told her,' I say. 'Last week, I finally told her how I felt. That night you caught us watching TV in your room? It happened then. You almost walked in to find us making out. Then last night... well, we kind of slept together.'

He grunts a laugh. 'No shit? I helped make that arrangement. Remember?'

I nod. I remember. 'Nah, River. Like we *slept* together. I'm in love with her.'

For a second, he stares at me. His eyes are locked with mine in a way that makes me feel like I can't look away. To see River, you'd think he was some Spicoli surfer dude. The love child of Ashton Kutcher and model Christopher Mason. But underneath that mop of blond hair and male model face lives a man fiercely protective of his friends and family.

'You *slept* with her?' he asks, his beer halfway to his lips before he slams it on the table, busting out the bottom, beer flooding our table.

As it pours into my lap, I jump from my stool, but River doesn't react, just continues to bore a hole through me with his glare.

'I don't think I heard ya right,' he says, standing from his seat, now watching me attempt to clean his mess.

Alright. He's pissed.

'You mean slept in the same bed because I moved back in. *Right?*'

I grab a stack of napkins from the table next to us. 'Come on, Riv. We've been getting closer, and things just hit that point. If you were ever home, you'd have known. But *no*, you disappeared to your own fucking world and left me to be the one there for her. What'd you expect to happen?'

He practically growls at my words implying he's at fault for this. I knew those wouldn't go over well, but if he wants to throw a fit over things the other's done wrong, let's go there.

'She's my sister, man!' He says it under his breath

and through clenched teeth, but only because his parents are headed our way.

'It's not what you—'

'Boys!' Penny interrupts, helping me wipe up the table with the napkins she's carried over. 'What are ya, six years old and spilling your drinks again?'

River shoots me a shut-the-fuck-up glare. So, he's not thrilled. Message received.

'Slip of the hand,' River lies.

'We wanted to let you know we've decided to go to dinner instead,' John says. 'You guys want to join us?'

'You two go. Dax and I got some shit to discuss.'

Penny's eyes meet mine immediately. *Hollyn?* she mouths.

I shake my head, refusing to answer. How the hell does she know everything? Am I that easy to read?

'Next time,' John says, patting me on the back before the two of them leave. Penny turns before they exit, giving me a discreet thumbs up. Jesus.

'Come on, Dax. You're serious about this?' River continues our conversation the moment the front door closes behind his parents. 'You fucked Hollyn?'

'Can ya *not* say it that way?' I ask. 'It's not like that. I'm in love with her.'

'Bro code, dude,' he says. 'Bro code.' He repeats it with a fist on his chest, disappointment in his voice.

After a moment of him considering my words, he heaves a sigh. 'Time out,' he says, motioning the hand gesture. 'I need a fresh drink. Wanna shot? I feel like we need shots for this.'

'Sure.' He's not wrong.

I sip my beer as he stands across the room at the bar, taking a single shot without me before carrying five more to the table. Good god, he's gonna get me drunk. He lines up the shots between us, making himself comfortable on the barstool, before making eye contact.

'Why isn't she here?' he asks, pushing a glass my way with one finger. 'I'm already up one. Your turn.'

I grab the glass, downing the shot, sitting the glass on the table in front of me. 'This was my responsibility. Also, you're kind of an ass to her at times.'

'Now you're going to lecture me on how I should treat my sister? Must I remind you I'm her *younger* brother and being an ass is my fucking job?'

'No, it's not. Your job is being there for her. Protecting her. Not hurting her feelings. You could have gone a little easier when you told her why Summer dumped you last night. That wasn't her fault. It was yours.'

This isn't mine and River's first fight. In high school, we got into it over something I don't even remember, and we literally tried to kill each other in the backyard. Our parents didn't even notice until he came home with a busted lip, and I came home with a black eye. When you grow up as close as we did, you argue shit out sometimes. He's mad now, yeah. But this isn't the final nail or anything.

He has no response, just points at the shots. I grab another one, downing it and setting the glass back on the table before shoving one his way.

'Shots were *your* idea,' I remind him. 'You gonna fall behind?'

His eyes never leave mine as he downs the shot, slamming the empty glass on the table.

'This isn't brand new, Riv. We've been going through the motions of discovering this since I picked her up at the airport. I told her how I feel, and we want to see where it goes.'

'*We?*'

'You think I'd be talking to you about this if I didn't *know* she feels the same way?'

'After a *month?*'

'We've known each other our entire lives.'

He stares at me, no emotion on his face.

'I even ended things with Sydney.'

'This is gonna make me seem like I have feelings,' River says, rolling his eyes, a smirk on his face, 'but

Hollyn means everything to me. No matter what stupid shit I do, I know she'll be on my side without a doubt. Maybe I'm an ass to her sometimes, but she's no fucking angel. I'd never intentionally hurt her feelings.'

'Then we have that in common.'

He stares at me, his arms crossed over his chest for what feels like forever. He points to the shots. Rarely do I drink, but I grab a shot, down it and softly set the glass on the table.

'I can't give her up, so you'll need to make your peace with this.'

'You ever hurt her the way Professor Fuckface did, I'll kill you,' River says, his face stone-cold sober. 'I mean that.'

'I'd be concerned if you didn't.'

He shoves the last shot my way. This time just thinking about doing it makes me wanna puke. I down it, turning it upside down and setting it down.

'If you two break up? What am I supposed to do then?'

I shake my head. How do I answer that when I don't even want to consider it? 'I guess we'd sit down and talk again.'

'You know if you two got married, we'd be brothers.'

'We're not even close to saying that word.'

He laughs, shaking his head. 'Well, congratulations on boning my sister, man. But since your impending drunkenness is on me, I'll order you an Uber tonight. What do you want to drink?'

'Water,' I say as he walks away towards the bar. I'm four shots and a beer in. There's no way I'm going balls to the wall drinking then home to Hollyn. I want to be conscious for night number two with her.

I pull my phone from my pocket while River's gone, sending Hollyn a text. She was nervous for tonight but knew she could torment River into submission if she needed. Those two never grew out of their teenage years when around each other.

It was touch and go, but he's cool. We can commence the bedroom sharing. If you wanna?

The three dots of her typing appear almost immediately.

I wanna. You know where to find me.

28

HOLLYN

Friday Night – At the Rooftop Garden...

This week, the show is filming in Portland. Since we're down to the final three, we're filming the results as we find them out tonight.

'Hey, Daxy,' Celeste says in a sing-song voice.

Cutesy *and* ballsy. Who calls a guy they hardly know by a childish nickname? I've slept with him multiple times, and no way would I call him Daxy as if he's five. Nope. Not even in the throes of passion will that come out of my mouth.

'Celeste,' he says with little emotion.

'Did you get my last email?'

He nods, his hand suddenly on the small of my back. 'I did get your email,' he says.

'What do you think?' She looks between the two of us.

'I think we're competitors on a show so drinks probably wouldn't be appropriate.'

She asked him to have a drink with her? We're in a rooftop garden with an open bar. This wasn't private enough? CeCe is something else. Then again, she thinks he's single. Maybe he is? *No. Hollyn, stop obsessing. You're creating a problem where there isn't one. If you ruin this before it's even started, you'll regret it.*

I glance around the rooftop, looking for any familiar faces that can help me not panic. It's bad enough I'm still thinking about the stupid text from Sydney last weekend. I didn't ask him about it since it wasn't my business, and he didn't mention it. I don't know if I want to know.

'Hey.' River's voice stops my head.

Thank god. Never in a million years have I been so glad to see my annoying little brother. I can't stand here overthinking every possible problem *or* be the jealous other woman. *Again.* I can't. I just got out of that kind of relationship.

'Is this your boyfriend, Hollyn?' Celeste asks, an

almost relieved grin on her face as River stops by my side. She takes a step closer to Dax as if she's claiming her property.

'You two are adorable together,' Celeste says. 'Don't you think?'

Dax nods, his eyes on me, his smile slowly growing. 'They sure are.'

River and I exchange glances, him shoving me an arm's length away from him.

'Gross.' He gawks. 'She's my sister. So, *no*. We are not *adorable* together.'

'He's your *brother*?' Celeste asks, now eying him from head to toe.

I glance at Dax, who laughs under his breath. Is this girl just hard up for any guy or what? I guess that makes me feel better.

'You seem a little desperate, honey,' River says matter-of-factly, reading her silent stare. 'Can I get you a drink?' he asks her, taking advantage of his previous words.

'No. Thanks,' she says, sticking close to Dax.

'*I'll* join you,' I say to River, glancing back at Dax, who nods as if he understands.

'As my *sister*,' he shouts to Celeste. 'She'll join me as my annoying sister.'

'She gets it, Riv,' I say, pushing him away from her towards the bar.

'What's up with her?' He requests two beers from the bartender.

'She's got the hots for Dax.'

'Of course she does,' he says, obviously unimpressed. 'Seems like everyone around me has the hots for Dax,' he says, lowering his chin, giving me a classic *what did you do*, dad look. 'Why didn't *you* tell me?'

'You two have this stupid bro code thing going on, so he felt like he needed to be the one to break it to you.'

He nods, taking the beers from the bartender and handing me one. 'Keep talking.'

I let out a groan. 'I was afraid you'd think I was getting myself into another mess. You know, because of how fast things have gone.'

'You do like to move in with guys quickly, don't you?'

'Shut up. Dax and I *aren't living together* living together.'

'No...' He drags out the word. 'You've slept in his bed every night this week, and practically all your shit is in his room. But nah, you're *definitely not living together* living together.'

Oh my god. Did I do it again? Move in with a guy

too soon? *What* was I thinking? This is exactly what I swore I wouldn't do.

'Stop panicking,' Riv says, reading my mind. 'It was a joke; I didn't realize you're already in your head.'

I turn towards him. '*Am* I going too fast? God, Riv, I'm gonna ruin this. I don't want to ruin this. I like him.'

River rests a hand on my shoulder. 'He loves you. Relax.'

'You *really* think he does?'

'He's always loved you, Hols. *I* don't get it, but I guess the heart wants what it wants and all that shit. What kind of spell did you cast?'

'Ha-ha.'

'I think maybe you should figure out how you feel about him and tell him before it goes too far. He's already all the way in this, so don't make him have to get over you twice.'

'Why didn't you ever tell me he had feelings for me?'

'It's not my place. That was his thing. I figured if he was serious, he'd tell you. It was probably just a crush he'd grow out of if he couldn't.'

'And you didn't think him going to therapy and changing the way he did after I left indicated him being pretty seriously damn heartbroken?'

River shrugs, sipping his beer. 'Dax's feelings aren't really my thing. We're guys. He was alive; I figured he was good, and you claimed to be happy. What should I have done?'

'Saved me from wasting eight years of my life with the wrong guy.'

'Tried it. You're stubborn as fuck.'

I tilt my head, unable to disagree since I know this.

'For what it's worth, I trust Dax with my life. I know him better than he knows himself at times. He's serious about you, Hols. Personally, I think you'd be an idiot to let him go. He'd never hurt you. In any way. That I know.'

A grin grows on my face. When did River get so grown up? He was mad Dax and I went there, and now he's suggesting I never let him go. I'd trust River with *my* life, so I know he'd only say this if he meant it.

'*Never* tell him I told you this, but you're the only girl he's ever loved. Every woman he's been with has been physical and casual. I don't think he's ever had a real relationship.'

'Really?' He's never told another woman he loved them? Only me?

'Oh, god,' he groans. 'Don't tell me I'm somehow helping him woo you now?'

'It's sweet, Riv. I had no idea.'

'Cause your head is always up your ass or in the storm clouds hunting for the next lightning strike. Here's a word of advice, open your eyes in this relationship. I trust Dax about a thousand percent more than Professor Jizzstain.'

Ew.

'But please, pay attention this time around. Don't pretend things are A-OK if they're not. Talk to him. Dax enjoys using his words like a grown-up. Fight shit out. Tell him when something's wrong.' He sighs, glancing at me with a serious look on his face.

'I don't want to beat the hell out of my best friend, Hols. I'd choose you over Dax in a heartbeat. That's my job as your brother. But can you try your damndest to not let it ever come to that?' he asks. 'For my sake?'

This is the nicest conversation River and I have had in a long time.

'You're a good brother, River. I promise I won't come between you two. Where would I be without you?'

'Probably still at the airport,' he says through a laugh. 'Talk over. Otherwise, I may have *actual* feelings in public, and nobody wants that.'

I laugh, looking at the people mingling around

us. The secret of who my mom is is officially out there and she's in her element with the production crew. I wouldn't be surprised if she's pitching ideas at them right now. Rebecca, Dax's mom, who my own mother calls Bex, is at Mom's side, chattering away with whoever is with them. They've been best of friends since we were little kids. I wonder how they'll react to Dax and me together?

My gaze stops at Mercy, now standing in front of Dax, the two of them having what seems to be a serious conversation. I walk their way.

'Hey!' Mercy says when she spots me, suddenly halting their convo. 'I have a great idea. I just mentioned it to Dax, and *he* disagrees.' She rolls her eyes. 'But what the hell does he know?'

'What is it?'

'You need a good lawyer.'

Dax nods, giving me a concerned look. 'Mercy thinks you should sue Tristan.'

'I know exactly the lawyer to do it too. Sydney! I called her, and she agreed to see you tomorrow.'

'*Tomorrow? Sydney?*' I ask, shocked at her suggestion. She made an appointment? With Dax's Sydney? I can't do that. It's weird.

'I uh – I... I...' I glance to Dax.

'Hols,' he says softly. 'I broke things off with Sydney.'

'You did?'

'I did.'

'What's happening here?' Mercy asks, her eyes following our words.

'Dax and I kinda—'

'He rang her bell.' River finishes my sentence as he walks up with the worst words ever.

Dax bursts out a laugh.

'*Shut. Up*,' Mercy says. 'And everyone knows but *me*? What the hell, Hols? I thought we were cool? No more lying, you said.'

'We are good. River needed to know first. You were next.'

She crosses her arms over her chest, cocking her head. 'Fine. That's an acceptable reason, considering how immature River is. I'm sure he needed the extra words and Dax's gentle touch.'

Dax and River both roll their eyes.

'What happened to you two going slow?' she asks.

'The heart doesn't always agree with the head. My intentions were good.'

'But her loins were on fire,' Dax adds with a goofy grin, now taking my hand in his.

I shrug.

Mercy stares at the two of us.

'Well, this is uncomfortable,' Dax says. 'I'm going to save myself and run to the bathroom. You good?'

I nod.

Mercy waits until he's out of hearing distance. 'I can't believe you did him.'

'I didn't *plan* on it. It just happened.'

'They're sharing a bedroom,' River says, ratting me out before lifting his beer to his lips.

'You *moved in* with him? Like *officially*?'

'I didn't even realize that I'd done it until River pointed it out ten minutes ago. We haven't made anything *official* yet. He hasn't even called me his girlfriend. I didn't really know what I felt beyond knowing I was feeling something.'

'Well, what was that something?' she asks.

'I uh...' I look at River then back at Mercy. 'I think I'm in love with him.' I shrug again like I just can't help it. And it's not a lie.

She softens. 'Really?'

'Really, Merc. *Love*. It's so... *big*. And scary, considering what I'm just getting out of. I haven't even told *him* yet.'

'You haven't told him? What in the hell are you telling me first for? Go. Tell him. It's what he's wanted to hear since he was a kid.'

'You think I should tell him *now*? In the middle of all this?' I throw an arm out, reminding her where we are.

'I think you should tell him now, mid-stream.'

'*What?*' I burst out a laugh.

'Hols, my father is in prison. My mom disappeared when I was a baby. Besides Edie, there's never been a lot of love flowing in my direction through life. So, yeah. Take it from the girl who's had very few people say it to her and who's said it to even fewer. *Tell him. Right now.* Barge into that men's room and announce it to every guy there.'

I laugh nervously. I don't know. In the *men's* room? Either he'll think it's cute, or he'll think I'm as weird as they come.

'OK.' I hand her my beer. 'I'm gonna walk in there and say it before I lose my nerve.'

'Good,' Mercy says, now sipping my beer. 'Go.'

It takes me a moment to convince myself to take a step, but I'm finally walking across the roof towards the bathrooms. Swarms of butterflies race through my chest, making it hard to breathe. I'm about to tell Dax – *annoying, dorky neighbor kid Dax* – I love him. I didn't expect this.

How is my life about to change? I can't even picture it. I turn the corner, stopping in my tracks. What the—? No, no. My heart feels as though it's caving in on itself. For a split second, I panic in a way that feels like sudden death but somehow manage to turn before they notice me and run across the roof.

I thought he was different. Now he's proving Mercy's warnings right by kissing Celeste behind my back? Is this just my life now? Choosing guys who don't choose me in return?

29

DAX

Moments Ago...

'You're so vague in our conversations. I'm constantly wondering, do you like me? Don't you? But I get it. You're a man of few words. I don't mind doing the talking. I want to know you, Dax. Intimately. What do you say to that?'

Celeste has me cornered by the bathrooms.

'I say no thanks.' I try to walk around her, but she throws herself at me, pressing against me and planting her lips on mine.

What the hell? I grab her by the shoulders, gently moving her away from me. Movement catches my eye, and my heart drops as I see Hollyn's back as she runs away. Fucking hell; she didn't just walk up on that, did she?

'You ever heard of asking permission?' I ask Celeste. 'I'm with Hollyn.'

'Yeah, I know, as childhood friends,' she says.

'No, Celeste. I love her. My answer to you will always be no because of that. Get it already.'

I take off running in Hollyn's direction. 'Hollyn!'

'What did you do?' Mercy asks as I pass her.

'Hols!'

She shoves open the door to the stairwell, sprinting down the flight of stairs, the door slamming on me right as I get to it.

'Hollyn, stop!' I yell as I yank open the door. 'What you saw wasn't was it looked like,' I say as she disappears through the next door.

'Damn it,' I groan, running down the stairs.

I'm five seconds behind her, just a few steps from plowing through the door to the hallway, as an older woman moseys her ass through.

'Come on!' I yell, causing her to jump to the side. I get through just in time to see Hollyn slip into the elevator as the doors close.

'I thought you were better than him. But you're just another asshole,' she says, her voice wavering as the doors slide closed too quickly for me to stop them.

No.

I run through the next stairwell door and down the stairs as fast as possible. There's no way I can make it to the ground before her. I'm seven floors up, and I've got no way in to the building from here besides the ground floor. How the fuck did I let this happen?

Finally, I get to the ground level, slamming the door open and checking the elevators. No Hollyn.

'Did you see a blonde woman run through here?' I bark at security.

'What is going on?' Mercy asks as she and River step out of the second elevator.

'Fucking Celeste,' I growl. 'She's been emailing me about hooking up, and she cornered me by the bathrooms and kissed me. Hollyn walked up on it. I stopped it *immediately*, but of course, she didn't see that part.'

Everything around me seems to move a hundred miles a minute, but I'm going in slow motion.

Mercy's face drops. She calls Hollyn on speaker, but it goes straight to voicemail. 'She was trying to find you to tell you she's in love with you!' she says, trying her phone again.

'*What?*' I lace my hands on my head, my heart feeling as though it's free-falling through me to the concrete below, imploding upon impact. 'I made her cry. She called me an asshole. She's probably somewhere, making this into something it isn't, panicking. What do I do?' I ask River. His face is pinched. 'I *didn't* kiss, Celeste. I'd never do that to Hollyn. You *know* that,' I remind him. 'You *have* to help me.'

I can barely breathe, and I doubt it's all from sprinting down seven flights of stairs. The growing lump in my throat feels like it may put me out of my misery and suffocate me at any moment.

'Mercy, get security to help you check every floor. Maybe she got off when someone else got on.' River taps the alarm on his keys, his car beeping to life along the curb just outside the building. 'We'll go look for her. Call me if you find her.'

I stand in front of Mercy. 'Please, Merc. I know you don't trust me, but I love her. I can't lose her. Make sure she knows the truth. *Please?*'

She nods.

I grab River's keys from his hand, running to his car and jumping into the driver's seat as he scrambles for the passenger side.

'I never said you could drive,' he says, strapping on his seatbelt.

'I never asked.' I start his car, pulling out a little recklessly. 'This will crush her, Riv. After Tristan's bullshit.'

'You're not like Tristan; she knows that.'

'She just said I was like him.'

Those words felt like a sword through my heart. I don't want to be anything like him, and now she thinks I am.

I slam through the gears as I drive a couple of blocks from the building, River grimacing with each grind. This car is his baby, and I'm abusing the hell out of it.

'Maybe I should drive?' he asks, holding onto the dash as I turn a corner. 'Come on, Dax. You're freaked out you're gonna lose her, but ya won't.'

'You don't know what she's been through.' I slow at every alley, every doorway. 'She can't handle this right now. *How* did she just disappear?'

'There's no way she got this far. She's got to be in the building. Pull over,' he commands.

I pull over at the next open spot, slowing the car to a stop along the curb, dropping my head against the steering wheel until River practically yanks me from the car to take a breather. I've destroyed her. She'll never trust me again. This is easily the worst thing that could have happened. It's why I was so quick to cut things off with Sydney. I know what Hollyn's been through, and she thinks I've just let her down in the same way he did.

30

HOLLYN

Moments Later...

'Hollyn?'

I hear Mercy's voice as I stand at the end of the hallway on the sixth floor, staring out the window into the city. My breathing has finally slowed after what felt like imminent death for a few moments. A resident got into the elevator as I fled, so I slipped out and have been here ever since. It feels like forever, but it's probably only been ten minutes of me staring out of this window and wondering how I get into these messes of relationships.

'Thank god,' she says, relief in her voice as she catches her breath while grabbing her chest as though she's having a heart attack. 'I've just run through five other floors searching for you, and you know how much I enjoy running for fun. *What* are you doing here?'

'You were right about him.'

Here I thought he wanted me and only me, but he was talking to Celeste the whole time. Like I was his back-up plan. Sounds familiar.

'I wasn't right about anything,' she says, stopping at my side. 'You know as well as I do that's hard for me to admit.' She goes quiet for a while, still catching her breath.

'He loves you,' she says gently.

'Not really.' I sigh, blinking away tears. 'We've been together, what, a week? And I catch him kissing someone else. That's not a good sign. Maybe Tristan was right? I'm not enough for anyone.'

'It's not true, Hols. Dax *didn't* kiss Celeste. *She* kissed him. He stopped it immediately; you just walked up at an unfortunate moment.'

'And you believe that?'

She sighs heavily, nodding her head like the words she's about to say pain her. 'Yeah. I believe him. Over the last couple of years, I've spent practically every weekend with Dax, and I've never seen him like this. He's devastated. The guy ran down seven flights of stairs looking for you. *Seven*, Hols.' She lets out a chuckle.

'I don't know a single man who'd do that for me. Not even Edie if the building was on fire and he's my only family.' She points to the window. 'Look!' She turns me to the window with her hands on my shoulders, pointing at the block below us.

Dax and River are standing on the sidewalk a block up. Dax is pacing back and forth, his hands clasped on top of his head as River walks with him.

'Does that look like a guy that just voluntarily kissed another woman cause he wanted to?' She shakes her head. 'No. It looks like a guy who's afraid he's just lost everything he ever wanted.'

I stare at River's face because Dax has got his back to me. River rests a hand on Dax's upper arm. I can tell their conversation isn't lighthearted. The two converse until River opens the passenger side door and Dax gets in.

'I don't know,' I cry, what's left of my heart falling to pieces in a way it hasn't before. 'I don't understand what happened?'

'The only way to clear that up is to talk to him. Please, Hols. I know I've had many opinions about

Dax, but I've most certainly given you the worst advice in the world. For that, I'm sorry. I'm way too cynical about love. We both know this. But in the last fifteen minutes, I just watched Dax's entire world crash around him, and his emotions are real. Maybe I've yet to experience it personally, but I know love when I see it. He loves you. You have to believe me,' she pleads. 'You have to believe *him.*'

I glance over, wiping tears from my face. 'I've spent nearly a decade dealing with this kind of thing. I don't want to do it again, Merc. I'm tired of always being second. I deserve better.'

'Dax *is* better. He's not going to do you like Tristan did.' She slips her hand into the crook of my arm, leading me towards the elevator.

'If you hurt this much right now, imagine what he's feeling. He did nothing wrong, and he's terrified he's just lost his opportunity with a woman he's loved his entire life.'

'Why am I so insecure?'

'Because Professor Dickstain did some serious fucking damage. Dax knows that.' She presses the elevator button on the wall. 'Promise me something.'

The elevator doors open and Mercy presses the ground floor button as we walk in.

'Promise me you won't compare every move Dax

makes to Tristan. The two aren't even on the same planet for comparison. Tristan is gone. And sayo-fuck-ing-nara if you ask me. You fell in love with someone else. That's scary. Especially as quickly as it happened. But you know Dax, and you know he's a good guy.'

My stomach turns as the elevator drops floors.

'Remember when you thought dickweed was going to propose, and we talked about how you'd know if it was right?'

I nod, wishing I didn't have to think about him for another second.

'I said you'd feel it in your bones or some shit, and you pretty much guffawed at that.' She laughs. 'We both did.' She fidgets with a ring on her middle finger as she speaks.

'I feel this in my bones *for* you, Hols. Tell Dax how you feel. All of it. Insecurities, fears, hopes, dreams, everything. He'll never use it against you like Tristan used to. You can trust him. Even with your heart.'

The elevator doors slide open, revealing River and Dax walking through the front doors. Dax looks awful, his head down as he walks by River's side.

'Dax,' Mercy calls his name.

He looks up with a pained stare as he notices me. 'Hollyn.' His voice drips with relief.

Mercy steps out, holding the door. I don't move,

my feet apparently glued to the floor, so he jumps in and hits all the buttons on the panel.

'Hols,' he says when the doors close. 'I'm *so* sorry you saw that. I stopped her immediately.' He takes the step to me, hesitantly touching my hand.

'I love you, Hollyn. You have to know I'd never hurt you.'

All the feelings racing through me surface at once into a panicky relieved sob. Dax doesn't waste a second, wrapping his arms around me, holding me tighter than he ever has.

'I'm sorry,' I cry into his chest. 'I just—'

'No,' he says. 'You've got nothing to apologize for. *I* do. I handled the situation terribly. I thought if I blew Celeste off, she'd go away. That was wrong, and I'm sorry.' He moves a hand to my neck, the pad of his thumb grazing over my skin as he stares into my eyes.

'I know trusting me won't come easily for you. I'll be patient, I promise. I just need you to know I'll never do what he did to you. *Ever.*' He kisses my forehead gently. 'There will never be another woman because I've only ever wanted you.'

The door dings open on floor three. Dax turns, slamming the door closed button, leaving a man looking confused in the hall.

'Kind of in the middle of something,' Dax tells him somewhat apologetically. 'Wait for the next.'

'Dax.'

He turns to me, worry still in his eyes.

'I'm in love with you.'

A grin grows on his face.

'But I'm scared. I'm coming out of what I now see as an emotionally traumatizing relationship. Yet somehow, from the moment you picked me up at the airport, I've fallen headfirst into you.'

'What did you say?'

I look around the elevator. 'I'm scared?'

'Before that.'

'I said, I'm in love with you.' I repeat the words he clearly needs to hear again. 'I'm in love with you, and it feels nothing like I thought it did.'

A weird half laugh, half relieved sigh leaves his lips as he kisses me gently. 'I love you, Hols. I've never said that to anyone else. Only you.'

'Really?'

'Really. I'm a little scared too. I've never done any of this before. Relationships have never been my thing, as I've pined over the same girl my whole life. I lost her once, and today I almost lost her again. And in all the confusion I realize she's everything to me. *You're* everything to me, Hollyn.'

I can tell he means every sweet word and I am speechless so I nod like some wordless loser in love.

He presses his lips to mine, an arm around my waist. I've never cried through a kiss that makes my insides burn like a campfire, but apparently, it leads to the frantic we-need-to-fix-it-now-before-these-doors-open elevator kiss you only see in the movies.

After a moment, he pulls away, laughing to himself as he points to the elevator ceiling above us, leaning his head against mine. One of my mom's most famous ballads, now considered elevator music, plays softly through the speakers.

'*Never* tell her,' I say.

'I promise.' He holds me tight. 'I thought I'd lost you. I've never been so scared, Hols.'

'I felt like I was dying,' I say, my arms around his neck. 'And only a small part of that was from the panic attack.'

Mercy's right. He's not comparable to Tristan in any way. Dax is a good man. I believe him when he says he'd never hurt me. I'd be an idiot not to throw myself at him. He makes me happy in a way no one else ever has.

31

DAX

Moments Later...

'We don't have to go back to the roof if you're uncomfortable. I'm cool if you'd rather leave here and never deal with *Battle of the Blossoms* again.'

'But what about your dad's shop?'

'I'll figure out something else. You come first, Hols.'

She thinks on it for a moment, the two of us standing in the hallway outside the stairwell leading to the roof full of our family and friends.

'No. This is important to you. Which means it's important to me. You come first too, and you've earned this opportunity. Let's finish the show.'

I hold her hand tightly as we walk up the stairs to the roof, all eyes on us as we come outside. Jillian grins, waving us over. The walk across the rooftop is a tad nerve-racking considering every head is turned our way.

Here we go. If our relationship was secret before, it's not now.

Leo, Celeste, and their assistants are standing near Jillian already like they've been waiting on us.

'I hear you had a bit of a hiccup, but things are good now?' Jillian asks, glancing between Hollyn and me, her gaze moving to our hands, which are intertwined in a way that makes my heart race every time.

I nod.

'Alright then!' Jillian says. 'Who's ready to celebrate our top two?'

Most of the people here are our friends and family and the ridiculous hoots and hollers from the Matthews make me grin. I pull Hollyn's hand to my chest, holding it in both of mine, attempting to breathe through Jillian's announcement.

'Leo!' Jillian says his name excitedly. 'Congratulations. You got the most votes this week.'

I blow out a breath. Thank god. Win or lose, I won't be alone with Celeste. Honestly, I kind of hope I lose. I'm over it. I just want to go home, make up with Hollyn, and move on with our lives. I'll figure out how to deal with the shop. Maybe it's just not meant to be?

'Celeste and Dax.'

Even Jillian using our names in the same sentence makes my skin crawl. Hollyn grips my hand even tighter.

'Celeste, darling. Hard lessons were learned today. We have rules for a reason. You'll be going home this week because you didn't follow those rules.' She doesn't sugar-coat it one bit. Not even when Celeste bursts out crying, her sister comforting her.

Did the truth come out while I was searching for Hollyn? She never lifts her head as Jillian speaks. Are they punishing her? It sure seems that way.

Jillian's gaze moves to Hollyn and me. 'Something's changed with you two,' she says with a grin.

I glance out at our friends and family. All their eyes are on us, most of them with goofy grins on their faces as they aren't just finding out the results tonight.

'I uh – I came to this show based on my skills as a florist, and I think I'd rather focus on that, not air our personal life if that's alright?'

Jillian nods. 'I only ask because our viewers have

taken quite an interest in you two. We don't need to discuss anything besides the fact that you're in our final two. You got only a dozen votes less than Leo.'

Our families cheer like they're at a Super Bowl as I pull Hollyn to me, kissing the top of her head. The top two. Wow.

'Before we disperse, I want to say one thing. One of you has stood out to me over the last few weeks.' Jillian walks our way, stopping in front of Hollyn. 'Hollyn, I've seen so much growth in you. In one of our interviews, you were asked what you wanted to do with your life. You answered with "I don't know".'

Hollyn nods.

'I'd like to make a suggestion. You've partnered with one of the best florists on the west coast. And in a matter of weeks, I'd never have guessed you hadn't been in this business as long as he has. I think you're a florist, Hollyn. You have an eye for it, and you and Dax work so well together I wouldn't feel right leaving here not suggesting you make this a partnership. You two are going places. I feel it in my bones.'

Hols' gaze moves to Mercy, the two of them smiling at Jillian's words. Maybe an inside joke? I don't know. I don't get it. But I agree with Jillian completely. Hols has developed an eye for flowers.

'Thank you,' Hollyn says to Jillian. 'A partnership with this one would be amazing. But I'll let him decide that. I'm just happy to be a part of this competition with him. Because of the show, I got someone important from my past back in a way I'd never imagined. I have no regrets.'

'We're thrilled to see the four of you in Seattle next week! We've got two lovely couples for each of you to work with, and they're very eager to meet you,' Jillian says with a clap, genuine excitement in her voice. 'Congratulations!'

Before we can think, our moms are standing in front of us. The grins on their faces say they aren't here to only congratulate us for our big win.

'You did it!' Mom says, pulling me in for a hug.

'Looks like maybe they've done more than just make the top two,' Penny announces.

'Mom!' Hollyn says with a gasp.

'Is it true? You and Hollyn?' my mom asks, her hands on my shoulders as she looks up at me.

'It's true, Mom.'

'Well,' she says with a sigh. 'I always suspected.'

'You did?'

She nods her head. 'I've only seen one man look at a woman like you've always looked at Hollyn. Your father. It's one of the things I've missed about him the most. But you two, you're reminding me of things I haven't thought of in years. Good things. Sometimes love takes time. Never waste a second.'

'Did you talk to River?' Penny asks, interrupting us with logistics.

'Yes, he did.' River lifts his beer to his lips. 'Congratulations, man.' He extends his hand to me. 'Both on making the top two *and* somehow not killing me or my car during the death ride earlier.'

'Sorry about that,' I say, taking his hand. 'I panicked I'd lost the most important thing in my life for a second.' I glance at Hollyn, who bites her lip to rein in her smile. 'We're good now.'

Dr John approaches us very straight-faced. He stops before us, his gaze moving from Hollyn to me. Honestly, I'm a little nervous about the words that are going to come out of his mouth.

'Congratulations, Dax. Your dad was my best friend, and I know he'd be proud of you just like I am.'

'Thank you.'

He turns to Hollyn, a forced clenched-teeth grin plastered on her face.

'I'm proud of you too, Hols. You set aside your problems, big as they seemed, and you put someone else's happiness ahead of your own. That's the daughter I remember before her teen years hit, and she decided we were the enemy. Welcome back.' He opens his arms; Hols immediately bursts into tears.

'*Women*,' River says, now standing next to me. 'They cry too much.'

32

HOLLYN

One Week Later – At Seattle Airport...

'Hello, Seattle,' I say, irritation I hadn't intended in my voice.

The closer we got to this trip, the more worried I've been. I don't know if I'm more afraid to run into my old life or that the whole city is bad luck, and will somehow curse me, causing me to run away alone this time too. Please, no.

'We can turn around and go home right now if this is too much,' Dax says, lugging a bag behind him.

'I'll get over it. For now, we're here until you've

won this thing.' I slide my hand into his, my other hand on his forearm.

'Where is Enrique?' he asks, glancing around the cars in front of us as he parks our suitcase. He pulls his phone from his pocket, searching license plates. 'There he is. If it's not Iglesias, I'll be disappointed.'

This last week has easily been the best week of my life, truthfully. Dax can't keep his hands off me and does anything to make me smile. Which honestly, isn't hard. I'm seeing all those things I thought were just 'nice' back when we were teenagers, and suddenly, they're the most heartfelt, romantic things anyone's done for me. I genuinely don't know how I didn't see it back then. Maybe I was just too young and immature? Who knows? Who cares? We're there now.

He slides his hand down my thigh, sensing my wavering anxiety. 'I'm right here with you, Hols. Nothing's gonna happen. I promise.'

I grab his hand, holding it tight as I stare out the windows. Raindrops slide down them steadily. Not exactly happy-as-a-daisy weather for a floral competition that was supposed to be held outside but is now urgently setting up in a fancy hotel downtown. Here's to hoping the saying that the rain on your wedding day is good luck is true.

'Is there anything you miss about Seattle? We can go, make a new memory to replace the old?'

I glance over at him, flashing him a thankful grin. 'I've never been happier than where I am now. No need to dredge up old feelings while we're here when we can make a brand-new memory.'

Dax lifts my hand to his lips, looking out his window at the city we're driving into.

I literally can't think of even one place I'd want to visit from my time here. All I want to do is put all this behind me to tell you the truth. The money included. If I never see it again, lesson learned. Don't invest in the wrong life. In every way.

'Any idea what we'll do today? We didn't really talk about it last night.'

'We can't seem to get any talking done at night,' he says as if it's a mystery. 'I love it. But no. No ideas. Figured why stress about it when we have to give the couple what they want, and they aren't telling us that until later this afternoon.'

I nod. 'You've got this, that I'm sure of.'

'*I've* got this?' he asks. 'We're a team. *We've* got this. What are you worrying about, Hols? I know it's something.'

A sigh leaves my lips. 'This has been the best five weeks of my life and it's almost over. I'll have to find a job when we're done with this competition. Where am I going to work? I don't even have a car. I can't put all this on you.'

'What would you say if I asked you to keep working with me?'

'Keep working with you?'

'Yeah. If I win, I'll have the shop to get ready, and I've been busier than ever since the show started. I could use some help, and I'll pay you. With *actual* money, not just favors in the bedroom.' He winks, making me laugh.

'You want to be my boyfriend and my *boss*?' That doesn't seem smart.

'Your boyfriend?' he repeats the word we haven't really discussed.

'I just – I feel like that's where this is headed.'

'I'll never be your boss,' he corrects me quickly. 'I'd love to be your boyfriend and your business partner. Multiple people have said it. We work great together. We see each other's visions, and when we don't, what we compromise to turns out even better. I've been a one-man show for a long time, and the last month has been more fun than I've ever had doing this. That's because you've been by my side. I don't want it to end. Maybe we run this business together?'

'Are you asking me to be your work wife?'

He laughs, nodding his head. 'Be my work wife *and* my live-in girlfriend? I know it seems fast, but is it really?'

'There's that undeniable charm again.'

'Undeniable, meaning your answer is yes?'

I nod. No wasn't even an option, truthfully. 'I truly can't think of anything else I'd want to do.'

Our Uber driver, who sadly was not Iglesias like Dax had hoped, pulls up to the Edgewater Hotel, which sits on the water in downtown Seattle. I've never been here before but have admired it from afar. It has views to die for and I can see why they'd choose the place for the big finale. It's beautiful.

McKenzie is waiting for us at the front desk. 'Hi, you two.' She grins, pointing at our hands, which are firmly gripped together. 'I've got to say that this romance happening on our time has been a pleasure to watch. I can't say I'm even a little surprised either. I was rooting for you the moment I met you.'

'You could have told us,' Dax says with a laugh.

'The final two,' she says as we check-in. 'You nervous?'

'Yes,' I say. 'We're a little nervous.'

'Understandable. Listen, I talked to Celeste; she spilled everything. We want to apologize for what happened back in Portland, via email, whatever. To *us*, it seemed ballsy. To *her*, she was playing a game, attempting to knock another team off theirs. To you two, it almost disrupted your real life. That's not OK. To make it up to you, we've sent up a gift. It's waiting in your room, and you can use it at any time. It's the least we could do.'

That's what Celeste said? She was just playing the game? I call bullshit on that. The way she looked at Dax never said 'I want you eliminated'. It screamed, 'I want you in my bed'.

'What do you think they did?' I ask Dax when the elevator doors close on us a few minutes later.

'I know what *I* did, but I've got no idea what *they* did.'

I glance over at him. He did something? The man already brings me flowers daily. What could he have possibly done?

'What *you* did?'

He shrugs, the elevator doors opening and him leaving me behind before he can answer.

'Dax,' I say, following behind him. 'What did *you* do?'

When he reaches our door, he slows, stopping and handing me the keycard in his hand. 'Go ahead.'

'You know I hate surprises.' A detail he's desperately trying to change.

'Not this one.'

I slide the key into the door, turn the handle, and step in. The smell hits me first: sugary, powdery, flowery. Thousands of flowers fill the room. On every surface. Of every color. Every kind. It looks like the flowers we're to use for the weddings have accidentally been delivered to our room. I glance back at him, now standing in the doorway watching me witness this.

'Seemed fitting. Ya know?'

I bite my bottom lip through the grin, causing him to drop his gaze with a chuckle. 'We've only got a couple of hours, Hols. I don't know if that's enough time.'

'Thank you,' I say, hugging him, my head on his chest.

'I'm hoping to make up for every time some asshole has not brought you flowers.'

'Well, it's working because just when I think I couldn't possibly love you more, you go and do something like this.'

'Maybe I'm better at this relationship thing than I thought.'

He notices an envelope between vases of flowers and flashes it my way. Our names are written across the front.

'The show's gift?'

He nods. 'Remember that massage you wanted eons ago? Here it is.'

I take the coupon he's handing me. 'A couple's massage? Does that mean we have to get naked in front of strangers? Cause that's going to be awkward. For *them*.' I laugh. 'You can't keep your hands off me when I'm clothed.'

'For good reason,' he says, now looking into the envelope he's still holding. 'Hols.' His voice drops. 'There's something else in here. For you.' He hands me the paper, folded into thirds, my name written across the front in black ink.

I open the paper, something falling to the floor as I do. 'Thank River and your dad.' I read the written words aloud, looking at the floor for whatever dropped out.

A check. Dax and I exchange looks as I kneel to grab it. Tristan Wells is printed at the top. My heart pounds as I look at the amount. One hundred thousand dollars. *More* than he owed me.

'Oh my god.'

Dax steps up to me, looking at the check. 'He gave the money back.'

'He gave the money back,' I repeat under my

breath, dropping onto the bed behind me. 'But why? How?'

'I don't kn—'

Knock. Knock. Knock.

Dax and I look at one another. He raises a single eyebrow as he stands from the bed, walking to the door and peering through the peephole as though we're in the middle of a horror film. He drops his head with a laugh, opening it to reveal River and my dad.

'Whoa.' River walks in, uninvited. 'Talk about bringing your work home with ya. Somebody is looking to get laid tonight,' he says obnoxiously as if I'm not his sister.

'River,' Dad says sternly.

Riv shrugs, giving me a sly grin as he and Dax shake hands like they haven't seen each other in weeks, even though it's been three days. We thought he'd left town for something to do with the documentary which means we've had the apartment to ourselves during that time, and I learned what River meant when he told me Dax cleans after sexcapades. He sure does. Hot pink dishwashing gloves, dancing to ridiculous pop music, and it's way hotter than I expected it to be.

'*How?*' I ask the two of them. 'How'd you convince him to give it back?'

Dad kisses my cheek like he used to when I was a kid. 'It was nothing a couple of baseball bats couldn't convince him of.'

'Guy likes his kneecaps,' River adds.

'You *beat* it out of him?' Dax asks, his eyes wide. 'Should I be on the look-out for cops?' He shuts the door quickly, locking all the locks.

'Nah.' Dad laughs, patting Dax on the back. 'I let you have the last hit with that tool. It turns out a visit from my lawyer, and the two of us were enough of a threat. You might also be happy to hear Victoria dumped him when she found out what he'd done to you. The cheating, stealing, lying, it was too much for her and she threw the ring in his face.'

'It was epic,' River says.

She dumped him? The smile on my face is slowly growing. I don't know why that makes me feel good. It probably didn't feel great for her, but I bet it made him miserable. I'll take that victory any way I can.

'And,' River says, 'I filed a complaint with the college the day you got back into town. I told them the whole story. They already had an investigation in the works, and this week, they fired him.'

I don't know where I'd be without River. Never in a million years did I expect him to grow up to be such a goofball with a heart of gold. He's exactly who you want on your side in life.

Without warning, I hug him. He grunts a laugh, his arms extended at his sides. 'You've done so much for me. I don't know how to thank you.'

He rests his hands on my back with a sigh. 'How about you start by not ruining my shirt by bawling into it and smearing your make-up on me? You know I'm not great with crying women, Hols.'

I laugh, stepping away from him and wiping my eyes.

'I'd deposit it fast,' Dad says. 'Never know what he might try.'

'Now we drink!' Riv says, lifting a finger into the air as though he's had an epiphany. 'Shall we?' He and Dax head to the room door.

'Can I uh – Dad? Can I talk to you?'

He looks surprised but nods. 'Sure, sweet pea.'

I glance at Dax. 'We'll catch up.'

'What's going on?' Dad asks when the room door closes.

'Mom suggested if I got the money back, I should invest it in something I believe in.'

'Your mother is a smart woman.'

'Yeah,' I agree. 'Thing is, there's a chance Dax may not win today. He's in this to earn the money to buy back Robert's shop and use it as his own. If he doesn't win, would I be totally crazy to believe in *his* business enough to buy the place?'

Dad pulls the chair from the desk, turning it towards me and sitting down. His face is somber as he considers what I've said.

'You want to date him *and* invest in his business?'

'Earlier, he asked me to work with him as his partner. I've never been happier than I am right now, so I want to. I think him wanting to do this in the same place his dad did is so... endearing.'

Dad nods as though he agrees. 'Family meant everything to Robert. I see that in Dax. I also see Dax surpassing his father in this industry already. I think his business would be a great thing to invest in. Both personally *and* financially.'

My dad has always been the most soft spoken of my parents. When you're married to a pop star, *she* leads the show. Dad brought up the back. We'd go to him first when River and I were in trouble. He'd smooth things over before we said a word to Mom. And if we disagreed, he'd give us advice on handling things. He never lectured. He used to say, 'Sometimes it takes time to find the right words, and it's always worth the wait.'

'You sure you love him, Hols?'

'He's given me everything since I came back. A place to stay. Something to do so I didn't feel like a total failure in life. He listens without judgment. Makes me laugh even when I don't want to. He made himself my bodyguard.' I laugh under my breath. 'He's loved me his entire life, and like the selfish girl I was, I never saw it. Until recently I didn't even know this feeling *was* love. Dax has changed me, Dad. I want to be a better person because of him. He makes me so happy, even when he says nothing at all. I'll never be able to pay him back for all of it as long as I live. So, to answer your question the long way, I'm sure I love him. I want to do this. For us.'

An ear-to-ear grin greets me as I glance up at my dad. He wipes one of his eyes – I get my over-emotional cry-at-everything side from him.

'Your mother's wedding vows weren't that good.'

We both laugh. I'm pretty sure my mom's wedding vows were lyrics from a song she later recorded, inspired by him. The exact same song that was playing in the elevator recently.

'I think it's a great idea. Dax is going places. Anyone who knows him can see that.' He pats my knee. 'I don't know that he'll accept that kind of gift easily, though. He's never been one to ask for help so you may want to really consider how you tell him. If today doesn't go in his favor, I'll make a few calls, and we'll get it all settled.'

'Thank you,' I say as he stands from the chair, pushing it back where it goes. 'For everything, Dad. I know I haven't been the world's greatest daughter, and I've made some humiliating mistakes. I hope maybe we can move past it?'

'Of course we can. Now, let's get a drink. You're buying, right?' He flicks the check still in my hand.

'Definitely.'

33

DAX

Two Weeks Later...

'Hols, I lost. We don't need to have a party.'

Yep. Two weeks ago, Leo won *Battle of the Blossoms*. He earned it. To compete, we'd have needed a dozen more people helping us. I still don't know how he got it all done. His team covered the floor of the ceremony with flowers – thousands of them.

Hollyn and I didn't do terribly. We hung a variety of blue flowers from the ceiling like raindrops, then did a flower-covered patio umbrella as an altar of sorts. It was gorgeous, but Leo's was breathtaking. We gasped when we walked in to see what he'd done. I played off the weather outside; he created the outside the couples wanted to begin with. He deserved to win, and I've genuinely got no hard feelings.

Am I depressed about it? A little. But I'm also proud. In two short years, I've created a suddenly thriving business and have been named one of the top florists on the west coast, right behind Leo. I'm good with that.

I'm mostly depressed someone bought my dad's shop after we got back. Kevin sold it right out from under me the second he learned I'd lost. It wasn't to 'Jeremy'. Though part of me hoped it was.

'I have a surprise for you,' Hols says. 'Do you trust me?'

A smile grows on my face. 'More than anyone in the world. But I thought you hated surprises?'

She cocks her head. 'There's this guy,' she says casually. 'He's changing my mind about a lot of things. Here.' She tosses my car keys my way.

'Where are we going for this surprise?' I ask Hollyn as we walk to my car.

'Penny Candy Records.'

'Am I gonna regret this?'

Hollyn's been worried about me since Seattle. It's sweet but unnecessary. I might not have won the show or got my dad's shop, but what I ended up with is a thousand times better.

'Not all of it,' she says, flashing me a coy grin.

It doesn't take us long to get to her mom's shop. I pull up behind her mom's car, but Hollyn takes off across the street when she gets out before me.

'Hols!' I call after her, locking my car with the click of a button. 'Where are you going?' I follow after her. 'Why are you walking so fast? Your mom's shop is back there.' I nod towards the building behind us as though she doesn't know where it is.

She stops, turning to me in front of my dad's old shop. 'We aren't *actually* going to my mom's shop. We're going to yours.'

'Mine?' I ask, confused. 'What do you mean?'

I watch as she silently pulls a key from her purse, sliding it into the front lock and turning it, the door popping open. I look from her to the now cracked open front door. Completely puzzled.

'How did you—'

'I did something,' she interrupts me, her nose scrunched in a way I've learned means she's nervous. 'I hope you're not mad. But when you lost the show, my heart broke. I couldn't let you lose the reason you entered to begin with. My mom said that if I could get my trust fund money back, I should invest in something I believe in. There's only one business owner in this town I believe in enough to invest that kind of money into. So, I bought the shop.'

'*You* bought the shop?' I ask, follow her inside, my hand now on my head as I walk away from her, looking around the place. 'Are you serious?'

'Serious as a heart attack,' she says with a laugh.

She's standing in the middle of the dark room, a ray of sunlight pouring in through a tear in the paper over the windows, illuminating her from behind. She's so lovely; I'll never get over it.

'When you asked me to be your business partner, I thought what better way to say yes than putting in a contribution. So, if you'll still have me, I'd love to run this place with you.'

All I can do is nod, the emotions guys usually try to hide from new girlfriends coming at me full speed.

'You didn't lose your fifty grand; it's waiting for you in my account, and we'll use it to fix this dump up. *And—*'

I burst out an overly emotional laugh. 'There's *more*?'

'Just one more thing.' She pulls her phone from her pocket, tapping the screen before handing it to me. 'I bought that.'

The photo is a neon sign; the words 'The Flower Boy' stare back at me.

'The letter L is a single stem rose for your dad.'

As the tears begin to flow, I wrap my arms around her, holding her tight, my chin resting on her head. 'I can't believe you did this. I don't know how to thank you, Hols.'

'I can think of many bedroom favors,' she says with a laugh.

'Ew. No, you promised.' River's voice makes me break into a laugh.

'You invited your brother?' I ask, releasing Hollyn.

'*Actually...*' She grimaces, turning towards the back-office area where River, Jake, Brynn, John, Penny, Mercy, and my mom appear. 'Everyone wanted to be here for this.'

She offers me the key to the shop. 'Welcome home, flower boy.'

EPILOGUE

DAX

Ten Months Later...

'Oh,' Roger says as I walk to the door. He never gets less creepy. 'What's the occasion?'

'Wedding,' I say, knocking on my front door.

'Yours or someone else's?'

'My mom's.'

'Mazel tov!' he says, throwing his hands in the air like he and my mom go way back.

For the first time in a long time, I've been invited to a wedding as more than just a florist. My mom met the second love of her life a few months ago, and they decided not to waste any time, so they're getting married tonight.

Obviously, Hollyn got her own invitation, but she agreed to go as my plus one too. It's kind of a given, considering we've spent practically every moment together since the day I picked her up at the airport a year ago. Looking back, that was easily the best day of my life.

Today will be the second. I need everything to be perfect. So, like the weirdo I sometimes am, I snuck out of the apartment without Hollyn knowing twenty minutes ago and changed in the back of my delivery truck. Being over six-four and trying to change in a truck isn't the easiest. But I did it, and I'm now standing at my front door, flowers in one hand.

'Dax? We should have left ten minutes ago. *Dax*?' I hear her say as she walks through the apartment, finally opening the door, a surprised grin on her face. She glances behind me as if she's expecting someone else.

'What are you doing?' Her eyes move from mine down my shirt, the phrase *Once and Floral* written across the front. She smiles, before inspecting the navy-blue floral print suit jacket I secretly bought a couple of weeks ago.

'Hols, you look beautiful.'

That's an understatement. She's beyond beautiful. She's wearing a navy strapless fitted dress which falls just below her knees, her hair pulled over one shoulder. I don't think she's ever been prettier than right now.

'You act surprised, but I tried it on for you last night. You literally took it off me.'

Before she tried the dress on last night, she was lying on our couch in tiny pajama shorts, a stained T-shirt, her hair messily piled on top of her head, glasses instead of contacts, and a dab of toothpaste on what she claimed was an incoming zit. She looks the complete opposite right now, and I was more than hot for her then.

'I remember. It's not the same as seeing the finished product, though.'

I'd avoided her pretty much the entire time she was getting ready so that I could have *this* moment. I want to remember every second of this day, starting now.

'What is this?' she asks, her hand on the arm of my jacket.

'Leo.'

He searched it out. Somehow he has a way of finding the most ridiculous floral print men's suits, so I figured he was the best person to ask for a recommendation. I didn't buy the matching slacks. The jacket seemed obnoxious enough.

'I can't believe I'm going to say this, but I love it. It's totally you.' She steps out of the doorway, pressing her lips to mine, then patting my chest. 'You're too handsome for your own good.'

'That's what River tells me too.' I wink.

She rolls her eyes playfully. I bet there will come a day that she'll wish she didn't choose her brother's best friend as her partner in life but I hope it's a long way away.

'These are for you, gorgeous.'

'Where exactly should I put them?' she asks, swinging open the door, displaying the many flowers on every counter, table, and surface. I've brought her flowers every day for the last month. It's all a part of the plan.

'Our place is full of pretty things, yet none of them can compare to you.'

She bursts out a laugh, grabbing her bag. 'You sure know how to make a girl feel good.'

'Only you,' I tell her as she steps onto our porch with me, locking the door behind her.

We're partway to the venue when she reaches across the center console and grabs my hand.

'You nervous about this?'

'A little.' I pull her hand to my lips, glancing over at her. She flashes me a smile. I don't know why I'm so nervous. I've never loved someone so much, and I know she feels the same.

'It'll be great, Dax. I think she really loves this guy.'

'Yeah. Me too.' She has no idea we're having two different conversations.

When I pull into the lot, she doesn't wait for me to get out of the car to open her door, probably because I'm a little frozen in place now that we're here. Once she's stepped out, I reach into the inside pocket of my jacket, feeling for the loose ring floating around. A ring I paid for pretty much with flower boy perfor-mances. Every. Single. Weekend. There are so many videos of me floating around YouTube it's embar-rassing.

'Hello?' Hols knocks on my window.

'Sorry.' I step out, grabbing the bouquet I made for my mom from the back seat. She didn't want anything over the top. No roses, but nothing extravagant, either. Just like the wedding. Simple, sweet, and with only the people closest to the couple.

I take Hollyn's hand as we walk into the venue, an ornate house on a property landscaped to the hilt. Ponds, weeping willow trees, wildflowers, twinkle lights, even a fire pit for s'mores-making under the stars.

'Finally,' River says, standing with his dad off to the back of the room. 'Your new step-sister is making me feel dirty in a *real* good way.'

'Gross. Can you not violate her before I've had a chance to get to know her?'

He glances over at her, lifting a single shoulder. 'Maybe?'

'Wait a second,' Jake says, now at River's side. 'Something's different.'

The two of them stare at me, their eyes lingering on my jacket.

'What in the hell are you wearing?' River asks.

'Curtain if I had to guess,' Jake says with a smirk.

'Can you guys leave him alone?' Hols says. 'He looks ridiculously handsome in floral prints.'

River groans. 'Good thing someone still lies to you.'

'Seriously, you two hate it?' I ask, pulling the lapel with my free hand.

'Don't let them pick on you,' Hols says, 'or I'll create the sister code.'

'And what would that entail?' River asks.

'*Not* boning your best friend's step-sisters.'

He rolls his eyes.

'*Hollyn*.' Dr John says her name like she's a little girl, swearing when she shouldn't.

'You should find your mom,' she says to me.

'Right, I'll see you in a few.' I kiss her lips, walking away from her right as Mercy walks up, leading her away from me. The two of us make eye contact, and she flashes me a smile.

Mercy and I haven't always gotten along, but things have improved. I can appreciate that she loves Hollyn as much as I do, and I honestly couldn't imagine our lives without her in it. She's helped me tremendously with this plan, and she's quite possibly as excited as I am.

I walk through the house, towards the bridal suite, knocking twice. Mom asked me to walk her down the aisle since her father is long gone. Of course my answer was yes. She seems happy, and that's all I've ever wanted for her. Plus, her marrying Mick means she'll never be alone again.

'Finally,' Brynn says as she pulls open the door. 'Did you take the bus?'

'I'm *ten* minutes late.'

'Dax!' Mom interrupts us, looking at me through the mirror she's standing in front of.

'You look beautiful.' I kiss her on the cheek, handing her the bouquet. 'You nervous?'

'Not at all,' she says, cool as a cucumber. 'I've waited years for this.' She turns my way, now adjusting my jacket. 'Are *you* nervous?'

'Yes,' I say. 'Very, *very*.'

'She loves you, sweetheart. There's no way she'll say no.'

A detail I'm putting all my faith into.

'Shall we get this party started?' I ask, extending my elbow to her so I can escort her down the aisle.

Mercy plays violin as we walk down the aisle and Mom is as excited as I've ever seen her. Once the ceremony gets under way, Hollyn sits at my side, her hand in mine, a grin on her face as she watches Mom and Mick tie the knot. She has no idea what I've planned.

The wedding goes off without a hitch and the guests move to the backyard, where lights hang from the trees, creating a soft glow against the quickly setting sun. A fire burns in the pit, soft music plays, and food is served buffet style. Even a freaking swan paddles through the small pond, something I didn't plan.

I glance around, finding Mercy and lifting my chin her way. She nods.

'Can I grab you another glass of wine?' I ask Hollyn, who nods, handing me her glass as she talks to her mom.

This is it. The moment I've waited my whole life for.

'Mercy, I'm *not* single. I don't qualify for the bouquet toss.'

I can hear them talking from the bar, which is only feet from where they are.

'You're single till Dax puts a ring on it,' Mercy says. 'Do you never listen to Beyoncé?'

Hollyn glances back at me as I make my way towards her with wine. We've talked about catching the bouquet and who qualifies. It was kind of a set-up to see if I could pull this off. After scouring the internet for romantic, surprising ways to propose, Mom suggested I ask her today because our delightfully overly involved friends and family wanted to witness it.

I flash her a smile as I stop in front of her. 'You two talking about me?'

'Yeah,' Mercy says. 'Welcome to Dax network. Where it's all Dax all the time over here.' She rolls her eyes.

I shake my head with a laugh.

'Hollyn doesn't want to join me for the bouquet toss because she's obsessed with you, even though she's not *technically* unavailable.'

I laugh. Mercy and I have talked endlessly about

what to say, but I should have known she'd improvise in an insult wherever she could.

'What are the bouquet toss rules again?' I ask, as if this isn't my business. I know all the rules.

'To qualify, a certain finger must be ringless,' Mercy says, lifting Hollyn's hand. 'Hols' finger is lonely as they come.'

I laugh under my breath. 'Maybe we should fix that?'

Hollyn's head snaps to me. 'How would we fix that?' she asks, now looking at me with her brow furrowed like she's not following.

'I dunno...' I hand Mercy the wine I was bringing to Hollyn. 'I was thinking with this.' I reach into my jacket, pulling the ring out and dropping down to one knee.

'Dax, what are you—'

At first, she's shocked, her eyes moving to the ring then back to me.

'Oh my god, is that a—' She glances at Mercy, then back at me. '*Shut up*. We haven't even talked about this. Are you *serious*?'

I nod. I've been thinking about what to say during this moment for a couple of months. I even talked it over with River and Jake. I took exactly none of their ideas either. I also remember nothing I scripted, so I'm going rogue.

'One year ago, you thought you were on your way to meet your future husband. It turned out you were; it just took a broken heart and plane ride to get to me. You're the only woman I ever want to do life with, Hols, and I'm kind of hoping I could ask you an important question?'

I take her left hand in mine, lifting it to my lips momentarily, ready to slide a ring – an *actual* engagement ring – onto her finger and officially take her out of the bouquet toss.

She nods, a hand now on her chest.

'I'll bring you every flower in the world if you blow off this bouquet toss and marry me instead?'

* * *

Hollyn
Seconds Later...

Oh my god. Tears are already starting to fall as it sinks in that Dax is knelt in front of me, asking me to marry him. I stare at the ring he's offering me, his eyes wide, his face nervous. *This* is what this moment is supposed to feel like. Not a part of me is worried. My ass isn't sweating. My head, heart, and loins are all on the same page. And I somehow feel my answer in my bones?

'You want to marry me?'

'More than anything, Hols.'

I nod my head, hardly able to speak as his words sink in.

'That's a *yes*?'

'Yes!'

'Yes?' he asks as if he's still not sure.

'Yes, Dax, I want to marry you.'

The smile on his face is one of relief and exhilaration as he slides the ring onto my finger. He stands, his hands on my hips as he kisses me, our families now cheering from the sidelines. I wrap my arms around his neck, looking at the ring over his shoulder.

'I can't believe you kept this a secret.'

'Oh, *everyone* knew,' he says with a laugh. 'Jake and River helped pick the ring. Mercy had a script she wandered away from. I asked your parents for permission. I ran my proposal by my mom yesterday. Everyone knew but you.'

I laugh. Of course they did.

'You made this perfect. I didn't even question my

answer. I just *know* you're who I want to spend my life with.'

'Finally.' He grins, staring into my eyes, looking happier than I've ever seen him. 'Cause I've always known, Hols.'

'I'm sorry I took so long to get here.'

'You're right on time, gorgeous.'

And that's how the boy next door unexpectedly swept me off my feet and restored my faith in love. He's perfect, my family no longer hates me, and I feel like I'm home in so many ways. I didn't know life or love could feel like this. I have him to thank for that. Let the wedding planning begin.

A NOTE FROM THE AUTHOR

Thank you so much for reading *He Love Me He Loves Me Not*. I hope you love this group of friends and their wacky families as much as I do because both Mercy and River are getting their own books and I can't wait for you to read their stories as well.

As always, if you loved the book (or even if you didn't – honest reviews welcome) I'd like to ask you to please leave your review on Amazon. It doesn't have to be much, just a line or two. Thank you in advance. Reviews help authors so *so* much more than I can explain.

Want to say hello? I'd love that! I'm all over social media (my phone and I are in an intimate relationship at this point...) and I would love to hear from you. Follow, friend, email or subscribe to my newsletter to keep in touch and never miss an update. Stop by my website https://aimeebwrites.com for info on how to keep in touch.

PLAYLIST (BY SCENE)

'Peace of Mind', Imagine Dragons
 'I'm Too Sexy', Right Said Fred
 'Anxiety', JVKE
 'Maybe You're the Problem', Ava Max
 'Hurts Like Hell' (feat. Offset), Madison Beer
 'Dear Miss Holloway', easy life & Kevin Abstract
 'Caution', Cuco
 'I Love You Always Forever', Betty Who
 'I Saw Him Standing There', Tiffany
 'Live, Laugh, Love', Abe Parker
 'Deep End', Dayglow
 'Late Night Talking', Harry Styles
 'Better Days', Neiked, Mae Muller & Polo G
 'Bad Guy', Simply Three

'Trust Issues', Emei

'Cassiopeia', Sara Bareilles

'Maniac', Conan Gray

'Hero', Mariah Carey

'Where the Sidewalk Ends', Garrett Nash & Scott Helman

'Sucker', Jonas Brothers

'SexyBack', Justin Timberlake

'Crush', Tessa Violet

'Boy Problems', Carly Rae Jepsen

'I Like You (A Happier Song)' (feat. Doja Cat), Post Malone

'Lucky Star', Madonna

'Am I Talking Too Much?', OSTON

'Overwhelmed', Royal & the Serpent

'Ocean View', easy life

Knockin' Boots, Candyman

'Crazy in Love' (feat. Jay-Z), Beyoncé

'Catching Feelings' (feat. Phony Ppl), Drax Project & SIX60

'Ooh La', Josie Dunne

'About Damn Time', Lizzo

'Sticks and Stones' (feat. Charlotte Sands), JORDY

'I GUESS I'M IN LOVE', Clinton Kane

'Dream Girl', Anna of the North

'Who's In Your Head', Jonas Brothers

'Perfect', Ed Sheeran

'Hollaback Girl', Gwen Stefani

'That's the Way Love Goes', Janet Jackson

'If I Could Turn Back Time', Cher

'What a Man Gotta Do', Jonas Brothers

'Nervous', John Legend

'Fall', Big Time Rush

'Sit Next to Me' (Stereotypes Remix), Foster the People

'Plot Twist' (Remix) (feat. Hailee Steinfeld), Marc E. Bassy

'This Is What Falling In Love Feels Like', JVKE

'Please Don't Go', Mike Posner

'The Exit', Conan Gray

'All the Man That I Need', Whitney Houston

'On Top of the World', Imagine Dragons

'Falling like the Stars', James Arthur

Best Feeling, Alfie Templeman

'How Long Will I Love You' (Bonus Track), Ellie Goulding

ACKNOWLEDGMENTS

This book is for all my dedicated readers who stuck by me through tough times, waiting patiently for another book. Life got in the way for a while, but I hope you love this series as much as I loved writing it.

To my early Beta readers (the folks who volunteer to read when the book is absolute shit and tell you what could make it better without making you want to sink into a hole and give up, those are your true friends), Andie Newton, Brook McCoy, and Christina Boyd. Thank you, appreciation isn't enough.

A special thank you to Andie Newton who continually talked me up during submissions when things seemed bleak. She's talked me down off ledges that felt too scary to face. She pulled over while driving to squeal with me on the phone when I got an offer. She's right there anytime I need her whether that be to talk writing, nonsensical girl talk, or allowing me to bounce ridiculous lines and ideas off her without telling me I'm a super weirdo (well, *most* of the time...

lol). You're the best, girl! Without you I may have given up this dream completely. Thank you. <3

To my amazing team at Boldwood; there aren't words. Y'all know my story and have made this easy, painless, and fun. This book is better because of all of you. I'm *so* excited to continue publishing my daydreams with you.

MORE FROM AIMEE BROWN

We hope you enjoyed reading *He Loves Me He Loves Me Not*
If you did, please leave a review.

If you'd like to gift a copy, this book is also available as an
ebook, digital audio download and audiobook CD.

Sign up to Aimee Brown's mailing list for news,
competitions and updates on future books.

https://bit.ly/AimeeBrownNews

ABOUT THE AUTHOR

Aimee Brown is the bestselling romantic comedy author of several books including *The Lucky Dress*. She's an Oregon native, now living in a tiny town in cold Montana and sets her books in Portland. Previously published by Aria, her new series for Boldwood is full of love and laughter and real-life issues. *He Loves Me He Loves Me Not* is Aimee's first book with Boldwood.

Visit Aimee Brown's website: https://aimeebwrites.com

Follow Aimee Brown on social media:

twitter.com/aimeebwrites

facebook.com/authoraimeebrown

instagram.com/authoraimeeb

Boldwood

Boldwood Books is an award-winning fiction publishing company seeking out the best stories from around the world.

Find out more at www.boldwoodbooks.com

Join our reader community for brilliant books, competitions and offers!

Follow us
@BoldwoodBooks
@BookandTonic

Sign up to our weekly deals newsletter

https://bit.ly/BoldwoodBNewsletter